RAW

A JAKE MORGAN MYSTERY

DEAL

With Compliments

Rick Gadziola

ECW Press

Published by ECW PRESS
2120 Queen Street East, Suite 200, Toronto, Ontario, Canada M4E 1E2

NATIONAL LIBRARY OF CANADA CATALOGUING IN PUBLICATION

Gadziola, Rick
Raw deal : a Jake Morgan mystery / Rick Gadziola.

(Jake Morgan mystery series)
ISBN 1-55022-636-3

I. Title. II. Series: Gadziola, Rick. Jake Morgan mystery series.

PS8613.A398R39 2004   C813'.6   C2003-907311-4

Editor: Michael Holmes
Cover and Text Design: Tania Craan
Cover illustration: Gary Doak / Photonica
Production & Typesetting: Mary Bowness
Printing: Gauvin Press

This book is set in Serifedsans and Minion.

The publication of *Raw Deal* has been generously supported by the Canada Council, the Ontario Arts Council, the Ontario Media Development Corporation, and the Government of Canada through the Book Publishing Industry Development Program. Canada

DISTRIBUTION
CANADA: Jaguar Book Group, 100 Armstrong Avenue, Georgetown, ON, L7G 5S4
UNITED STATES: Independent Publishers Group, 814 North Franklin Street, Chicago, Illinois 60610

PRINTED AND BOUND IN CANADA

ECW PRESS
ecwpress.com

For Susan, Paul and Marie, who I pray will always be there.
And for Stella and Walter, who couldn't be.

"I used to go to the horse track every day of the week. Now I only go when it's open."

— Anonymous gambler

Chapter

"Go ahead . . . hit me."

The little guy sure had balls. I knew if I hit him again I'd bust him. One part of me wanted to offer some friendly advice. Another said finish him, now. He was sweating profusely as he fumbled with a long, thin black cigar. I noticed his hand shaking ever so slightly as he lit it off the one he was just finishing. He puffed hungrily, like a baby on a pacifier, and bits of ash floated this way and that.

"Yeah, come on, hit 'im, for chrissake!"

The bleached blond was draped all over him. She had one arm hooked through his, slobbering into the glass of rye she held in her other. She was a full size twelve shoehorned into a skimpy size ten, and she wore heavy gold earrings the way a hot air balloon wore sandbags — and I suppose they served the same purpose.

"Look, friend," I said. "Are you sure you —"

My body tensed as I sensed McClusky come up from behind. Before I could look over my shoulder, he jabbed me with his damn pen. I hated when he did that. Sometimes, in the heat of excitement, he forgot which end was which.

His hot breath tickled the hairs on the back of my neck. "Flush the little asswipe outta here, Morgan," he whispered. "He's stinkin' up the place." Underneath McClusky's rough exterior was an even rougher interior, and although I couldn't see his face, I didn't need to be psychic to know he wasn't smiling.

"Come on, schmuck, gimme one!" The little guy wiped his brow with the sleeve of his brown polyester suit. "But no faces, huh?" He winked at his rent-a-date and gave her breast a playful squeeze.

"You're the boss." I reached across to my left and gave him my best shot. It was a queen.

"Shit," he hissed. "The bitch of spades."

Blondie threw her drink across the front of my shirt. "You rotten prick!" she screeched, licking drops of rye from her charm bracelet.

Christ, I hated when they did that. I counted to ten by fives and collected the jerk's 800 bucks.

Defiant, he ripped his cards in half and whistled the pieces at my head. "Way to go, dickhead!"

Enough was enough. I reached across the green felt of the blackjack table and grabbed the twerp by his tie. My other arm was extended behind me, and I was just about to launch when McClusky gripped me by the wrist.

"Cool it, Jake," he said calmly. "It's your last week, and it's not the way to go outta here."

I took a couple gulps of air and counted to ten again, this time by twos. McClusky was right. I finally had a ticket out of this moronic job and it would be stupid to ruin it now.

Security was fast approaching through the crowded aisles, so I shoved the little pissant in their direction. I tossed his remaining chips at the blond bimbo, who dropped half of them to the floor.

"Go change your shirt, Morgan," McClusky advised. He patted me on the ass like a coach would his quarterback. "You did right, Jake." I uncurled my lip and unfixed my stare.

"Yeah, thanks." I turned and walked away, fondling the three, black hundred-dollar chips I had palmed from the pile I'd tossed to the blond. A donation to my stress relief fund.

The Oasis Hotel's casino was the biggest in Las Vegas, about the size of a football field. To get to the dealers' break room I had to walk from one end zone to the other. The route led past the poker room, soon to be my new home. It was packed. It was wonderful. I took a moment to savor the sights and sounds.

One of the advantages of the poker room was that it was always busy. Nothing was more boring than being marooned on an empty blackjack table. Standing there like an idiot with my hands behind my back gave me too much time to think. Not a good thing.

Poker, especially hold 'em poker, was quickly becoming America's favorite gambling pastime. The old, cigar-smoke-filled, backroom joints had given way to clean, lavish card rooms. More than half the states had legalized card rooms, either in swank surroundings like California, New Jersey, or New England, or on Indian reservations and riverboats.

And most of the poker players had a different outlook. At blackjack, you could always tell from a player's face if they were losing. It was them against the house. At poker, even a lot of the losers would keep their cool. Losing it would be a show of weakness, and in a tough game, where half the table consisted of local pros, they'd feed on emotions and "tells" like a school of piranha feeds on helpless prey.

As I gave the room a last wistful look, I heard my name being called.

"Hey, Jake! You still on for our game a week from Saturday?"

Kenny was a poker dealer here at the Oasis and hosted a game for a bunch of the guys every couple of weeks at his place. It was supposed to be friendly, and for the most part it was. But last week I got caught in a session with two guys on tilt. The game turned into a wild shoot-out, and when the smoke cleared I was out one paycheck and part of my next. I swore I'd never play again. But that was last week.

"I'll be there," I told him, stroking the chips in my pocket. "And you'd better make sure those two yahoos are there, too!"

"Atta boy, Jake," he grinned. "You can't keep a good man down." He patted me on the back, like a banker with his best customer. "So when do you start dealing in the poker pit?"

"Another week and a half. I've got one more shift of BJ, then I'm taking a few days off."

"That's great." He glanced down at the wet stain on my shirt. "Hey buddy, you got a drinking problem?"

"Nah, just a problem with drinkers."

"Well, don't think it'll get any better in the poker room. I almost lost an eye once. Cards can really sting when some asshole whips them at you for filling some other guy's inside straight."

"Yeah, but at least I'll get to sit down while I get abused," I laughed. "And I get to keep the tokes I earn instead of sharing them with a hundred other dealers."

"True, very true." He glanced down at his watch. "Gotta run, Jakester. I'm dealin' a one-three Omaha game with a bunch of outta town fish." He rattled the chips in his pants pocket. "They can't play worth a damn, but they're sure havin' a good time!"

·

When I arrived at the dealers' room, I took a few gibes regarding my sartorial splendor from the gang sitting around the big-screen TV. Then I found myself a quiet corner in the adjoining locker room, peeled off my shirt, and soaked it in cold water. I was lucky she had been a hard drinker.

Mix would have made it worse.

It wasn't the first time I'd had a drink thrown at me, and it probably wouldn't be the last. At least this one had the courtesy to hold onto her glass. Not like the hotheaded Colombian I had my first month dealing BJ at the Oasis.

The Juan Valdez impersonator had been drinking up a storm and betting large and loud to impress a hot number hanging on his arm. Apparently I was the reason for his bad luck, and he wasn't shy about telling me, and whoever else could hear, what a stupid gringo I was. When he was ready to pack it in and take the Charo look-alike upstairs to play "peel the banana," he slapped down a five thousand dollar chip and announced it was his final bet. I smiled inside when I gave him two eights. His date gleefully encouraged him to split. He got two more eights, a few threes, and a deuce. By the time he was finished splitting and doubling down he had another thirty-five large spread out on the table in crisp hundreds. I never saw the glass coming after I busted him with my own twenty-one. If you look closely at my right eyebrow, you can still see the scar.

When security arrested him he claimed I'd laughed at his misfortune. I, of course, insisted he was mistaken.

It had only been a smirk.

If a year in Las Vegas had taught me anything, it was that people turned weird when they arrived here, almost as if they had tripped and fallen into the "Fountain of Stupid" when they landed at McCarran International.

It was a psychiatrist's dream come true. Mind you, it could also be a coroner's nightmare.

You wouldn't find it in any tourist guide or travel brochure, but in the past year, 417 tourists had died while visiting their Mecca of Madness — more than one a day.

With the constant razzle-dazzle, the lack of sleep, the free booze, the strain and stress of gambling, it was no wonder so many of them ended up in the cardiac ward of Sunrise Hospital.

I wrung out the shirt and held it up for inspection. The guy staring back at me in the mirror looked tired, strung out and dejected. Vegas could do that to you. She was a costly siren.

But she was still my kind of town, which probably accounted for the sparkle in the recesses of my baby blues. A good gambler trusts his gut instincts. And I *was* a damn good gambler. A good judge of character, no. Fiscally responsible, uh-uh. Domestically inclined, nope. But sit me down at a card table and I felt like a fox in one of the Colonel's chicken coops.

Still gazing in the mirror, I pressed gently on the discolored pucker of skin just beneath my left shoulder. I placed two fingers against the wound and measured the distance from the bullet's entry point to my heart. Two inches, the surgeon had said.

Who said Jake Morgan wasn't the luckiest guy in Vegas?

Chapter

Feeling better now that I'd cleared my head and changed, I joined the rest of the gang in the break room. I called McClusky and told him I was ironing my shirt and would be back for my next turn. He warned me not to be late. I grabbed a corner of an empty sofa, plunked my ass down, and picked up a copy of the *Daily Racing Form*.

All around me the sounds of music and television shows fought for my attention. Many of the dealers were involved in various forms of card games, which never ceased to amaze me. A few sat quietly and read books. The rest of them lounged around, trying to cram three cigarettes' worth of smoke into their lungs during their twenty-minute break.

I was still analyzing the first race at Hollywood Park when I felt the cushions shift ever so slightly. A heady scent of lavender wafted in the air.

"Hello, Jake."

There were only two voices I knew that could sound so long and lusty and lush. And since I didn't know Kathleen Turner, there was only one woman it could be. As I lowered the paper, my heart began to hammer and my mouth went dry.

"Rachel?" I stammered.

I knew I couldn't be dreaming, because I'd never play such a cruel joke on myself, even sleeping. Rachel Sinclair was a showgirl in the Oasis' main showroom, the Sultan's Tent. I'd met her exactly three and a half times. The first was to present her with a white rose and to ask her out. She'd thought about that for a moment, then said she was sorry but she was busy. The next two were because I couldn't take no for an answer, but no was exactly what I had got. The half was two weeks ago, when I'd waved hello to her in the hallway and she'd walked right by.

I cleared my throat. "Rachel."

She smiled saucily, crossed her sleek, sexy legs and pondered me for a moment. "Hello, again, *Mr. Secret Admirer*," she purred.

"My admiration was a secret?" I asked.

"Well, no, but flowers *and* champagne? They're absolutely beautiful!" She gave me that damn look again. "I know my promotion in the show was reported in most of the papers, and I appreciate the congratulations, but it really wasn't — hey, how did you get my home address?"

Damn, that was right. I'd read the other day that there had been a shake-up in the cast. "Ah, the flowers and champagne . . . right."

"Three dozen long-stem roses!" she exclaimed. "*And* Dom Perignon."

Some tourist must have caught her show, enjoyed a few fleeting fantasies, sent her the gifts, and returned home to the boonies.

I folded and tossed the paper behind the sofa. "What can I say? I'm a helluva guy!"

"Are you?" She leaned back into a comfortable pose, placed an arm on the back of the sofa, and tucked a loose strand of blond hair behind her ear. "Would you like to go out tonight?"

I considered looking behind me to see if she was talking to someone else.

"Excuse me?"

"Would you like to go out with me tonight?" She gave me a soft smile.

"You mean, like on a date?"

She laughed lightly. "Actually, it would be more like a business date."

Now it was my turn to smile. "A business date?"

"Let me explain." She shifted slightly and tucked her legs under her. "Valentine's invited us to the show tonight. His own private table. He wants me to watch Leona — you know, to get an audience perspective for when I take over for her."

Christian Valentine was the featured star of the show, Las Vegas' hottest property. He had Harrison Ford's looks, Tom Jones' voice and the personality and libido of a German shepherd in heat — no offense to German shepherds. He packed them in twice a night, six nights a week, singing and wiggling his ass on stage. Big deal. For a million a month I'd get up there and wiggle my ass, too.

"Hold the phone." I raised one bushy eyebrow. "You said *us*. Valentine invited *us*?"

She bit softly on her lower lip. "You used to be a cop, right?"

Now both brows rose. "How the hell did you know that?"

"You've got that look . . . and after you asked me out, well, let's just say I had you checked out."

She was right, I *had* been a cop, but it wasn't something I liked to talk about. "You had me checked out, did you?"

"I wasn't sure about you the first time we met. This town attracts all types. I don't go out with anyone until I know what I'm dealing with."

"Well, obviously I made a big impression. You shot me down every time."

"Cops can be scary, too," she said softly.

I certainly couldn't argue with her about that.

"So what does my being an ex-cop have to do with Christian Valentine?"

"I'm not sure." Rachel blew out a light puff of breath. "I know I mentioned you to a few of the girls, might have mentioned it around Valentine, too. He's always hanging around backstage trying to catch a peek of the new talent in the dressing room. Last night he came up to me after the show and asked if I ever went out with that cop guy that had been asking me out. I told him no. That's when he said I should watch the show from the audience. He asked me to bring you along," she said, turning her palms up. "That's it."

It wasn't exactly what I'd had in mind when Rachel first caught my eye, but at least I was getting up to bat.

"Well, it's hardly a Romeo and Juliet beginning," I said, giving her my best smile. "But let's hope it has a better ending."

Rachel's sigh came with a slight warning. "Let's take it one step at a time, okay, Jake? For now, I'm doing this because Christian Valentine asked me to. We'll see where it goes from there. But please, if we meet Valentine, be on your best behavior. It's my ass on the line — the chorus line."

"And what a fine ass it is."

She got up, handed me a slip of paper, and gave me an admonishing look. "Pick me up around eight." Then she surprised me by leaning over and giving me a peck on the cheek.

"Lights and siren?" I asked.

Rachel Sinclair studied me for a second, shaking her head. "Cops . . ." She turned and walked away, with every male eye in the room following her and a few female eyes, too.

Yep, mighty fine.

Chapter

The corner of Las Vegas Boulevard and Flamingo Road was packed. Two or three hundred cars were aimed in all directions, waiting for what had to be the longest red light in the world. I drummed my thumbs against the steering wheel to the beat of Carlos Santana, thinking about the irony of my being asked out by Rachel Sinclair. The whole thing smelled funny, especially the Christian Valentine bit, but my instincts told me to take the ride and just see where I ended up.

The light finally decided to change from red to green and I headed south along the Strip. At Tropicana I made a right, heading west. The pattern of two- and three-story condominiums broke for a mile or so, past open desert fields that lay in dusty rest, waiting for the eventual development that was swelling the city. Up ahead were the lights of Rachel's subdivision. I gave the engine a little more gas. The beat-up Chevy shuddered for a moment, and so did I.

I made another right down a neat main road. The developer must have had a Caribbean fixation as all the streets were named after islands and West Indian capitals. I took the Grand Bahama Way traffic circle around to San Juan East and turned down Grenada. By the time I pulled into Rachel's driveway on Martinique, I had a strange craving for a rum punch.

"Thatta girl. Hold it with two hands, one around the base and the other up around the top." Rachel had said she was new at this and I was guiding her along. "Okay, good. Now put it between your legs and wiggle it around with your thumb and forefinger until you feel it start to move. That's it!" I encouraged her. "Now squeeze."

Rachel bit her lower lip and squinted. "Like this?"

"That's good," I said, relaxing into the soft confines of the sofa. "You've just about got it. Keep going. Back and forth, back and forth."

The nervous strain showed on her face. "I can feel it coming. Now what do I do?"

"Okay, get ready," I told her, moving back a bit.

The bottle popped all of a sudden and the cork bounced off the ceiling, hit the far wall, and flew across into the drapes behind a love seat.

"You did it!" I got out of the deep sofa, took two glasses off the tea wagon and set them on the table. "Here, let me."

"No, Jake," Rachel insisted. "You supplied the champagne. I'll pour."

I sat back knowing I should level with her about the flowers and champagne, but why spoil the mood? Rachel was still in jogging pants and a UNLV sweatshirt, but she looked great. Her thick blond hair was freshly washed, and there was a clean, just-bathed scent to her exquisite body. Her nails were polished blood red.

My wardrobe consisted of my favorite suit, Bugatti tie and my Perry Ellis underwear, the outfit I wore for really big occasions. I hadn't been able to decide between colognes, Stetson or Tuscany, so I had splashed on a bit of both. I smelled like a cowboy in a spaghetti western.

Rachel filled both glasses and handed me one.

"To us," I said, ever the optimist, clinking her glass with mine.

She rubbed a finger lightly around the edge of her glass and looked across at me. "I thought this champagne was to celebrate my promotion . . ."

I flashed a smile a Hollywood orthodontist would have been proud of.

"To Rachel Sinclair. May your rising star burn long and bright, a lodestar to those around you."

"Thanks," she said, smiling back. "So tell me, what's all this mystery about you being a cop back in Boston? Why did you leave?"

I took a long drink. The celebratory mood had just dimmed. "I didn't really have a lot of choice."

"The copy of the employee file I read said there was an honorable discharge."

"Believe me, Rachel, it wasn't that honorable."

"Tell me about it."

"No."

She studied my face over the rim of her glass. "Bad?"

"Bad enough." I held out my glass and she poured one more.

"Did you enjoy being a cop?"

I watched the bubbles work their way from the bottom to the top of the glass. "The job itself was fine, I guess. Unfortunately I've always had a problem with authority figures and rules and regulations. It was funny in a way."

"How's that?"

"I could enforce a lot better than I could follow."

"And you got yourself into trouble?"

I sat farther back in the sofa, alone with my thoughts and angry with myself for bringing back the memories.

"But you don't like to talk about it."

"No."

We sat and talked for another fifteen minutes, and I managed to change the subject around to her. I found out she was from Minneapolis, had majored in dance, had come to Vegas via Reno, where she had started in the chorus line of a small production. Rachel shared the house with two other dancers she'd worked with once at the Rio. She was twenty-eight, eleven years younger than me, and had been living in Vegas for just over two years. Being promoted to star alongside Valentine was the closest she had come to being considered a feature attraction.

Rachel glanced at her watch. "We better be going." She finished off what remained in her glass and headed for the stairs. "Give me ten minutes to slip on a dress and fix myself up."

I watched her take the stairs two steps at a time.

There certainly wasn't much to fix.

Chapter

We were standing in the roped-off VIP line just outside the Sultan's Tent showroom. It wasn't much shorter than the regular line. The only difference was the maître d' would expect a bigger tip for seating us.

Rachel looked absolutely stunning. She was wearing a slinky crimson number, designed by some French guy whose name I couldn't even begin to pronounce. I had to give the man credit for knowing how to frame a work of art. The dress was hemmed high, accentuating her dancer's legs, and cut amazingly low. The display of her magnificent chest had attracted a lot of attention from the men we'd passed and a few icy glares from the women on their arms. You could read from their envious looks that they questioned whether she had been surgically enhanced.

I'd be lying if I said the thought hadn't crossed my mind.

"Excuse me, Jake. I'll be back in a minute," Rachel said. She slipped between two rows of slot machines and headed in the general direction of the ladies' room.

As I watched her go, I noticed a young couple standing near the cashier cage a few yards away. The girl was five or six months pregnant; he was a big strapping kid with a buzz cut that screamed military. She was crying openly while he just stood there like a deer caught in high beams. I had seen the situation a hundred times before. As a matter of fact, I'd been there myself.

"How could you, Bobby!" she wailed.

Bobby didn't answer; he just shook his head.

"That was everything we had." She dabbed at her eyes with an already damp tissue. "How could you do that to us?"

"I'm sorry, baby." He dropped his head, staring at his shoes. When he looked up again his eyes were moist. "I just . . . I couldn't believe his luck . . . I just thought . . ."

"You didn't think at all, Bobby. Now what are we going to do? We haven't even got gas money to get home!" She searched around in her purse and found a fresh tissue.

The couple in front of me must have caught her last line. They laughed, and I overheard the word *losers*.

I reached into my pants pocket and asked the guy behind me to hold my spot. I walked up to the couple, bent down to the heavily patterned carpet, and stood again.

"Excuse me, Miss?"

She looked at me and sniffled.

"I think you dropped these." I handed her two black chips.

She held them for a moment, then started to hand them back. "I'm sorry. I didn't — "

"Hold on, Charlene," Bobby said.

She turned to him. "Shut up, Bobby."

"When you opened your purse," I explained. "I think they may have fallen out."

Charlene studied my face, biting lightly on her lower lip.

Bobby glared at me and said, "What the fuck?"

I folded her hand around the chips. "Go on," I said softly.

"Hey, maybe you didn't hear — "

I reached over and put my hand on his thick shoulder. "Look, Bobby. Your lady here seems like a real nice woman. And I know you're a smart guy 'cause you're with her. But right now she's going to go up to that cage and cash out. If I see you even look at those bills, I'm going to make you feel even more sorry than you already do. Do I make myself clear, soldier?"

A couple of veins popped on his neck, but he didn't say anything.

"Go home," I told her.

"Thank you," she said. "Thank you so much."

She grabbed Bobby by his shirtsleeve and went to cash in the chips. As she walked away, she turned and gave a little wave.

I didn't bother waving back.

Chapter

Rachel was returning as the line began to move forward. Her every step exuded an air of grace and confidence, and I couldn't take my eyes off her. I felt like the luckiest guy alive. She came up beside me and started to thread her arm through mine.

"By the way," she whispered, "they're real."

I hoped I wasn't blushing. "As a proper gentleman, I, of course, have no idea what you're talking about."

"Yeah, right," she laughed lightly. "Some cop you were."

"Cops are usually allowed to frisk."

"*Ex-cop,* then." She gave me a saucy smile. "And I'm not cuffed."

"Kinky," I replied. "Very kinky."

"Ms. Sinclair!" The maître d' lifted Rachel's hand to his lips. His fingers were long, the nails polished to a sheen. The diamond on his pinkie caught the light. "How good of you to join us," he said, smiling at Rachel and ignoring me.

I wondered if he had to practice his act in front of a mirror before each show. He clasped his hands to his chest and gave a brisk bow.

"I understand congratulations are in order, Ms. Sinclair."

When he finally finished rolling his r's, Rachel said, "Thank you very much, Franco. It's nice to come in through the front door for a change. Oh, and by the way, this *proper gentleman* beside me is Jake Morgan."

Now he had to look at me, whether he wanted to or not. He was in his early forties, maybe younger, with the square-shouldered build of an ex-boxer. His skin was olive-colored, his eyes dark, knowing and as sharp as a salesman's opening line. He had a full head of black hair, slicked back, parted in the middle, and a thin, well-kept pencil moustache. And while you couldn't call him sleazy, it helped that he wasn't standing in the entrance to a strip joint.

Franco extended a hand the size of a small roast and I took it cautiously. "Mr. Morgan," he said curtly.

I never trusted anyone with sweaty palms, and Franco's were as wet as a baby's diaper.

We were escorted to our seats. Unlike most showroom tables, which were long and narrow and ran perpendicular to the stage, ours was crescent-shaped, private and faced the curtain.

I dug into my pocket for the obligatory big tip and came up with a dollar bill. Before I could reach in again to find what I wanted, Franco snatched the single out of my hand without looking at it. He bowed slightly, clipped his heels Gestapo-style, and was gone.

"What a jerk," I said, figuring I'd just saved nineteen bucks.

"Oh, come on, Jake. Relax. He's just air and flair."

The VIP menu was the same as the not-so-VIP menu and in a way I was glad to see that. We had a limited choice of duck à l'orange or roast beef with Yorkshire pudding. Since nobody in their right mind came to a Vegas showroom to have duck à l'orange, we both ordered the beef.

A young Mexican waiter took our order and politely asked if we wanted drinks with dinner. Rachel ordered a vodka martini and I asked for the coldest beer he could find. He smiled and hurried off.

Our drinks and dinner came and went. The talk was polite and occasionally playful but hardly the soft, romantic, filled-with-promise conversation I had hoped it might be. Still, the night was young.

Eventually the lights dimmed, but not fully. The huge room was three-quarters full and people were still filing in. A band was located off to the side, about twenty feet up. The string section began tuning while the brass blew some light riffs.

The maître d' came back down the aisle, aiming a tiny flashlight in our direction. A very classy lady followed.

Franco must have finally noticed the size of my tip, because he gave me a wicked glare. Then he smiled at Rachel and said, "Ms. Sinclair, Mrs. Yolanda Valentine." He lit a candle hidden in a floral arrangement on the table, snapped his flashlight off, did the Gestapo thing again, and left.

The two of us tried to stand.

"Please," Mrs. Valentine said. "Sit."

We sat and introduced ourselves. Mrs. Valentine insisted we call her Yolanda. She reached back casually and slipped off her embroidered jacket. Rachel had pointed out a similar one in a hotel shop window we had passed on our way in. It was almost the same price as a car, and not a twenty-five-year-old Chev either — more like a brand-new Buick.

Yolanda Valentine tossed the jacket carelessly to the side. She wore some kind of black chiffon gown that hugged close to her body in great big bunches. The extravagant pearl necklace matched the earrings as well as the baubles on her fingers and wrist.

Word was the Valentines had been married almost twenty-five years, so that put her somewhere in her late forties, maybe early fifties. She was trim and fit-looking, with what appeared to be energy to spare.

"So, Rachel," said Yolanda, reaching into a colorful, sequin handbag. "I understand you're taking Leona Carter's place."

Rachel nodded. "That's right."

"Good part," Yolanda confirmed, removing a cigarette from a silver case. "I've seen you dance many times." She tapped the cigarette lightly against the case and looked Rachel in the eye. "You were very good."

"Thank you," said Rachel.

Yolanda fitted the cigarette into a sleek silver holder. "The promotion was certainly well deserved," she added warmly.

Rachel flushed. "Thank you, again."

I reached for one of the hotel matchbooks on the table and offered Yolanda a light. She held my wrist to fix the match, but my hand was as steady as William Tell's.

Yolanda studied me briefly over the flame, then blew out the match with a warm, seductive puff.

"So tell me, Jake Morgan," she said, finally remembering to let go of my hand. "What is it that you do?"

"I'm a dealer," I replied. "Here at the Oasis. But I just got promo —"

"Really," she said, cutting me off. "How nice . . ." She turned to get the waiter's attention, and when she did her large pearl earrings swung out wildly. Even though they were damn near as big as golf balls, I remembered my promise not to embarrass Rachel and didn't yell, "Fore!"

Yolanda ordered a bottle of champagne, Rachel requested tea. Another cold beer was fine by me. When the drinks arrived, Yolanda asked us to join her in a toast to Rachel's promotion.

Rachel blushed as our gracious hostess poured three flutes of bubbly. I began to reconsider my preconceived dislike of the Valentines. Maybe I had them pegged wrong. I picked up my drink and we clinked glasses all around. The band eased into a soft number and the lights dimmed even more.

"Did the two of you have dinner?" Yolanda asked, already pouring herself a refill.

"Yes," I answered. "Roast beef."

"Good?" she asked.

I made a face by wrinkling my nose, then held my hand out and flipped it from side to side. *"Comme çi, comme ça."*

The opening number began.

Yolanda smiled and stabbed her cigarette out. "Well, as the saying goes," she said over the rising music, "one doesn't come to a Las Vegas showroom for the roast beef!"

Chapter

The first part of the show moved at a breathtaking pace. Animal acts with leopards, lions, and elephants; Elvis, Madonna, and Liberace impersonators; jugglers catching chainsaws and swords; half-naked dancers; and my favorite, a guy spitting ping-pong balls fifty feet in the air and then catching them again in his mouth. I had a hard enough time with beer nuts at the bar.

I learned Rachel's old part had been in the bare-breasted and scantily clad portion, and I was terribly disappointed I had never caught her act before. She'd still be in the show, but the more important her role became, the more clothes she'd be allowed to wear. To top it off, Leona's part had a major song-and-dance routine in Valentine's half of the show. And what a show it was.

I had never seen Christian Valentine perform an entire set before. Sometimes, during breaks, I would sneak backstage, and occasionally I caught Valentine. But I had never heard him so strong and resonant. On this night he was the consummate performer. I could actually feel the notes in the glass I was holding as he glided from one octave to another with ease.

His stage presence was something to behold: immense, sleek, powerful, filled with a passion that I had not realized he possessed. He went into a rendition of "It's Not Unusual" that would have made Tom Jones stand up and applaud. He gyrated and humped about on the apron of the stage, straining his skintight pants to the point of popping, splashing the fanatical women in the front row with beads of sweat from his open-necked shirt.

"Christ," murmured Yolanda to no one in particular. "What an ass-hole."

Our host was working on her second bottle of champagne and her second pack of smokes, and I couldn't help but wonder if she was as fit as I had first thought.

"Pardon?" I asked, not sure if I had heard her correctly.

Yolanda rubbed her cigarette out and shook her head. "Look at him," she said with disdain, "prancing and posing out there as if he were some twenty-year-old teenage heartthrob."

Not sure if that counted as an oxymoron or not, I decided to let it pass. She was reaching for another cigarette, so I struck another match. It was the last one in the book. I made a mental note to check if a person was a chain-smoker before setting any lighting precedents in the future.

Yolanda blew a trail of smoke out toward the stage. "Tom Jones does-n't need a rolled-up sock to impress the front row." Some distant memory brought a smirk to her face, and I wondered if she was speaking from personal knowledge. She filled her glass and tipped the empty bottle into the ice bucket.

Two dead soldiers. At this rate, the hotel might have to call for rein-forcements.

"You're kidding about the sock, right?" I asked, checking Valentine's crotch closer. I looked over at Rachel. She nodded and mouthed the word *wardrobe* to me.

The remainder of the set passed without incident. When the show ended, the audience gave the entire cast a polite ovation, but when Christian Valentine came out from behind the curtains they stood and went absolutely wild. Especially the women. I was mighty impressed.

The houselights came on and the band played softly as the customers made their way out of the showroom. Rachel excused herself to go back-stage.

"Do you like to gamble, Yolanda?" I asked, trying to make small talk.

She stabbed out her umpteenth cigarette in the ashtray and sipped at her fresh cognac. "No," she said, shaking her head, then trying to focus on me. "I hate to lose." When she said the word *lose,* it came out rhyming with *rouge.*

We were alone in the huge room now, except for our waiter who was cleaning up in preparation for the midnight show. The lights were on and I could see where Yolanda must have been one heck of a looker back in her twenties. She was still an attractive lady, but on closer inspection she appeared a trifle worn.

I wondered what Rachel would look like at her age. She was fast approaching thirty and I was pushing forty — not exactly a May/December relationship. Hopefully she found slightly older men appealing.

As I was racking my brain trying to think of something to say to Yolanda that wouldn't be nosy, or impolite, a deep laugh broke the silence of the cavernous showroom.

Christian Valentine and Rachel came out from behind a burgundy vel-vet curtain. He had one hand fondling Rachel's shoulder and the other lovingly around a flute of champagne.

It was hard for me to tell which he was enjoying more.

As they approached, Yolanda Valentine slid over to make room. The table was built to seat four comfortably, but Yolanda was so close to me we could have squeezed in six. Her warm thigh and friendly calf were pressed tightly against mine, and if I hadn't had a mild buzz building from all the free booze, I probably could have made more room. But I didn't.

Christian Valentine helped Rachel slide into the seat, then he came over and shook my hand and told me how pleased he was to meet me. I tried not to be obvious as I checked for "wardrobe" evidence. He leaned toward Yolanda and gave her a peck on the cheek. He didn't seem to be such a bad guy.

The entertainer knocked back his drink in one long pull and then said to his wife, "Hey, honeybunch. I didn't know you were coming tonight."

"It was one of those last-minute things," she explained.

Valentine appeared to think about it for a moment. "You know I've told you to let me know when you're going out."

"I'm a big girl," she said sweetly. "I can take care of myself." She blew a loud trail of gray smoke in his general direction. "Besides," she continued, "I was bored out of my mind sitting around the house."

"That's not the point," he said sternly. "The point is, we have rules."

"No we don't," she argued politely. "*You* have rules."

"Whatever," he sighed. "We'll talk about it later. Right now, I need a refill." He picked up a spoon and tapped his glass loud.

"Hey, Chico!" he barked. "How 'bout some vino, *por favor*?"

From the hurt look in the boy's eyes, I could tell his name wasn't Chico.

"Yes sir, Mr. Valentine," he said meekly, making his way slowly to the kitchen.

Valentine seemed pleased with himself. "These Mex kids love it when a gringo talks their lingo." His face lit up. "*Gringo lingo*. That's a good one!" He was still laughing as he unwrapped the gold foil band from an impressive-looking cigar.

The fresh feeling that I'd just had about him began to sour with his every word.

Valentine was wearing an expensive white silk shirt, loose-fitting and open to the navel. Two or three gold chains were buried beneath a thick growth of chest hair. He was tall and well proportioned, bigger than he appeared on stage. His wavy black hair was freshly washed and sprayed.

His skin was pink and wrinkle-free, well kept, I thought, for a man his age. I figured he had to be fifty, maybe fifty-five, almost old enough to be my father. Now I wasn't exactly out of shape, but Valentine was in good enough condition to make me feel a bit envious. His wife's chummy leg resting against mine made up for it.

While the girls made small talk, I watched Valentine as he carefully clipped the end of his cigar. When he finally finished, he lit it with a gold Dunhill lighter encrusted with diamonds and blew an obnoxious cloud of smoke my way. He held the cigar out, admiring it.

"Cuban," he said, pointing it in my direction for approval. "Spics know how to roll a good stogie." He pulled another from a gold case and offered it to me.

"No, thanks," I said, politely. "I grew out of most of my oral fixations."

He stopped in mid-puff. Rachel kicked me in the shin. Valentine put on his serious face and studied mine. I studied him right back. He looked over at Rachel, back to me, and then exhaled with a gusty laugh. "Oral fixations! That's a good one."

Yolanda said "Jesus Christ" under her breath, barely loud enough for me to hear. She finished her cognac, wrapped a paper napkin around an unfinished glass of champagne, and excused herself from my side.

"Where you goin', hon?" asked Valentine.

Yolanda had a solemn look on her face. "I've got things to do." She nodded politely to Rachel and me, then turned and left.

The waiter arrived with the champagne and a fresh bucket of ice. Christian reached into his pocket, gave the kid a handful of small change, and told him, "Gratzy ass, Chico."

When the waiter left, he added in a lecturing tone, "You don't want to give them too much. It only encourages more of them to sneak over the border."

I began to wonder what the hell I was doing here feeding this maniac's ego. Then I remembered Rachel.

"I see," I said, proud of keeping it at that.

"So, what did you think of my show, Mr. Morgan?"

"It was good. Very enjoyable. I've seen parts of it before, but I really liked the guy with the ping-pong —"

"Could you hear me okay up here? I've had a bit of a sore throat last couple of days and thought I might lose a bit off my high octave."

"You sounded fine." I chewed lightly on my lower lip, getting the urge to start smoking again. "These were great seats."

"Well, as long as you could hear me."

He poured himself a glass of champagne and waited for the bubbles to settle. "Mr. Morgan," he said, dipping his finger into his drink and running a circle around the rim of the glass until it started humming. "I was wondering if you and I could have a little powwow."

A tiny smile passed over my lips as I realized he really talked this way. "Sure. Shoot, Kemosabe."

Valentine looked up from his drink and over to Rachel, then over to me again. "No, I mean just you and me. You know, *mano a mano.*"

I glanced over at Rachel for help. "Well, I thought I'd drive Rachel out to —"

"Come on," he laughed, tapping ash from his cigar. "You two lovebirds can get together later." He reached into his pocket and pulled out a silver Navaho money clip embedded with a highly polished green stone. He slipped a fifty from a gaggle of others, opened Rachel's fingers, put the bill in, and closed up her hand.

"Sweetheart, be a doll," he said, patting her clenched fist and smiling magnificently. "There's cabs out front, and you're a big girl. Can you loan me . . ." He glanced in my direction.

"Jake," I prompted sullenly.

Rachel thought for a moment. I prayed she would save me from such cruel punishment. But she didn't.

"Right." She picked up her purse and gave me a kiss on the cheek. "Thanks, Jake. Maybe we can get together again sometime. 'Night, Christian," she said as she left the room.

Valentine gulped down the last half of his drink and stood. "Great girl," he said. "Come on, Jake. Let's go up to my suite. It's a lot more comfortable."

He lifted the hundred-dollar bottle of champagne from the bucket and turned it over so it bubbled out into the icy water. "You don't want the dishwashers getting into the good stuff," he advised me. He turned and walked away, circling his hand for me to follow.

Regretfully, I kissed off any thoughts of the romantic conclusion I'd envisioned for the evening. I pulled a twenty from my pocket and left the tip on the table, surprised to find Yolanda's expensive silk jacket still on the seat. I draped it over my arm and caught up with Valentine.

"Tonight's your lucky night, Jake!" he told me.

Something told me the last thing I was going to get tonight was lucky.

Chapter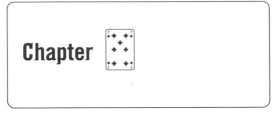

"Have a seat, Jake."

After hanging Yolanda's jacket in the foyer closet I sat as instructed in a chrome tubular chair that didn't look at all supportive or even remotely comfortable. As it turned out, it was. But I wasn't.

"Drink?"

"Cold beer," I answered. "If you've got one."

Valentine chuckled. "If I've got one. That's good."

The white walls and pale gray carpet made the room light and airy. A bust of Valentine mounted on a marble pedestal sat in front of a wall filled with splashy abstract paintings.

When he turned the sculpted head counterclockwise, the wall of paintings vanished quietly into the ceiling. An elaborate, well-stocked bar appeared in its place.

I considered applauding.

"Any particular country?" he asked.

"Pardon?"

"Any particular country you prefer your beer from?" He pressed a button on the bar and another portion of wall slid away, this time to the side. A vast selection of bottled beer stared back at me. Valentine waved an arm toward the inside.

"Thirty-seven for you to choose from," he boasted.

"Look, Mr. Valentine," I said. "I'll take whatever you pick." I glanced down at my watch and wondered where Rachel might be. "Besides, I thought we came here for a . . . a powwow."

"Right you are, Jake." He chose a bottle at random, flipped off the cap with an opener, selected a glass from a rack above his head and brought both to me. "Right you are."

The beer was cold, unpronounceable and from Africa.

A loud metallic click broke the momentary silence, and I froze. Unexpected noises made all cops skittish — even former ones. A glassy-eyed Asian girl appeared in an open doorway. She didn't say a word, but I heard the sounds of roiling water coming from the room. A vast, circular bed lay empty behind her, its pink satin spread trailing onto the carpet. A mirror of equal size and shape aimed down from the ceiling.

But the scenery in front was far more compelling: glossy black hair down to her hips and a wisp of silk that left nothing to the imagination.

"Mitsou!" Valentine barked sharply, like one of the animal trainers in his show. "Back to your room!" He glanced at me, shaking his head. "Gimme a sec', Jake."

At the bar, he read the back of one of the bottles, slid aside another panel and punched a set of numbers into a display on a wall safe. The door clicked open. After rummaging around for a minute, he came out with a small plastic bag. He tucked it into his shirt pocket, shut the safe, and excused himself again.

Something told me Mrs. Valentine would not be amused.

Being in such fancy surroundings, I bucked tradition and poured my beer into the glass and took a sip. It wasn't bad.

We were on the thirty-fourth floor, corner suite, floor-to-ceiling windows down both sides. I got up to browse.

The music room next door was lined with black-and-white photos of Valentine shaking hands with, or embracing, just about everybody who was anybody in show business. Studying them closer, I noticed he had the same smile in every picture. Practice does make perfect. A white baby grand piano sat on a raised platform overlooking the living room.

All the rooms I had seen so far were the work of a very good designer. Everything was coordinated: pastel colors, carpeting, walls, furniture. But the collection of medieval weapons and pieces of statuary scattered around the suite were superficial enough to have been Valentine's doing. Swords, lances, crossbows and blowguns lined most of the walls.

In college, I had gained a certain appreciation for ancient weaponry and Greek mythological art. But I had also been taught that art appreciation was like respect: it couldn't be bought — it had to be acquired.

The statuary was impressive, though somewhat out of place considering the rest of the suite. Apollo stood appropriately at the entrance to the music room, Zeus and Hera near the door to the bedroom, and Cerberus in the middle of a bank of windows overseeing the flashing neon of the Strip. A dark painting of Medea hung on a wall by itself.

I poked around here and there, admiring the art and the view. I tried to spot my building but couldn't.

Christian Valentine came out of the bedroom and closed the door with a gentle pull. "Sorry about the interruption," he said with a sheepish grin. He walked over to the bar, poured a healthy serving of cognac from a crystal decanter and took a large, manila envelope from the safe. He started toward me, noticed my empty glass and brought me another beer. This one was from Yugoslavia.

"Look, Mr. Valentine," I said, sitting again. "It's not that I don't appreciate your hospitality, I do, but . . ."

Valentine squeezed the two brass strips together and opened the envelope. He fished around inside and passed me the contents.

"Jake, I want you to check into something for me." He sat in a peach-colored, wingback chair, elbows on his knees, head tilted down, his sharp black eyes aimed firmly at my baby blues.

He passed two sets of papers to me. The first was composed of a number of gruesome photos and headlines from grocery store tabloids announcing the untimely deaths of a number of Hollywood favorites over the years. The second was a collection of weird, threatening letters with glued-on words from newspapers and glossy magazines. After sorting through them the way a poker player studies his cards, I said to him, "Okay, I give up."

Valentine gave me a disturbed expression.

"Hey, I'm sorry," I said. "But I don't see what this has to do with me. You'd be better off with the police." I handed the papers back to him but they were refused.

"I can't go to the cops with this," he exclaimed as if I should have known better. "There's a lot of what you could call . . . *discretion* required here." He raised an eyebrow at me. "I don't need any more attention from the media, Jake, if you get my drift."

I got his drift all right. "You mean your wife."

Valentine finished off his drink and made his way back to the bar. "Come on now, Jake," he said, pouring what appeared to be a double, maybe a double and a half. "Don't tell me you fish off the same dock, day in, day out." He sipped loud on his drink and stood in front of the bar, ankles crossed and a stupid smirk on his face.

"Look," I said, standing up slowly. "There's nothing I can do." I put the glass down. "Go to the police."

Valentine made his way over unsteadily. "You were a cop, right?"

"Yeah, right," I said, staring hard out the window. "Now I'm dealing downstairs as part of an elaborate undercover assignment."

Down below, a police cruiser was running interference for a fire engine and I could hear both sirens howling even from way up here. Then again, maybe the warning was meant for me.

"Let's just say I couldn't take the bullshit," I told him. "Or the discipline. I'd just as soon leave it at that." I turned to go. "Thanks for the beer."

One of Valentine's hands clamped my shoulder hard. "But Jake, that's exactly what I'm looking for."

I removed his hand and dropped it to his side. "Not a good thing to do," I warned him, with the help of a cold stare.

"Jake, Jake, Jake," he chided, easing me back into the chair. "You're too sensitive. You gotta learn to relax."

When he pulled his chair closer to mine, I figured we were finally getting around to the powwow.

"Jesus Christ, Jake. Didn't you read that stuff? Somebody out there wants to kill me if I don't pay up!" He wiped a hand across his lips. "Half a fuckin' million! Sure, I can go to the cops if I want to. But I can't afford the publicity. If I call in those bozos, the story'll get out for sure. Listen, Jake," he said in a serious voice. "I'm willing to pay for discretion."

The way I figured it, half a mil to Valentine was probably about twenty hours of singing to audiences that loved him. For me, it was about twenty years of dealing cards to people who ended up hating my guts. And although I didn't think half a million was so bad a restitution for his years of indiscretion, I decided to keep my mouth shut, for now.

After exhaling sharply through his nose, he spoke softly, as a father might to a son who doesn't understand. "Listen, Jake. I don't want anything official done here. Just sniff around a little. I'm 110 percent sure that whoever it is, is right here in the hotel or casino."

Valentine brushed the pile of paper in my hand. "This ain't fan mail! And you know it'll never stop there. They always come back for more. I just need someone to nose around a little, that's all. Find the asshole who's tugging on my leash. I'll take care of the rest." He found the room to chuckle. "I know people who can plug assholes."

"I'm sure you do," I agreed. "So why not get them involved now?"

"Jesus H. Christ, Jake," he cried, shaking his head as if I'd just peed on his carpet. "These people I know don't have brains like me and you. They're all muscle. Shit, I've got plenty of connections. I even know about you." He pulled a white index card from the envelope. "Let's see. You'll be forty next year; born and raised in Concord, New Hampshire. You went to Southern Maine, majored in math and art . . ." He thought about that for a moment, then said, "That's a strange combination."

"You should see me paint by numbers."

He pointed down at the sheet and continued. "Minored in ancient history. Dropped out in your senior year, joined the army for a two-year stint and then honorably discharged. After that it was twelve years with the Boston PD and then another honorable discharge." He slapped the paper and smiled. "You've had more discharges than a wino with VD!"

It was obvious he wasn't used to reading. Especially when drinking. He was pointing at the words and they were coming out slurred. But give him credit, he had done his homework.

"And now you're here," he continued, waving at the window and the neon lights outside. "Lost Wages, Nevada. Home of every derelict, loser, hooker and part-time pimp that got their ass reamed on their way from New York to L.A." He picked an ice cube from his drink and chewed on it. "Shit, I even know that your real given name is . . ." He rummaged around in the envelope. "I know it's in here somewhere . . . real funny one, too . . ."

"Okay," I said, wanting to change the subject. "You've made your point." I swirled the remainder of my beer around in the bottom of the glass. "So you know all about me. So what?"

"Jake, I'm not just any entertainer. I'm a *star*! I've made a fortune and

I'm damn good at what I do. I'm the *best!*" He flung his arm out for emphasis and lost the rest of his drink.

"But fuck it," he continued. "I'm not paying a dime to some lousy blackmailer. I'll see him dead first."

Now that I'd had some exposure, I realized big stars were just like candy bars; most of them were nutty, but some were nuttier than others.

I stood, shaking my head. "You need professional help."

"Dammit, Jake! I told you I don't want a professional. I want you!"

I walked by the window to return my glass to the bar and couldn't help but look out to see if there was a full moon. As luck would have it, there was.

"Being a dealer, people around here have seen you before. They won't think twice about you hanging around the hotel. Or, now that I've gotten you closer to Rachel, even backstage. Just nose around. Whoever's sending me this crap will probably get scared off when they hear somebody's asking questions. And if you find 'em and they don't, well, like I said, I'll have someone take care of the son of a bitch."

He took a great big breath and blew it out loudly through his mouth. "Jake, what do you make? Four or five hundred a week? I'll pay you two-fifty a day just to ask questions in your spare time. Keep your day job. I don't care. Just give me a couple of hours a day for a week or two. What do you say?"

Two-fifty a day for a couple of weeks would put more than three grand into my account. Added to what I had in there wouldn't put the total over four, but still, the thought was enticing.

"I don't think so, Mr. Valentine. Thanks anyway."

He leaned both arms on the bar and I swear I heard his smile click into place. "Chrissake, Jake. You haven't even got five hundred bucks in the bank. If nothing else," he reasoned, "do it for the money."

He really did have connections. "What gave me away? The suit?"

Valentine picked at a spot on his snifter, deep in apparent thought, then he reached back into the safe and pulled out another envelope. It looked like he was playing his ace.

"Come on, I don't want to see any more letters," I said in a tired voice. "Let me try and explain it to you in plain, simple English." I stared at him, eye to eye. "Number one: I can't help you. I'm not qualified for this kind of thing. Hell, I wouldn't even know where to begin. And number two: I don't want to help you. The only reason I'm here talking to you at all is because Rachel asked me to. And number three? Sure I need the money, but I don't need it this bad."

I started for the door. *"Adios, amigo."*

As I walked by him, he pulled out two torn pieces of an eight-by-ten glossy and fitted them together on top of the bar. He gave them a lengthy examination, so I glanced over.

It was a publicity shot of him and Rachel, announcing her upcoming move in the show. The two of them were smiling brightly, arms around each other's waist. They wouldn't have been smiling quite so radiantly if they'd known someone was going to scrawl *Death to you and the bitch* across their photo in bright red lipstick.

He *had* played an ace. And it just about completed his hand.

"Jake, I'm gonna give you one last chance. Do what I asked. You'll make yourself a few bucks and I'll even make sure Rachel treats you right."

I gave him a wary look.

"No, I don't mean like that! I mean I'll make sure she spends some time with you backstage and around the cast and crew. I'll get you in the door, but the rest is up to you. Play your cards right and you could fill that inside straight yourself. And besides," he continued, glancing down at the photo again. "I'm apparently not the only one being threatened here."

He had me there. To cover my anxiety, I went to the bar, pressed the button that opened the fridge and grabbed a cold Molson's. Before I opened the bottle I held it against my forehead to forestall the migraine I felt coming on. I couldn't care less about Valentine, but I was concerned about Rachel. I wasn't exactly sure where the two of us might go, but I knew it wouldn't be far if I didn't have Valentine in my corner. He was dealing the cards in her career game.

"Okay," I said, twisting off the cap. "It's five hundred a day — plus expenses — and a grand up front as a retainer."

Valentine smiled and reached into his pocket. "Two-fifty a day and there shouldn't be any expenses." He peeled off five one-hundred dollar bills and fanned them across the bar for effect. "Shouldn't take more than a week or two, right, Jake?"

I drank thoughtfully, straight from the bottle, and pondered my predicament. Eventually I picked up the bills from the bar and weighed them, then I folded them in half and put them inside my jacket pocket. I clinked his glass with the edge of my bottle.

"Right, boss."

Chapter

I woke up late the next morning with my head throbbing mildly. As I stared at the ceiling fan circling above, I couldn't decide if the pulse was the result of the booze or a pact I'd made with the devil. I mulled over my decision to help Valentine and Rachel and, after a long, steaming shower and a cup of extra-strong coffee, felt ready to attack the day.

I didn't, however, feel up to clearing the mountain of garbage that was accumulating around the apartment. I knew I would have to tidy up soon. My cleaning lady was due in a few days, and I was always embarrassed to leave a disaster area for her.

It felt strange pulling into the staff parking lot on my day off. My first stop inside the Oasis was the gift shop, where I purchased a black spiral notebook and a couple of pens. Just to prove Valentine wrong, I kept the receipt for expenses.

The next stop was the Sports Book located at the far end of the casino. After squaring up with the cable company on my way to the hotel, I still had 380 of Valentine's bucks burning a hole in my pocket. I made my way through the crowded casino aisles, dodging children in bathing suits carrying Pokemon balloons tied to strings.

Vegas certainly had changed.

I finally arrived at the Sports Book and was elated to find the Bosox just nine-to-five favorites over Texas. Martinez was pitching for Boston and some no-name kid was on the mound for the Rangers. I rushed up to the window before the oddsmakers had a chance to change their minds.

"Curtis," I said to my fellow employee behind the cage, "gimme the Bo', and quick!" I peeled off four twenties and a crisp hundred and slapped them on the counter.

Curtis gave me a smile and laughed. "Jake, what the hell you doin'? Payday's four days off. You come into an inheritance?"

"Yeah," I smiled back. "Something like that."

"You're sure now?" he asked, fanning the bills for the camera above. "You haven't been running that well."

"Never mind. This is Pedro!" I felt a giggle building up. "In Fenway for God's sake!"

With my $180 working at nine-to-five odds, I'd make a hundred bucks clear and tax-free and almost be back to the five hundred Valentine had started me with.

Curtis punched up the slip on the computer and handed me my copy. He wished me luck.

"Luck," I told him philosophically, pointing at the betting slip, "is preparation meeting opportunity."

Rachel was in the dressing room with a few of the other girls from the show. She was wearing a bright turquoise spandex aerobics outfit and black stockings, her lean body glistening from a hard workout. She rubbed a towel vigorously through her hair and draped it around her neck.

Rachel noticed me and called out, "Jake, we were just talking about you."

The others smiled and said hello, except for Leona Carter, the girl whose part Rachel was taking. She was sitting by herself in a corner, facing a mirror and brushing her hair slowly as if it really didn't matter. I could see a trickle of tears in the reflection of the mirror and a tired, aged look on her beautiful young face. I asked Rachel if we could take a short walk.

"Leona's taking her leaving pretty hard," I said.

We were sitting at a table in the showroom, watching a dance routine by members of the chorus. Rachel was sipping on an orange drink.

"I don't know," she said thoughtfully, "some of it might be that, but I think it probably has more to do with what's going on inside her, being pregnant." She stirred her drink slowly back and forth with a hotel swizzle stick. "Raising a child on her own."

"That's tough. Especially in this town."

"In any town," Rachel answered sadly.

My head nodded in agreement.

"So how did it go with Christian last night?" she asked.

"He talked. I listened. He's a real piece of work."

"So what was the big mystery? Why did he want to talk with you?"

"Well, I found out what was making him so edgy."

I told her about the blackmail threats and his decision to keep things away from the media. I decided not to worry her with the photograph of her and Valentine.

"Jesus," she said when I had finished. "No wonder he's been looking over his shoulder so much and asking so many questions."

"Well," I said, "I think there might be a little more to it. He seems more worried than he should be over some juvenile-looking threats. I've got a feeling there are some other issues. Whoever's sending these to him might have something else on him he's not telling me about."

"And he thinks you can help?"

"Apparently."

I told her Valentine wanted me to keep my ears and eyes open, around the casino, the break room and even backstage. I explained that he might ask her to help me by allowing me to be with her occasionally around the cast and crew.

She thought about it for a moment and then said, "I guess I could . . . if he thinks it'll really help."

Not the ringing endorsement I had hoped for, but it was a start all the same.

I went on to explain that she should keep her eyes and ears open, too, and that she could call me with anything she might learn. I tore out a sheet from my notebook and gave her my number.

She looked at it for a moment, then folded it in half. "So, I suppose you're going to need my number, too?" she asked. "For professional reasons, of course."

"Of course." I gave her my hundred-watt smile. "I'll try not to abuse the privilege."

Rachel took the notebook and pen. "Yeah, we'll see . . ."

We watched the end of the routine in silence, then walked back to the dressing room. Rachel said she had to shower and change, and that maybe we could get together later for a drink if she learned anything from the girls.

I told her that would be just fine by me.

When she left, the dressing room was empty for the moment, the sounds of spraying water and girlish laughter echoing from around the corner. There wasn't much to do, so I figured I might as well start earning my pay. I decided to start nosing around.

On my way out I noticed a folded piece of paper lying on the floor beside Leona's chair. I walked over, picked it up and, like any good detective, nonchalantly lifted the corner. It read: *Meet me at the lounge. 5 p.m. Sharp!*

It would have been a most natural kind of invitation, except for the exclamation mark. I tucked the paper back again, wondering if it was the note that had been bothering Leona earlier. I checked my watch. It was just after four.

Backstage, I found a number of men busy at work, repairing and building and taking down sets. The stage manager, Murray Gladstone, was overseeing things. I had met Murray a few months ago at a poker game. He was short and stocky, late fifties, jet-black hair thinning at the temples and slicked back into what my old man used to call a "duck's ass." He was a happy-go-lucky kind of guy with a mischievous face and the disposition of your favorite uncle.

Murray pulled a pencil from behind his ear and checked off something on a clipboard. As he glanced around, he noticed me.

"Jake, long time no see!" A wide smile came to his face and he extended a hand. It was tough and calloused, and it felt as if I were shaking hands with an old leather baseball glove.

"Been playing in a game over at Kenny's place," I told him. "I meant to drop by to see you, but I've been working the swing shift last month or so."

Murray nodded, then he picked up a tool belt and strapped it on. He took a handful of nails from a box on the floor and dropped them into a pouch on his belt. "I work afternoons, take a few hours off, then come back for two shows. Don't get home until around two or three in the morning." He started tapping nails into what appeared to be the beginning of a garden trellis. "And that's only providing nothing goes wrong during the late show."

"That's why you get paid the big bucks, Mur."

"Yeah, right," he laughed. "So what's this I hear? About you and Rachel Sinclair."

News certainly traveled fast. And far.

"Ah, it wasn't like that," I explained. "She was supposed to watch Leona's part from the audience. And I guess she didn't want to go alone."

Murray looked up at me skeptically. "Yeah, and out of a couple thousand eligible bachelors around here, she picked an old fart like you?"

"Yep. I've asked her out three times in the last two months, but she kept turning me down. I think she might have been making it up to me. To tell you the truth, Murray, I'm really hoping it'll continue. I'd like to see a lot more of her."

"Can't blame you," he agreed. "She seems like a nice girl. Real pretty, too."

"Sure is," I said, hoisting a hefty power tool from his portable work bench. "What's this?"

"Jesus Christ, Jake!" he cautioned with a hand up in the air. "Aim that away." I did as I was told. "It's a nail gun," he explained, "for driving nails through heavy board or concrete." He was visibly relieved when I put it back on the bench. "It'll go right through a man."

I thought about wearing the nail gun in a shoulder holster for my last shift with McClusky. I wondered if it would fire pens.

"Murray," I said, "you see just about everything that goes on around here. Have you seen anything strange going on the last few weeks? Anybody acting out of sorts? Somebody bad-mouthing somebody else?"

Murray stopped his hammering. "Like what?" he asked, not looking at me.

"Anything," I said in a confidential voice. "You know, sour grapes over changes in the show, jealousy over who's making how much money, maybe a romantic liaison gone bad."

"Christ, Jake, half the goddamn guys in the cast are screwin' the broads in the show. The other half of the guys are screwin' each other!" He fitted two pieces of the trellis together. "Hand me that two-by-four, Jake?"

I passed him the three-foot length of wood that lay by my foot. He stood the trellis on the two-by-four and asked me to hold it for him. He took out some longer nails and began to hammer the trellis to its base.

"What about Valentine?" I asked nonchalantly. "Anybody making any waves with him?"

Up to now, Murray had been perfect in his aim. But as soon as I mentioned Valentine's name, he missed the nail completely and drove the hammerhead deep into the board beneath. He seemed to catch himself and resumed hammering properly.

"What about Valentine?" he asked.

"I don't know," I said, waving it off as if it didn't really matter. "Rachel mentioned she thought he'd been acting strange lately. As if something, or someone, was bothering him."

"Not that I've noticed, Jake. Then again, Christian Valentine and I don't exactly travel in the same circles. If you know what I mean."

"Yeah, well, I don't travel in those circles either," I said in agreement, "but if you see or hear anything, let me or Rachel know, okay? She's worried about him. Thinks it might affect her new part. If you can help me, it might go a long way with my winning some brownie points with Rachel."

Murray finally looked up at me. He appeared pale and beads of perspiration glistened on his forehead. "Sure, Jake. I'll see ya around."

The Camel's Hump was the closest thing to a lounge the Oasis had, so I figured it was the best spot to watch for Leona and see who wanted to meet her at 5 p.m. *Sharp!* I had left a note for Rachel with the security guard at the dressing room entrance saying that's where I would be.

The Hump was raised high and afforded a good overall view of the casino and two other bars. In the evening, a piano player crooned romantic love songs, and some of the most gorgeous ladies in the world could be found here — for a price. Hence the name, I suppose. Right now it was practically empty, and I was the cutest thing around.

It was a quarter to five and neither Rachel nor Leona had shown. I sat nursing a Bloody Mary all by myself.

The huge casino was beginning to fill with the late-afternoon crowd, the ones who had partied until dawn and were just now rising for scrambled eggs and a round of gambling to get back in the swing of things.

A large black woman playing one of the slot machines off to my right let out an ear-piercing shriek and I almost lost the rest of my drink. She started jumping up and down, screaming "I won! I won!" at the top of her lungs.

As a group formed around her to find out what all the fuss was about, I happened to notice Leona pushing her way through. She was running toward the front entrance as fast as her high heels and tight, silky yellow dress would allow. There wasn't time to finish my drink, or to let Rachel know, so I got up and tried to catch up with the fleeing woman.

By the time I made it out through the automatic doors, I was just able to catch a glimpse of bright yellow cloth disappearing behind a dirty brown cab door.

My car was way around back in the employee parking lot. Not that it mattered. The Chevy was well past her cab-chasing days.

I knew a real detective would hail the next taxi, so that's exactly what I did. One pulled up right on cue, and before it came to a complete stop, I jerked open the back door and jumped in.

The driver was a middle-aged, heavyset guy with a marine haircut. He wore a thin tank top that showed most of his hairy shoulders and some of his hairy back. He rolled an ancient cigar around between his thick, wet lips and looked around at me as if I were psycho.

Leona's taxi was pulling out of the driveway and heading east down Flamingo Road.

"Follow that cab!" I instructed him. Just like in the movies.

The driver dragged his damp stogie from the corner of his mouth to spit away a fleck of tobacco. "Where the fuck you think you are?" he asked. "New York?"

I dangled a twenty over the front seat and he grabbed it in one swipe of his beefy paw, then he spat out his window, slapped down the flag of his antique meter and began singing loudly: "Start spreadin' the news . . ."

He was no Sinatra, but he wasn't bad. There was a lot of hidden talent on the streets of Las Vegas. As we motored down Flamingo, in hot pursuit, I took out my book and jotted down a few more notes. I didn't have many clues to go on, but the expenses were starting to add up.

Chapter

When we started out I was afraid we might lose Leona's cab because of stoplights and turns, but surprisingly that wasn't the case. Even more surprising was that we never made a single lane change, much less a turn. I almost felt I wasn't getting my money's worth.

We drove for fifteen minutes straight down Flamingo, the cabbie having stopped singing, now concentrating on his driving. I had no idea where we were heading. There weren't any bars or hotels out here, just rows of condominiums and strip malls. Boring Las Vegas suburbia. I knew we would have to turn soon, because the road sign said Boulder Highway was just ahead.

Her taxi made a right at the highway and then a quick left. We followed as it rolled into Sam's Town, an Old West-motif casino, a tourist trap for the bus trade on the way to Hoover Dam and Lake Mead.

Leona dashed from her taxi and hurried into the door marked "Saloon." My taxi bounced over the numerous speed bumps like a fat man making love on a waterbed, and when we finally came to a shuddering stop, I paid the driver and followed her inside.

The saloon was bigger than it appeared from the outside. I made my way carefully to the bar to let my eyes adjust to the sudden change of light. An oldtime bartender, complete with arm garter and handlebar moustache, wiped at a spot on the bar nearby. I sat down, ordered a Miller Lite, and he nodded his approval at my choice.

It wasn't much of a bar, eight or nine stools and a handful of tables, but it looked out over a small casino of a dozen or so blackjack tables and a stage with more tables and a few booths. I wasn't surprised to see Leona there, but I was shocked to see Christian Valentine.

I sipped at my beer and tried to look inconspicuous, plopping silver dollars in the video poker game built into the bar top.

Although I couldn't hear what was going on at their table, I could see they were in a heated discussion. She appeared to be trying to reason with him. I could appreciate her dilemma.

For a minute I thought Leona might have something to do with the blackmail threats, except blackmailers don't usually start crying.

My new employer was making an emphatic point to her face with a finger, then he laughed and held his palms out and shrugged his shoulders. Leona wiped at her eyes with a tissue.

Valentine surveyed his surroundings, seemingly pleased with himself, and although I was well hidden by a wooden pillar and the natural darkness of the bar, I placed a hand over my forehead and contemplated their meeting, as well as the four-card straight flush on the video screen.

It really didn't make a whole lot of sense — Leona being the blackmailer — but I wondered what the two of them could be getting so worked up about. Whatever it was, it didn't make me feel any better toward Valentine. For a guy who had pleaded for help the night before, he certainly didn't appear to be the victim right now.

I punched a button to discard the lone spade on my screen. The king of diamonds smiled up at me, matching in suit with the five, six, seven and eight. The machine began paying off eighteen silver dollars, which crashed loudly into the aluminum bucket.

Certain both of them had heard the racket, I covered my face and peeked through my fingers. Valentine was standing at the side of their booth. He reached into his jacket pocket and pulled out a thick, white envelope. After tapping it on the edge of the table, he spoke to her with a serious look on his face, then he tossed the envelope toward her, turned, and walked away.

Thirty seconds later, Leona left too, shoving the envelope into her purse along with the soiled tissues.

It wasn't the time to approach either one of them, so I hung around the bar, had another Lite, and lost back my winnings plus another twenty of my own.

At the rate I was going, I'd need another part-time job to help me pay my way through this one.

Chapter

I tried calling Rachel at the hotel and found she had already left. When I tried her at home, there was no answer. On the way back to the Oasis, I stopped at the Mirage to contemplate the Leona–Valentine rendezvous over a fabulous all-you-can-eat buffet. The fact that I had a "comp" from the Mirage poker room made it even more fabulous. Not only was it free, but I got to enter the comp line, which was practically empty.

By the time I had finished a mixed salad and a couple of crusty rolls, I'd concluded that Valentine must have been paying Leona off for something. For what, I had no idea.

After a heaping plate of tasty chicken cacciatore and a couple servings of lasagna, I still hadn't come up with any answers. I picked away at a piece of apple pie and a caramel tart and still came up with nothing. The waitress came by with a carafe of coffee and a toothpick, and when she left I nonchalantly loosened my belt one notch. The Valentine and Leona get-together didn't make any more sense, but I sure felt better thinking about it on a full stomach.

Christian Valentine might have been paying me a good amount of money, but he sure wasn't being straight. He had sent me off on some kind of wild goose chase, and I wondered how much he was really holding back.

I found room for rice pudding and another cup of coffee, then I made my way through the casino and over to the Mirage's Sports Book. It was just after seven and, with the time change, the game should have been wrapping up back in Boston.

The board showed the Red Sox ahead five-nothing at the top of the eighth and I granted myself a congratulatory smile. Feeling as good as I did, I decided to walk back to the Oasis.

Pedro Martinez could do that to you.

·

The Strip was beginning to build with the Friday-night crowd driving in from California, and although the sun was still high over the Las Madres mountains to the west, most of the hotels had their neon flashing at full wattage.

The temperature was still hovering somewhere in the eighties, so I took my time walking and managed to make it to the Oasis without losing my dinner or breaking out in a major sweat. At the showroom, security advised me Rachel was out, and remembering she wasn't scheduled to be in the show for the next few nights, I went back out to find a pay phone.

Since I had lost all my change at the video poker game, I dug in my pocket for a bill. Seeing the Red Sox wager slip reminded me of the $280 I had coming to me. With the slip in my hand and a smile on my face, I decided to go collect.

Curtis was fanning through receipts at the counter, and when he saw me he shook his head sadly back and forth.

"Was it ever in doubt?" I smiled, wiggling the betting slip in front of me.

Curtis raised an eyebrow and pointed to the board behind him, which listed the scores.

"Ahh, don't tell me . . ." I said, peeking up at the board.

"Well, Fenway can do that to you, Jake!"

"No kidding." I bunched up the slip and tossed it into an ashtray and made my way to the lobby.

After trading a dollar for four quarters from a change girl in the slot area, I called Rachel at home. She answered on the third ring.

"Hello," she said tentatively.

"Rachel, it's Jake."

"Oh, Jake. Thank God it's you!"

I pumped my fist and silently mouthed the word "*Yes!*" Then I heard her sniffling and came back to Earth.

"Are you okay?" I asked.

She took the time to let out a long breath. "I've been robbed!"

Chapter Jack ♦

"You all right?"

We were standing in Rachel's living room, waiting for the police to arrive.

"Yeah, I guess so," she said with a shudder.

It was your typical boot-and-shoot, a quick hit by a couple of druggies who had probably already fenced whatever they had taken long before Rachel had even arrived home.

At least there didn't appear to be much damage. As a cop I had seen enough B&E's to know that the worst part could be the vandalism. In many cases, the perps would ruin everything they couldn't take. They would slash furniture and paintings, smash artwork and personal items, and break every mirror in the place, as if doing so would somehow make them invisible from their own consciences. If you were really unfortunate, you would find a surprise "dropping" in your kitchen or, worse, on your bed.

"Did they take anything?"

Rachel looked around the room, hugging herself as if she were cold.

"Not much." She bent over and picked up a fallen cushion and tucked it into the corner of the sofa. "Not from what I can tell."

She walked over to the wall unit and picked up a chrome photo frame that had been knocked over. It was a picture of an older couple arm in arm, smiling as they swung on a porch swing.

"I guess I shouldn't be touching anything," she said, looking at the photo for a long time before placing it in an empty spot on the shelf.

"Probably won't matter," I explained. "They don't dust for simple break-and-enters. They usually just take down a list of what's missing, see if you've recorded serial numbers like you were supposed to — which nobody does — and ask if you noticed any suspicious characters lurking about in the past few days."

She thought about that for a moment.

"Did you find how they got in?" I asked.

"Through the kitchen. The window on the back door is broken — *Jesus!* — remind me to get that fixed. I wouldn't be able to sleep knowing . . ." She glanced over at me.

"Don't worry," I said. "If you've got a hammer and some nails, I'll take care of it." I wanted to tell her I'd stay the night, too, but thought better of it.

She let out a sigh of relief. "It looks as if they took most of my jewelry, not that it was worth much. The CD player is gone and some of the good silverware . . ." She forced a smile. "All in all, I guess it could have been worse."

I gave her an encouraging smile back.

There was a sharp knock at the door. Rachel went to answer. I took a seat.

It took about a half hour, give or take a question or two. A young uniformed cop jotted down the information that I had outlined to Rachel. He had poked around the broken window and told her they wouldn't be dusting for prints. He did, however, bag a couple of cigarette butts left behind on the kitchen floor. Neither Rachel nor I smoked. Her roommates Cassandra and Amber did, but they were up in Tahoe for the weekend, and Rachel didn't think either one smoked French Gauloises.

After the cop left, I hammered a piece of plywood over the broken window. Rachel said she had to go back to the Oasis to catch the second half of the show. I offered her a lift, and during the drive I told her about my trip out to Sam's Town. She was as confused about the events as I was, and said she would make a few discreet inquiries with some of the other dancers.

We separated at the hotel, Rachel going backstage and me toward the Hump. I told her to page me if she learned anything from the girls. Remembering it was Friday night, I stopped by the Sports Book and picked up a parlay sheet and a *Racing Form* for the Saturday card at Del Mar.

The bar was crowded, but I found a table in the far corner and nursed a Bud Light, pondering the past performances in the *Form* without much concentration or excitement. In place of the piano player, a country band was now onstage. The singer began telling the audience how he learned about love in his daddy's '67 Ford pickup, and right on cue a couple of the working girls wiggled by and asked if I wanted to play a television game show with them. Their version was called "If the Price Is Right." Not wanting to give the girls a complex, I put a sullen expression on my face and told them I had just lost everything at the tables. They could relate to that and left me alone.

When the singer suddenly segued into a tale of how he'd lost his job, his girl, his boots and his dog, I folded up my *Racing Form* and made my way to the dealers' break room.

Break time must have nearly been over, because the front half of the room was filled with cigarette smoke. Holding my breath, I made my way through the usual banter and frivolity toward the nonsmoking area at the rear. A couple of guys said they had seen me with Rachel the night before, and gave me the thumbs up with a wink. I smiled and gave them the thumbs up back, but didn't bother winking.

Some of the dealers were reading, some were playing video games.

Others were watching any one of the many televisions. For one of the few times that I could remember, no one was watching the set that was permanently locked on ESPN; apparently truck-and-tractor pulls had lost their luster.

I took a seat on a sofa in the corner. In a few minutes the room cleared, first of people, then of smoke, and with nothing but the hum of the air conditioning to distract me, I unfolded my *Form* and fell pleasantly into a deep rumination.

By the time the next wave of dealers rolled in and lit up, I had decided to confront Valentine about his meeting with Leona. I had to find out what the envelope transaction had been about.

If Valentine was jerking me around, fine. At $250 a day I could be jerked, but I wanted to know for my own peace of mind. At least then I could tread freely and not worry whether I was really earning my money. Or that Rachel was actually in danger.

Suddenly the door to the room flew open, and McClusky's full figure filled the doorway. The coach did not look happy.

"Where the fuck is she?"

The group became quiet. Remote controls were picked up and television sets silenced. Cards stopped being shuffled.

McClusky surveyed the room and found who he was looking for. His target was sitting by herself on another sofa down at my end, sipping on a diet soda while reading a paperback by Ayn Rand.

"What the hell do you think you were doin'?" he bellowed, stomping his way toward her.

She looked up from her book, glanced left and then right, pushed her eyeglasses up on her nose, and gave McClusky a "Who, me?"

"Who the hell else do you think I'm talkin' to!" he shouted, towering over her trembling frame. "The goddamn soda machine?" To further his point he walked over to the machine. "If I was talkin' to the goddamn machine, I'd be over here!" His face was bright crimson. "And if the goddamn machine hadda done what you did out there, I'd be doing this . . ." He gave the machine a healthy kick with the toe of his shoe. Hard enough that I heard a coin drop in the return.

McClusky's victim sat stonily in her seat. "What did —"

"Shut up and listen!" he yelled, breathing deeply and trying to control his words. "Now correct me if I'm wrong, but you don't understand Arabic, do you, Kellerman?"

Kellerman shook her head and began to open her mouth, but she thought about it and just shook her head again instead.

"Then why the hell did you keep hittin' him? You gotta make 'em use the hand signals when they want another card, for Chrissake!" He scratched at the air with his index finger. "Even rich oil sheiks! *Especially* rich oil sheiks!" he bawled. "You hit him when he hadn't scratched the felt yet! Then when you busted him, he said he didn't ask for another card and the eye-in-the-sky proved he hadn't. The friggin' cameras pick up motion, Kellerman, not sound! Ten thousand bucks and you went by a verbal? If you hadda waited he woulda hit on his own and busted!"

"Well, I thought —"

"Who asked you to think? Dealers aren't *supposed* to think. You're robots, for Chrissake! Just do as you're taught."

A buzzer sounded giving the dealers their one-minute warning, and for a change most of them appeared quite happy to get back to work.

"Ten thousand dollars!" McClusky lamented loudly. "You broads . . . sometimes I just wanna —"

"You wanna what?" shouted back Kellerman, standing up to leave, folding back the corner of the page of her paperback.

McClusky's eyes bulged and his mouth flapped open two or three times. The dealers who were leaving held their place.

"Okay, I'm sorry. I made a mistake," she agreed, "and I'll try not to do it again. But cut this horseshit!" She pointed a long red fingernail at his nose. "You raise your voice at me one more time, or threaten me in any way, and I'll grab you by the nuts and haul your ass up to the Human Rights Commission so fast it'll make your fat bald head spin!"

Kellerman sipped loudly on the last of her drink and tossed the can into the recycle container beside the machine. The sea of dealers parted to let her through, then followed, leaving me all alone with McClusky.

He gazed down at me, shaking his thick head dispiritedly, then he pulled out a handkerchief, dabbed at his wet forehead and sat heavily on the sofa beside me.

"Christ, Jake," he sighed wearily, "what the hell's this business comin' to? Twenty years ago, hell, even ten years ago, I could've picked her up by the scruff of her neck and tossed her Femi-Nazi ass out on the street. Now, with all these chickenshit rules and regulations . . . it's just not the same."

"Times change, I guess."

McClusky attempted a halfhearted smile. "Mind you, you don't go back that far, do you? What is it, six, seven months?" He wiped all around his beefy face.

"A year," I confessed.

When he finished wiping he said, "That long, huh? Christ, time flies . . ." He tucked the handkerchief back into his jacket. "But you're one of my aces, Morgan. You go out and do what you're paid to do. I can always count on you to go on in and get the money. Not like some of these wimps . . ."

"Thanks, coach."

"Yeah, I hate to lose you to the poker pit. You're sure I can't change your mind?"

"Nah," I told him. "As much as I like working with you, I gotta move on. You know, all the chickenshit rules and regulations . . . I just think poker will give me a little more freedom. And I feel the need to strike out in new directions."

"Yeah," he winked. "I saw you last night with that Rachel broad. Nice catch, Ace!"

"Well, I haven't caught her yet," I laughed. "But I'm working on it."

"I saw her a couple days ago, walkin' through the casino, wearin' this real tight sweater. I swear to God, it looked like two puppies playin' under a blanket." He shook his head at the memory. "By the way, how come you ain't dressed? You workin' the graveyard shift tonight?"

"No, it's my day off. I'm just hanging around, checking the races, seeing what's happening."

"Oh, that's right. I heard you was working for Valentine, helping him out on something."

I didn't try to hide my surprise. "How did you know?"

"Down at the Deli," he answered. "I was havin' a coffee and Franco dropped by. You know Franco, don't you?"

"Yeah," I nodded. "But how would he know what I was doing?"

"Who, Franco? Christ, him and Valentine are tighter than a sixty-year-old virgin."

"They're two of a kind," I ventured.

"Not just that," he added. "They're both gin rummy fanatics. They usually get together and play between shows. Just about every night. Helps Valentine unwind, I guess."

The next dealer shift was filing in. McClusky lifted his weight off the sofa. He leaned over to me, whispering. "From what I hear," he confided, "Franco's into Valentine *big time*."

McClusky straightened and tried to do up his jacket. It took a few moments to convince the button to enter the hole, but, when completed, he seemed satisfied. He pointed down at my *Form*.

"Fuckin' ponies'll be the death of you, Jake. Save your money and put it away for the fall." He gazed off dreamily. "College football, now *that's* excitin'!" With that, he was gone.

Well, at least now I was getting somewhere. So Valentine and Franco were gin buddies. And Franco was in the red. I didn't know how much, but "big time" in private games usually meant at least five figures. In the casino pits, it usually meant six.

The only clocks you could find anywhere near a Vegas casino were in the dealers' break room, and the one over the door told me it was just before twelve. The second show was about to begin and I still had an hour before the self-proclaimed star would go on.

I had no idea who Christian Valentine might have up to his suite tonight for fun and games, but I decided to confront him sooner rather than later. And I wanted his undivided attention. If he wanted me to work for him, fine, but he had some explaining to do.

Not only did his rendezvous with Leona bother me, I wanted to know how serious Franco was into him. And while I was at it, I'd ask him if he'd ever had a run-in with Murray, the stage manager.

I tucked away the notebook and the *Racing Form* and made my way upstairs to Valentine's suite. On the way out, I stopped at the pop machine and took out the coin McClusky had dislodged into the coin return.

It didn't quite make up for my loss on the Red Sox, but what the hell, it was a start.

Chapter

The hotel and casino were packed. The lengthy check-in line snaked through the main foyer, overlooking the busy gaming area and conveniently whetting the appetites of the hungry gamers.

The Oasis, like all Vegas hotels, was architecturally designed so that one could not possibly enter and get anywhere without having to go through the casino. Even if you were only there to grab a bite or to see a show, they wanted a shot at your wallet.

Because the break room was at the far rear of the casino, I was able to circumvent the hordes of people milling about. It wasn't quite enough, however, to stop me from losing my newfound quarter to a greedy slot machine while waiting at the busy bank of elevators.

Being the only person going up to the penthouses made for a slow ride, but eventually I got there. The floor was quiet except for the hum of a vacuum being worked over the deep pile carpeting in one of the open rooms at the far end of the hallway.

At Valentine's suite, I could hear the light sounds of pop music coming from behind his door. There was no answer to my knock. I knocked louder. Still no answer.

It seemed too early for Valentine to be doing a number on some young wannabe, but maybe he was playing gin rummy and couldn't hear me over the music. I knocked even louder.

The noise attracted the attention of the maid who had been vacuuming and was now rolling her cart of linen and cleaning equipment my way. She was a large, Hispanic woman in her early thirties, wearing a smile, but suspicious all the same.

"*Señor?*" she interrupted. "*Perdone.* You have business with *Señor* Valentine?"

"Ah, yes . . . *Sí*, I do." I pulled out my hotel identity card and held it up for her.

"Oh, *Señor* Morgan!" she announced enthusiastically. She was holding both hands to her ample bosom and beaming a wide smile my way as if we were long-lost friends.

"Do we know each other?" I asked, pointing to her and then to me.

"*Sí*," she nodded emphatically, "you are *Señorita* Rachel's boyfriend and you are the one helping *Señor* Valentine!"

I couldn't have been more shocked if I had just picked all fourteen winners on an NFL parlay card. "What? How could you know?"

"*Sí, sí.* My brother, Emilio," she explained. "He work as waiter. In Sultan's Tent room. He tell me you with *Señorita* Rachel and *Señor* Valentine at show last night." She paused and gave me an appealing look. "He tell me you not like some people, not like *Señor* Valentine . . . Oh!" She held her palms against her lips as if she'd just committed blasphemy.

I shouldn't have been as surprised as I was, all things considered. The hotel wasn't any different from any other corporation with six thousand employees. Corporate scuttlebutt had a way of sifting down to the minions the way dandruff did to a black dinner jacket.

"Don't worry," I smiled. "I'm not here as his friend . . . no *amigo* Mr. Valentine." I glanced at my watch and then back at the door. "*Trabajo,*" I explained with a shrug. "Just a job."

The maid nodded sadly in understanding.

I knocked again. Still no answer. I gave the maid my most pleading look.

After studying me for a moment, she put her ear to the door, listening, I thought, to the music inside. She made a motion with her hands as if dealing out cards, then she turned. I thought she might leave. Instead, she took a clipboard from a hook on the side of her cart, glanced at her watch, and ran her finger down a column of room numbers.

A sly smile crossed her face. "Turn down bed!" She pulled a long silver chain from the pocket of her uniform. At the end of the chain was a pre-programmed computerized house key card.

I nodded my approval and let her by. She slid the card into the small black box on the frame of the door and it clicked open. She stepped inside and held the door as I followed behind.

The living room was empty. I called out over the sounds of the stereo coming from the partially open bedroom door: "Mr. Valentine. It's me, Jake Morgan." No one answered. I went to check the landing of the music room and the maid went to the bedroom. The landing was clear. As I turned to the bedroom, the maid let out a huge breath of air.

"*Dios mio!*" She turned quickly on her heels, crossed herself, and mumbled a prayer-like chant I didn't understand.

There was no resistance as I put my hands on her shoulders and moved her aside.

The door to the bedroom was open, and in addition to the stereo that blared from inside, the turbulent sound of the Jacuzzi could be heard.

"Mr. Valentine?" I called out, poking my head around the door. "Mr. Val —"

Christian Valentine wasn't taking calls. He was facedown in the bubbling hot tub with a bright-colored arrow embedded in his back.

Unlike the maid, I wasn't an overly religious man.

"Oh, shit," was all I could think to say.

Chapter

We had already disturbed any fingerprint evidence on the door when we entered, but I knew well enough not to touch anything else.

"Please," I said to the distraught maid, "go and get Security."

She nodded frantically and seemed happy to leave.

Nudging the door with my shoulder, I entered the bedroom and made the long trip to the hot tub. Valentine was totally nude and floating gently with the action of the water, his arms out in front of him, fingers splayed. I was surprised at the amount of blood. The turbulent water was crimson.

The room itself, despite the situation, was relatively neat. The bed was made and a clean and freshly pressed suit was laid out on a valet stand beside a gleaming pair of black shoes. There was a small table beside the hot tub, empty except for a thick white towel. Under the table was a glass with a broken stem. On the other side of the tub, lying on its side, was a bottle of Dom Perignon.

"Jesus," I muttered.

When the press heard about this, they would go bonkers. After all, Valentine was a star. A *mega*-star. Vegas would go absolutely nuts. My thoughts turned to Rachel and what a lousy break this was for her.

Two burly hotel security guards barged in. Apparently they weren't any more religious than I was. One of them, slack-jawed with shock, held me in check. The other stood open-mouthed and wide-eyed for a moment, then bolted off down the hall shouting "Holy shit" over and over as he ran.

Okay, maybe he was a little bit religious.

The next forty-five minutes were spent in an empty suite on the same floor, proving who I was to hotel security and then to the police when they arrived. Eventually I was led back to the now-bustling Valentine suite, where I was ushered into the music room and introduced to a very serious Lieutenant Oakley.

He was only about thirty-five, which surprised me; him making Homicide lieutenant so young. He was tall and heavyset, but the extra pounds he carried under the lightweight beige suit appeared firm where they needed to be. He was blessed with a square jaw and a rugged face, and he had sun-bleached hair that was beginning to thin. A simple gold wedding band on his left hand didn't fool me for a second; he looked tough enough to take on the devil himself — and maybe even beat him two out of three.

Oakley ordered me to take a seat and tell him my story. He listened and nodded and took down notes, glancing at me when I mentioned I had once been a cop. Not to be outdone, I took out my notebook, too.

"Where 'bouts?" he asked.

"Boston."

"Humph," he replied, not impressed. "These blackmail letters you mentioned, any idea where Mr. Valentine kept them?"

"Sure," I nodded.

We left the music room and I led Oakley to the bar. The suite was filled with uniforms and plainclothes, and the print boys were busy dusting and taking pictures. One of the young uniforms advised the lieutenant that the medical examiner had arrived.

I went over to the bust of Valentine and stuck a baby finger in each of its ears and turned the head counterclockwise. The wall of pastel paintings slid quietly into the ceiling and, except for Oakley, everyone appeared impressed all to hell.

Walking up to the bar, I rummaged amongst the bottles until I found what I was looking for, then I copied the set of numbers into my notebook. With the writing end of my ballpoint, I slid the hidden panel to the left and punched in the numbers on the display. The safe's door clicked and, again with the end of the pen, I swung it open. "Voilà!"

Still not impressed, Oakley motioned for the print boys. Another cop in a suit, this one older, came by just as I finished telling Oakley about the sweet young thing Valentine had warming up his bed during my visit. He didn't bother to introduce himself. "We're already on the hotel and elevator videotapes, Lieutenant."

Oakley led the detective and me back to the music room, then he handed the other cop his notebook and various pieces of my identification.

The detective glanced from my hotel employee card to my driver's license and then back again. He motioned for me to sit.

"So what gives?" he asked. "Is Jake your first name or middle name, or what?"

"Uh, it's a nickname actually," I answered defensively.

"So *this* is your given name," he smiled, holding out the license.

When I answered with only a nod, he turned to Oakley.

"That's a goddamn girl's name, isn't it, Lieutenant?" he asked incredulously.

Oakley shrugged his large shoulders. "Sounds like it."

"My old man was a big John Wayne fan," I explained weakly.

"Been better off with 'Duke' then," the old cop snickered.

Oakley left and went down to the living room. The other took a seat on the piano bench and told me to go through it all again. So I did.

When I finished, I sat back and tucked my notebook away in my shirt pocket. "And that's about it."

The cop scribbled a few notes, gave me a skeptical look, scribbled some more, then gazed at me reflectively, gently slapping the notebook on his thigh while he did.

Oakley's booming voice broke his thought, as well as mine. "Hey, Morgan!"

The lieutenant was leaning through the bedroom doorway, wiggling his finger at me. "In here, shamus," he said with a jerk of his head.

The bedroom was crowded. The photographers were just wrapping up, packing their equipment in large, black nylon shoulder cases. The print team was still dusting and taking pictures. Two paramedics stood smoking cigarettes near a bathroom door, staring up at the mirror over the bed and snickering over some private joke. Waiting somberly to my right were a young male and female. Both were dressed in dark gray outfits, hands behind their backs and looking very much like coroner's staff. Everyone appeared teamed up, including Valentine.

The medical examiner, a middle-aged, serious-faced Asian, had Valentine facedown on a shiny aluminum gurney, the bright red arrow now grotesquely accompanied by a long, silver rectal thermometer. He spread Valentine's cheeks, checking his reading, speaking into a small Dictaphone wired to his lapel. Apparently satisfied, he snapped off his clear latex gloves and nodded to the lieutenant.

"Okay, wrap it up, boys and girls," ordered Oakley.

The photographers and paramedics filed out. The couple from the coroner's office gave each other a curt nod and sprang into action. The print boys carried on with their business of tagging a large plastic bag with a crossbow inside.

"You or the maid touch anything in here?"

"Not a thing, Lieutenant."

Oakley nodded his approval. "Tell me again why you came up to Mr. Valentine's suite."

It was a standard police tactic and I went along with it.

"As I told you before, Lieutenant, Mr. Valentine asked me to look into something for him. I came up to verify some information and ask a few questions."

"Such as?"

The pair from the coroner's office had pulled a black body bag out from under the stretcher. They'd removed their jackets and rolled up their sleeves and were now trying to stuff Valentine unceremoniously into the bag.

"I wanted to know who might have it in for him. I wasn't really getting anywhere, so I thought he could put me on the right track, maybe save a little time."

My mind was already made up; I had decided I wasn't going to tell the cops everything I'd discovered. Talking with Murray Gladstone, the stage manager, had been just that — talk. And although I did think Murray had overreacted at hearing Valentine's name, I wasn't about to get him caught up in this unnecessarily. At least not until I talked with him again. Same thing as far as Leona Carter was concerned.

"To be honest with you, Lieutenant, I was more worried about my friend, Rachel Sinclair."

Oakley was writing in his notebook. "I don't like it when people I'm interrogating tell me that, Morgan."

I gave him a vacant expression. "What do you mean?"

"When they tell me they're going to be honest with me." He glanced up from his notes. "It makes me think that maybe they haven't been totally honest up until then." He gave me a hard stare. "You catch my drift?"

He was a perceptive son of a bitch. "Come on, Lieutenant, I put my time in too. Back in Boston. Once a cop, always a cop."

Oakley gave me a discerning look. "Hardly, Morgan. Now cut the crap and tell me about your friend."

"She's the same friend I told you about who was in the photograph with Valentine. You must have seen it. It had lipstick all across it. The photo was with the blackmail threats in the safe."

"Go on."

I explained about Rachel's home being broken into.

"So when I put two and two together, I thought I'd better see if Valentine knew anything about it, see if he had any ideas about the two events possibly being connected."

The coroner's people were having difficulties with Valentine. They couldn't lay him out on his back because of the arrow, so they had him facedown in the bag. The problem was they couldn't do up the zipper, not with the arrow sticking out the way it was.

"Hey, Lieutenant," the young man called out. "Is it okay if we break this thing off?"

"No. Leave it right where it is."

The young man seemed perplexed. "But I can't wheel it out this way. It's gotta be done up."

His female partner nodded her head up and down. "It's the rules," she concurred.

Oakley took in and let out a large load of air as he walked toward the stretcher. He fished around in his pocket and pulled out a Swiss army knife. He lifted some of the rubberized material and appeared to take a measurement with his eye. When Oakley was finally satisfied, he held a spot of the bag with one hand as he opened the knife with his teeth. He drilled a two-inch hole, then he reached in and tilted Valentine to one side and poked the arrow through the hole. He zipped the bag with a firm pull and tucked away his knife.

"Okay, roll."

The young man and woman looked at each other and shrugged their shoulders, then rolled as ordered.

Oakley leaned over to the table and picked up the towel to wipe his hands from the wetness of Valentine's body. As he unfurled the cloth, a playing card fell out and floated toward the floor.

I reached reflexively and grabbed the card, managing to grasp it by its edges, and handed the six of spades to the lieutenant.

His face hardened. "You shouldn't have tried that."

"It was nothing, really," I said modestly.

As impossible as it seemed, his face hardened even more. He glanced toward the two print boys who were dusting the numeric pad of the telephone. "This might be a very valuable piece of evidence, Mr. Morgan. You could have messed up the prints."

"Not by catching it by its edges, Lieutenant."

"That was pure luck."

"Don't be so sure," I boasted. "I've been handling cards since I was twelve —"

He cut me off. "Carl, tag this for me, will you?"

One of the men got up from his knees and walked over and placed the card in a plastic bag.

"You," Oakley addressed me firmly, "out here." He walked briskly from the bedroom to the living room.

Feeling like a puppy about to be disciplined, I followed.

"Sit," he barked.

"Thank God," I said, starting to feel very tired of Oakley and the whole investigation. I fell into the same chair I'd sat in the night before with Christian Valentine. "The way you were carrying on, I thought you were going to tell me to roll over and play dead."

Oakley took a large, clear plastic bag from the top of the bar and dropped it with a loud thud on the round mahogany table to my left.

"Let's get something straight," he said wearily, forcing his weight into the narrow confines of the wingback chair. "Maybe you haven't noticed, but I don't have a sense of humor. I don't even think I have a funny bone. So how about not wasting my time, or the good taxpayers' money, with your stupid wisecracks?"

I gave him a cold stare back but realized it wouldn't do any good. Instead, I picked up the bag labeled "Safe Contents" and started to rummage through. There were a few other items besides the blackmail letters: a couple of spiral notebooks — apparently everyone had them — a few faxes, some legal letters, a laminated map, a bunch of expensive men's jewelry. I picked out the smaller plastic bag I had seen Valentine take from the safe for his young Asian sex toy the night before and held it up to the light.

"I take it this isn't sugar, Lieutenant."

"Close," he replied. "Nose candy."

I gave him a reproachful smile. "No sense of humor, you say."

"Forget that other stuff. Just go through what you were shown last night."

"It's just as I told you, Lieutenant," I replied, pulling out the familiar manila envelope and spilling the contents onto my lap. "Valentine said he was being blackmailed and this here's the proof."

"Right." Oakley was having a problem with his attempt at a smile. "But that's not the point I'm trying to make."

For a man with no sense of humor, not even a funny bone, he appeared mildly amused about something.

"And what point might that be, Lieutenant?"

There was a brisk knock and a young black officer opened the door. "Lieutenant. There's a Mr. Contini here to see you. Says he's the owner of the hotel."

Oakley sighed and rose from his chair. "Show him in."

Julius F. Contini *was* the owner of the Oasis. Or at least it was his name on all the legal documents. One never knew who was really behind a one-billion-dollar hotel in Las Vegas, except for the Nevada Gaming Commission, but the word on the street was he was as clean as they come. I had never had the pleasure of meeting him personally, but I had seen him around the casino from time to time, usually when he was busy introducing himself to a group of high rollers from the Far or Middle East.

The door to the suite opened wide and Big Julie blustered through. The door would have to be wide; Julius Contini was pushing 300 pounds, all packed onto a five-foot-six- or -seven-inch frame. He was sweating profusely, a Big Julie trademark, and sporting his usual lit cigar in his thick, meaty lips. One of the hotel veeps must have rousted him from bed, because he wasn't wearing either one of his expensive toupees. Instead, he had his thin black hair parted and combed up from as far back as it would reach.

"Are you Oakley?" he bellowed breathlessly.

The lieutenant walked over and held out his hand.

"I'm *Lieutenant* Oakley, yes."

"Whatever." Big Julie didn't take his hand. "Just tell me this ain't happening!"

"I'm afraid it's true, Mr. Contini," said Oakley, taking back his hand. "Mr. Valentine is dead. It appears he was murdered."

"It appears!" he hollered incredulously around his wet cigar. "It appears? Jesus Christ! I don't believe it . . ."

Oakley put a sympathetic hand on Big Julie's shoulder. "Look, Mr. Contini, I know how you must feel. The two of you must have been very close, but until the coroner —"

"Close?" Big Julie pulled a bright blue hankie from his back pocket and wiped it across his forehead. "Me and Valentine? That's funny! The prick would take me for every cent I got if he could." He stuck his hankie and cigar back in their respective places and looked at his Rolex. "Jesus Christ, I got two thousand people filling up my showroom as we speak." He sighed heavily and reached deep into his pants pocket and came out with a small pill box, then he stormed over to the bar, filled a shotglass with water, and washed the pills down. He took a deep breath and let it out hard, like the wolf who blew down the house the three little pigs built. He reached over to a bright yellow telephone, lifted the receiver, punched in three digits and shook his head dispiritedly.

"Yeah, who's that? . . . Murray, it's Contini . . . Yeah, it's true . . . That's right . . . Murray, listen up. Get a hold of Gary, right away. Tell him to put that Ventura kid in . . . that's right, tonight's show. Pronto!" He tapped a large ash into the bar sink and added, almost as an afterthought, "Oh, and Murray. Tell him to throw a few more titties in the show." He plopped the receiver down, sweating even more.

Oakley asked him, "Can I see you in the other room?"

Big Julie walked around from behind the bar. "Yeah, sure. I guess." He seemed to notice me in the room for the first time and gave me a brutal double take. "This the guy who knocked off Valentine?"

"No." Oakley's lips squeezed tightly together. "At least I don't think so. Actually, he's one of your employees."

I rose half out of my chair and extended my hand toward him. "Jake Morgan. I work BJ."

Big Julie Contini started to raise his hand. "Pit boss?"

"Uh, no. I'm a dealer, but I'm moving into poker —"

"Jesus Christ!" He yanked back his hand and stomped off toward the bedroom.

Oakley turned to the officer at the door. "Brad, keep an eye on Dick Tracy here."

"Sure, Lieutenant."

He started after Big Julie, who'd already disappeared.

"Hey, Lieutenant," I called. "Remember? You were about to tell me what point it was you were trying to make when Contini came in."

Oakley stopped and turned around, the way Lieutenant Columbo did on television. "That's right, Mr. Morgan. I was." He pointed to the plastic bag on my lap. "The photograph. You know, the one of your friend Rachel and Mr. Valentine, the one you came up here to talk to him about?"

My face was blank, still trying to make out his point.

"The point is, Mr. Morgan, there is no photograph there."

He left the room. I glanced down at the pile of blackmail threats.

He was right.

Chapter

After taking a few moments to digest Oakley's little morsel, I went through the bag of evidence with a fine-toothed comb. The cops obviously weren't too concerned with me handling the goods because they knew my prints were already there from last night. I had read the death threats the night before and the jewelry, although impressive, wasn't what I was interested in.

One of the two notebooks was filled with names and telephone numbers. The other had a few names and numbers too, but the back pages were filled with row after row of crossed-out numerics. Sometimes the numbers rose, then suddenly dipped and rose again. Like some kind of score sheet. Many pages had names or letters at the top: Johnny owed $1575, Slim $800, The Colonel $3720, W $1280, Benny $145, and F $8400.

The majority of the pages contained drawings of a pair of dice. Visible on each die were corresponding dots signifying their respective numbers. Strangely, all the dots were made with simple circles, except for the top of each die, which had been designated the number "one." These circles had been filled in. Crap jargon had a name for that roll: "snake eyes."

Whoever carried this artistic-yet-unusual moniker owed the incredibly ugly sum of $39,500.

I had gambled enough to know what a win/loss record looked like. Unfortunately, most of mine had minus signs beside my name. But Valentine must have been very good or very lucky, because his record looked extremely positive. I flipped back through the pages of the book, over the names and initials and amounts owing. None of the names made much sense, except for F, who could have been Franco.

The faxes were from some firm named Simington, Simington & Smiley, listing numerous assets and property totaling a nifty amount far exceeding my dreams.

The map turned out to be a nautical chart of Lake Mead. It folded out to an impressive size and consisted of depth markings, navigational information, and lake-level contours. The chart appeared new and had been purchased at the Lake Mead Resort and Marina. The only things that stood out on the chart were two markings in blue ink: once again the pair of dice with its snake eyes filled in, and a bold circle around the depth marking of 410 feet in the middle of Boulder Basin.

The legal-looking letters were just that. The first was from a Frederick T. Wilson, an attorney located on Fremont Street, downtown Las Vegas. The second came from a large law firm in Los Angeles that carried a lengthy masthead of twenty to thirty names of partners practicing out of a prominent Sunset Boulevard address.

I was in the midst of deciphering the tangle of legalese and gobbledygook when Big Julie and Lieutenant Oakley came back into the room. They approached the door and shook hands.

"Thanks, Lieutenant."

Oakley gave him a just-doing-my-job nod.

"Well," sighed Contini, glancing at his watch, "I better go and check out this Ventura kid for myself."

The cop at the door let him out.

The lieutenant stooped over and took the jumble of papers from my hand and the rest of the evidence from the table beside me.

"Satisfied?" he asked.

"Look, I know what I saw."

"Oh, that's right," he said, tapping his forehead. "I almost forgot. You were some big-shot cop back in Beantown."

Enough was enough. As far as I was concerned, I had been more than cooperative. Now I was tired and pissed off. Two hours with Oakley and his boys was beginning to remind me of all the crap I'd had to take back in Boston. The hell with it. And the hell with Oakley. I got up to leave.

"Going somewhere?"

"I am unless you're going to charge me with something."

Oakley thought about that for a moment. "Yeah, I guess you can go."

"Gee, thanks," I said with mock gratitude.

The young cop at the door stood firm. I turned back to Oakley with a resigned look on my face.

"It's okay, Brad. You can let Mr. Morgan out."

As I stepped through the doorway, Oakley called out. "By the way, be sure and let me know if you're planning on crossing the state line for the next little while." He afforded himself a tight smile. "And Mr. Morgan. Have yourself a real nice day."

"Sure," I said. "What's left of it."

Chapter

When I finally got home, after checking backstage for Rachel, there was a message on my machine to call her. She answered in a distraught voice, said she knew it was late but would I mind coming over. I told her I would be there in forty-five minutes. I hustled and made it in thirty.

I managed to calm her down by telling her I would crash there if it would make her feel safer. The sofa was comfortable, but I imagined her bed would have been even more so. She had been nervous enough, what with her home being broken into and all, but the news of Valentine's death had her really spooked. Luckily she knew nothing of the photo of her and Christian. If she had, she might have slept as fitfully as I did.

In the morning we had a simple breakfast of toast and coffee, and caught up with the news on a portable television set in the kitchen. As expected, the local stations were having a field day with the murder of Christian Valentine. Even the networks had cut into their regularly scheduled programming, including CNN.

"There you are!"

A piece on KLAS-TV had me being interviewed last night in the busy backstage area of the Oasis showroom. The thought of how far-reaching these televised reports would be had turned me into a total nervous wreck. I stopped chewing my breakfast.

"Mr. Morgan," the energetic female reporter asked. "Can you tell us what brought you to the scene of the crime?" She shoved the microphone in front of my nose and pressed on her earphone, listening to the studio director cueing her for the next question she was supposed to ask me.

"No. Not really . . ."

The camera caught me clearing my throat, pulling nervously at my shirt collar and looking totally out of place.

She nodded her head sympathetically. "Yes, I see," she said. "I understand you and Christian Valentine were very close. His death must have come as a great shock to you."

"Uhh, no . . . and, umm, yes, it did."

The cameraman had panned wider. One of the elephants from the show was being led back to its cage by a colorful midget clown. The elephant's thick thigh gently nudged the two of us. The clown gave an exaggerated expression and honked a horn pinned to his patched jacket.

The ever-smiling reporter didn't miss a beat. "It's certainly a circus of activity back here, Mr. Morgan!"

"Yeah . . . a real circus."

The camera focused on the reporter's still-smiling face. "Back to you, Chet!" she beamed into the lens.

"Jeezus . . ."

Rachel looked up at me over her cup, and there was just a hint of a sparkle in her eyes. "It wasn't *that* bad."

"Jeezus. I'm going to pay for that. I just know it."

"I thought you did okay, under the circumstances. Now stop knocking yourself and finish your toast."

Rachel got up and started putting plates and cups into the dishwasher. "It's true what they say, though."

"What's that?" I sighed, reaching for my last slice.

A tiny smile came to her lips. "About cameras. You know, how they add ten pounds to a person."

I dropped the toast to my plate and pushed it across to her side.

"Are you going in to work today?" she asked.

"Yeah, I guess so," I answered glumly. "With Valentine gone, I won't have any extra cash coming in. Besides, it's supposed to be my last shift in BJ. McClusky would have my ass if I missed it."

Standing up, I took out my black notebook and tossed it on the table. "Hell, I can't even recoup the expenses Valentine said I wouldn't have."

Her face clouded and she bit her lip.

"I'm sorry, Rachel. I shouldn't have said that." I walked over and put my hands on her shoulders.

She took a deep breath, let it out, and put her arms lightly around me.

"This is all too close to home, Jake," she said softly into my shoulder.

We held each other like that for a moment. "I know it is. But don't worry. This Lieutenant Oakley is a bit of a tightass, but he seems to know what he's doing. I'm sure the cops'll get this figured out soon."

Rachel raised her head off my shoulder and looked at me. Her eyes were moist. "I hope so." She kissed me lightly on the cheek. "Thanks for being here for me."

⊡

I coaxed the Chevy along Jones Boulevard, alone and in no real hurry. It was just after ten and my swing shift didn't start until noon. The sun was bright and intense, but somehow it wasn't as bothersome today. Instead, it seemed to help melt away the memories of last night.

Rachel and the cast and crew had a meeting scheduled for three o'clock. I had told her I would drop by during one of my breaks.

There were two others I wanted to talk to: Murray and Leona. I figured once they had a chance to explain their actions in light of what had happened, I could put my mind, and the case, to rest.

I made a right down Flamingo, remembering to stop and pick up a couple of clean shirts from the dry cleaner. My last shift could be a memorable one, and I wanted to be prepared.

Billy, the ancient guard at the Oasis parking lot, flagged me down with both arms and leaned on my open window.

"Hey, Jake," he said, tilting his cap. "Some news, huh?"

"Yeah, Billy," I answered. "Is there much commotion inside?"

"You kidding?" he asked excitedly. "This is the biggest thing to hit town since the fire at the old MGM. It's all everybody's talkin' about!"

I let Billy reminisce about the good old days for a few more minutes, then I asked him, "Murray Gladstone come in yet?"

"Yeah, sure. Murray just pulled in a little while ago."

"What about Leona Carter?"

Billy checked his clipboard. "I don't think so, Jake. I been on since six this morning." He flipped through the pages. "Unless she came in durin' my break . . ."

An orange VW convertible tooted its horn behind us.

"It's okay, Billy. I'll check inside." With a clunk, I dropped the transmission into gear.

"Say, what's up, Jake?" he whispered conspiratorially. "I heard you were workin' for Valentine when this shit hit the fan. You think maybe Murray knows something?" He raised a bushy gray eyebrow and hoisted his security belt, trying to recapture part of his past.

The horn tooted again and Billy gave the impatient driver an annoyed glance.

Feigning a good-natured laugh, I told him, "No, it's nothing like that. I just have to talk to Murray about building some bookshelves for my apartment."

My foot came off the brake and the Chevy idled forward. "Gotta run, Billy."

"Yeah, sure, Jake," he said dejectedly, then just as suddenly his face brightened. "Hey, by the way," he yelled out, "I saw you on TV this mornin' . . ."

I waved my thanks out the window and picked up speed.

After entering the hotel through the employees' entrance at the rear of the complex, I headed to the dealers' break room to stash my laundry. As expected, I was the unwilling center of attention. My excited colleagues demanded a behind-the-scenes reenactment, so I gave them what I could, minus the "umms" from the television interview.

Apparently satisfied with my sketchy details, they went back to their card-playing and video games. The one-minute warning sounded. Dealers finished their games, extinguishing cigarettes and checking their hair in the mirrors as they filed out. I beat a hasty retreat to my locker, hung the shirts and left quickly, not eager to repeat myself to the next wave of dealers about to come in.

It was just before eleven and the casino was abuzz. Dress codes and regulations were relaxed during the day, and now you could find suntan-lotioned spouses in swimwear leading each other from game to game. One of the most successful methods of maintaining a busy clientele throughout the day was the lowering of the table stake minimums. During the warm mornings and slow, sunny afternoons, many of the betting minimums were dropped to five dollars. And if you looked hard enough, you might even find a one- or two-dollar game. But in the evening, finding a low minimum was as difficult as finding a virgin at a porno convention.

Murray was backstage applying a coat of white paint to the trellis he'd made yesterday. Members of his crew were busy off in the corner, hanging backdrops of scenery from thick ropes high above.

When he saw me, Murray placed his paintbrush across the top of the open paint can, tugged a small white rag from his back pocket, and wiped his hands vigorously.

"What in Christ's name is goin' on, Jake?"

"Who knows?" I said, lifting myself up onto a stool nearby.

Murray dropped the rag near the paint can and produced a pack of cigarettes from his shirt. I was grateful to see they were Marlboros and not Gauloises. He lit up, blew a stream of smoke, and offered me the package. I declined.

"I know he wasn't the most popular guy in the world, but son of a bitch, this is crazy!"

I told him I agreed. We talked for a few minutes, then I asked about the general atmosphere and the reactions of the cast and crew.

He pulled up another stool and sat across from me. "Yeah, I heard you was workin' for Valentine." He flicked a short ash to the floor and frowned. "You could've told me that when we were chewin' the fat yesterday."

"Come on, Murray. It wasn't anything like that," I lied. "Valentine was putting the squeeze on me to help him out. Said he'd been getting threats and that some of them might involve Rachel."

The missing photograph of Rachel and Valentine crossed my mind, but I thought it wiser not to mention it to anybody.

"I didn't want to take the chance, Murray. Not with Rachel about to be working so close to him."

He mulled that over for a moment, longer than I thought necessary. "You've really got it bad for her, huh Jake?"

I nodded.

Murray studied the end of his cigarette, as if he were trying to read something in the red ember. "You noticed my reaction to your quizzing me about Valentine yesterday, didn't you?"

I didn't answer him. I didn't think I had to.

We sat like that for a few more moments. When he finally raised his head to me, I noticed his eyes were wet and red.

"You don't understand, Jake," he said in a strained whisper. He clamped his mouth in a thin line and took a long, deep breath through his nose. "Christian Valentine killed my daughter."

Chapter

"Tell me about it."

We were sipping on strong Arabian coffee, sitting at a table in the far back corner of the Ali Baba Deli. It was a quarter past eleven and the room wasn't quite half full.

Murray was stirring his cup absently, despite having added neither cream nor sugar. After a few more laps around his cup, he stopped and pulled out his cigarettes. He lit it off the one he had going and left the pack open on the table between us.

He hadn't offered this time, but I was mighty tempted. I hadn't had a smoke for well over a year, and times like this made it hard to resist.

"It was twelve years ago," he began. "Sherry was nineteen and working the Playboy Club in Chicago. Doing real good, too. She'd moved out of our house in Jersey a couple of years before. First she started out on cocktails — you know, the bunny outfit and all — but eventually they had an open audition for some of the minor dancing-and-singing roles, and she got one of them. Small stuff really, but it was a start. The waitressing paid the bills — paid damn well as a matter of fact — but her passion was the dancing she was doing. She got paid for that too, but she would have done it for nothing. You could tell she really loved it by the letters she wrote the wife and me. She'd write us, or phone, every single week without fail."

A waiter came by, filled our cups with fresh coffee and asked if we wanted to order. We both shook our heads.

"By this time, Valentine had come into the picture. He'd been playing small joints in the Catskills and all over the East Coast for years, but now he was on his way up — way up. And I guess, in his eyes, Sherry was ripe for the picking."

Murray paused over the memory. Not wanting to lose him, I asked, "Valentine must have been married then. Didn't Yolanda ever find out and step in?"

"Nah. He always kept her as far out of the picture as he could. Just like he did here. She'd always been the breadwinner up until Chicago, but now he was starting to pull in some major bucks himself. He could afford to get rid of her, you know, send her off on trips, set her up in some pad far enough away so she wouldn't cramp his style. It must have satisfied her — she stayed with him.

"It was a few months later that Sherry stopped writing. We talked on the phone once in a while, but usually it was us who had to call. At first we just figured she was real busy. But there seemed to be more to it. She never talked with the same enthusiasm anymore. Not for someone who was always so energetic, so full of life. Well, after a couple of months of this, I got on a plane and went to find out for myself."

Murray reached for another cigarette. "I found out all right," he said, lighting his smoke. "When I knocked on her door, she was shocked to see me standing there. She'd been expecting Valentine. It turned out that her and Christian had been seeing each other for quite a while. Then I asked her about Yolanda.

"It was the all-time, classic story. Boy meets girl, girl learns he's married, boy promises he's getting divorced, girl believes him."

I nodded my understanding.

"I tried to convince her that Valentine had been feeding her a line, but she wouldn't listen. She said she loved him. She told me Valentine was going to help her with her career too, that he had promised to have her promoted to a starring role. It was all planned for the next couple of months.

"We hadn't seen Sherry for five or six months, not since she had come home for Christmas, but while I was talking to her, I started to notice things that had changed about her. Little things. There was an unnatural edge to her. And not just in her voice. She was distant, always going off on tangents and rambling on.

"She'd lost weight, too. Not a lot, but noticeable. And her face seemed harder somehow, you know, dark lines, puffy around the eyes. She explained she'd been dieting, trying to lose a few pounds for her upcoming role, and that she'd been training extra hard.

"I tried to be as gentle as I could, told her not to put too much faith in an unfaithful lover. She laughed for the first time that night."

Murray's cigarette lay in the ashtray burning itself into the filter. I reached over and put it out.

"Two months later, she was dead. Overdose."

Never knowing what to say in these kinds of situations, I didn't say anything. The lunch crowd line beginning to form at the door reminded me that my shift would be starting soon. I reached for my wallet and left five dollars on the table.

"Does — *did* Valentine know about this?" I asked.

"No, I doubt it. She was using her stage name at the time."

I was surprised he could have worked with Valentine, but I didn't say it. I didn't have to. He read my expression.

"It was a fluke that the two of us met up here. I was hired during the construction of the Oasis, three years ago. I'd worked for Contini at a hotel back in Jersey. When I read he'd bought into Vegas, I called him and asked for a job. He was glad to have me. My wife passed away the year before and it was a good time to make a move. I sold the house, moved out here. Valentine wasn't signed on as the feature until just before the Oasis opened last year."

Murray took a last sip of his coffee, picked up his pack of cigarettes and stood up.

"There's absolutely no question in my mind, Jake," he said in a somber voice. "Christian Valentine was responsible for Sherry's death and I hope he rots in hell."

Looking me straight in the eye, he added, "But no, I didn't kill him."

Chapter

Maybe McClusky *did* have feelings.

He had me working a hundred-dollar-minimum table and it was emptier than an Alaskan golf course in January. It gave me a lot of time to think. And I had a lot on my mind.

If it had been Murray's intention to gain my sympathy, he had. But if it had been his intention to make me believe he didn't have anything to do with the murder of Valentine, well let's just say I wasn't totally convinced. Sure, I hadn't cared for Christian Valentine any more than Murray had, but then again I didn't have his motivation. He had the worst kind of anger a man could possess: pent-up, restricted, simmering all this time. As far as I was concerned though, the cops would be doing their own investigations, Murray included, and they were a lot better at homicide than I was.

What was important to me was that I no longer believed Rachel was in danger.

My shift went rather well. An abundance of low-rollers casing the casino avoided me and my hundred-dollar table like mice avoid a rattlesnake.

McClusky stopped by and I thanked him for putting me on a dead game. If I hadn't known the old warhorse better, I'd say he almost began to blush. Helping out a peon probably wasn't one of his strong suits.

"Yeah, well, we gotta have it," he explained offhandedly. "Just in case."

"I appreciate it all the same," I said, trying to milk the situation for all it was worth. "It was a rough night. I'll probably have nightmares for weeks."

He let out a large sigh. "Yeah, that was really something you went through, Jake. You must feel like shit." He pursed his meaty lips and shook his head slowly back and forth, possibly remembering Christian Valentine in some better light than I had ever seen him.

"It was," I readily agreed. "And I do." It suddenly dawned on me that I might actually be entitled to some kind of employee compensation. Mental duress, that sort of thing.

"It sure didn't put the hotel in a very good light, either," he pointed out, thinking like the good corporate man that he was. "It was embarrassin' as hell."

"That's for sure," I agreed in my best corporate tone. "A big name like Valentine, that could really hurt us."

His two furry brows went up, forming an almost perfect M.

"Valentine?" he asked in an amazed tone. "Hell, people'll probably be comin' in by the droves now. I was talkin' about you on TV this mornin'!"

"It was that bad, huh?"

"Bad?" He looked around from side to side, then breathed hot air in my ear, saying, "It was so friggin' bad, Publicity and Promotions wanted you canned during our meeting this morning."

"Jeezus . . ." I muttered.

McClusky sensed my discomfort. "Don't worry. I cooled them off."

"Cops been around much today?"

"You kiddin'? They've been all over. Even showed up at our meeting. Contini told us to give them our complete cooperation. They're going to be interviewing everybody and anybody who had anything to do with Valentine. Some cop named Oaktree was headin' it up."

"Oakley," I corrected.

"Whatever. They started with us this mornin', lookin' to see if we had any leads for them to get started on — a name, a face, you know, anybody who might've held a grudge against Valentine. But Christ, by the time we'd gotten halfway around the room, they had to go out and get another notebook."

"Were there any?"

"What, notebooks?"

"Leads."

"Nah. Not really." He seemed to roll the recollection around in his head for a moment. "Lotsa names though."

"Had Contini settled down any? He was pretty shaken up last night."

"Yeah, from what I could see. Supposedly this Ventura kid brought the house down. Made Mr. Contini very happy."

"Should have seen him in Valentine's suite," I told him. "He was sweating bullets."

"I don't doubt it," McClusky grinned. "His ass was on the line with Valentine out. Now he can rest easy."

I found that hard to believe, for Contini. "He'll save a bunch on his bottom line. I guess Ventura comes cheap compared to Valentine."

He nodded his heavy head in agreement. "About one-tenth the price. And that's not even countin' what he had on 'the Policy.'"

McClusky made "the Policy" sound like "the Bible."

I asked, "What policy is that?"

"You kiddin'?" he asked incredulously. "Contini and the Oasis had Valentine covered with more insurance policies than Liberace had candelabras. He'd have made a small fortune if Valentine had just broken an arm or a leg." McClusky's eyes seemed to glaze over. He shook his big head. "I can't even imagine what the death benefits will pay."

"My name come up at all?"

"I told you. They wanted you canned."

"No, I mean after that. With the cops."

"Yeah, sure," he replied evenly. He gave me a quizzical look. "What the hell did you do to that lieutenant anyway? He pumped us pretty good about you."

Obviously I was gone but not forgotten. "I sure hope somebody vouched for me . . ."

"You're still my ace, Jake," he said, starting to turn away. "My number-one shooter." He gave me a big wink over his parting shoulder. "But you owe me."

If I was going to owe anybody in this town it might as well be McClusky. He wouldn't break my kneecaps like a lot of others might.

At least I didn't think he would.

"By the way," he said. "If anybody even attempts to sit down, remember, you call me for relief. Until you're back on track." He jabbed me from behind with his pen. "You got it?"

"Got it, Coach."

Chapter

My last shift was going great. All I had to do was stand at my table like one of Madame Tussaud's wax pieces. Between rounds, I went back and relaxed with my shoes off in the break room.

During the current break, I noticed a mangled copy of the *Daily Racing Form* on one of the tables. In the excitement of the killing last night, I had forgotten all about the killing that I was supposed to make myself at Del Mar today. I picked up the *Form* and leafed through it.

Yesterday, I had made a number of notes while waiting for Leona Carter to meet her mystery writer in the Camel's Hump. One had been a reminder to check a three-year-old filly carrying the auspicious name Morgan's Dancer. It was scheduled for today's sixth race.

The past performances were not encouraging. In twenty-one cheap claiming races to date, Morgan's Dancer had managed to finish in the money twice: one win and one show. The sixth was an allowance race featuring fillies, many of which were multiple winners. Someone had noted the morning line odds in the margin. Morgan's Dancer was a whopping twenty to one.

I reminded myself that a good gambler bets with his head, not his heart. And without further Valentine subsidizations to fall back on, I'd have to learn to curb my gambling habits somewhat. At the very least, I'd stay away from dubious long shots — even if the horse's name might seem appealingly prophetic.

Deep down I knew I was due. Valentine's words of the night before hadn't gone totally over my head. Here I was jet-skiing toward forty and still without any substantial savings to speak of. The two hundred and change I still had in my wallet from Valentine nearly matched what I had in my account at the National Savings and Loan. Something had to give. I'd been down to meager scrapings before and always bounced back. Gambling was a series of peaks and valleys, potholes and smooth highways, turbulence and tranquility. The hard part was keeping the peaks in sight as I drove down that tranquil, smooth highway.

I made a promise to myself. From now on, I'd strive to be the Disciple of Discipline. The Master of Modicum. The Prince of Prudence.

At worst, the Allah of Alliteration.

Having set my sights, I perused the *Form* in search of a favorite.

After another round of staring off into space in the casino, I left for a thirty-minute lunch break. It was now a quarter to four. I passed by the Sports Book and put fifty bucks on the nose of a horse fittingly called Wise Sage, in the sixth at Del Mar. It was five minutes before post and Wise Sage was the heavy favorite at two to one. It wasn't money in the bank, but it was the closest thing to it. Morgan's Dancer was way up to thirty to one.

I grabbed a chili dog with all the fixings at a take-out near the gift shops and ate it on my way backstage in hopes of catching up with Rachel.

Security advised me that the cast and crew were still in their meeting. I asked the guard about Leona Carter. He motioned me back toward the dressing room area.

I followed the sounds of classical music coming from the wing. The showroom and stage were dark, except for a single spotlight that shone center stage. Leona Carter was dancing alone, dressed in a plain gray sweatsuit, performing simple, graceful moves in ballet fashion. Her eyes were closed, head tilted back. A light sheen of perspiration gleamed from her forehead. I stood aside and waited.

The concerto wound down. Just before the final sustaining note, Leona spun gently on the toe of one foot, timing with perfection an exaggerated bow to the empty chairs and vacant booths. She walked to a portable cassette player and pressed a button as the strains of the next arrangement began. Total quiet filled the room.

I stepped out from the wing area. Leona turned suddenly, hearing my footfalls. Not sure if she remembered me from the day before, I reintroduced myself as I entered her small circle of light. I complimented her on her dancing. She thanked me via a modest smile.

Leona stepped on a switch nearby. Three or four houselights snapped on. She reached behind the now-silent cassette player and came up with a small blue towel.

"I'm probably good for another two thousand miles," she announced, wiping the towel lightly across her brow. "Or five years. Whichever comes first."

"Beats my Chevy," I told her.

"So I've heard," said Leona with a faint grin. "I guess you're looking for Rachel. They're in the convention hall. West wing." She glanced down at the slim silver watch on her left wrist. "Shouldn't be too much longer. They've been in there for almost an hour now."

"Actually," I told her, "I was looking for you."

She was appropriately surprised. "Me?"

"I was wondering if we could talk for a few minutes."

"I guess so." She carried her towel to the apron of the stage and sat with her long legs dangling over the edge. I joined her.

"You're not in the cast meeting," I said. "How come?"

"It's a revamp session," she explained. "Most of my routines were with Christian. Now that he's gone, I'm gone."

Although a solemn appearance took shape on her delicate face, it didn't make Leona look anything like a murderer. I was having a hard enough time even picturing her as a blackmailer.

"I was winding down anyway," she continued. "What with me pregnant and Rachel taking over in the next couple of weeks . . . well, there was really no point in me being there."

"Are you leaving the production?" I asked. "Permanently?"

She nodded her answer. "I might come back," she said in a soft tone. "Later. But for now, well, they've got a policy here at the Oasis. All the girls have to sign it if they want to work." She smiled tenuously, patting her still-firm abdomen. "With all the rigorous training and the risk of injury, the hotel isn't about to take any chances with a pregnant dancer. After the baby, who knows . . . if I can work my body back into shape . . ." She toyed with a thin silver chain that hung from her watch. "But I'd really like to spend some time with the baby though."

The topic of Christian Valentine's murder hadn't come up yet, and I was mildly surprised. It seemed to be foremost on everyone else's mind. Certainly on mine.

"It was too bad about last night," I prodded.

Leona nodded.

After my recent faux pas with McClusky regarding my local television debut, I felt it might be wiser for me to be more specific in my line of questioning. "About Valentine, I mean."

"Yeah . . ." Leona toweled the back of her slender neck. I noticed a long red scratch, just beginning to heal, on the inside of her right forearm. "He kept the place packed."

We sat there for a while, saying nothing more. She obviously wasn't going to offer any of the information that I was looking for. I decided I might as well go for the direct approach.

"Was that all he was?" I asked. "A meal ticket for the cast and the Oasis?"

Leona turned her head to me. "What do you mean by that?" She sounded wary. Her look was hard once again.

"Nothing personal," I said. "It just seems everyone I've talked to reduces his demise into dollars and cents. Mostly dollars. Even the media are having a field day with this. They're treating the whole thing as if it were some kind of carnival, with Christian Valentine as the main attraction."

She was still holding her gaze, though it seemed to be softening. "And the tabloids haven't even arrived yet . . ."

"Exactly," I agreed. "My pit boss figures we'll draw better than ever because of this. People will be coming from all over to take pictures to show their kids where Valentine did his last gig. Like Elvis and Graceland. Publicity and Promotions are probably working on a souvenir postcard as we speak. Even Contini had me fooled last night, worried like he was. But it was just crocodile sweat. He had a showroom to fill. And a casino to pack after the show. Now I hear he's got a hot new kid to take over and enough insurance to make forgetting Christian Valentine as easy as forgetting Tiny Tim."

My voice had been getting louder as I spoke. I could hear my words echoing faintly from the back of the room. I said, a little softer, "I haven't seen much, if any, real sorrow."

"What about you?" she countered, with visible reproach. "Weren't you just another one making good on Christian's money and draw? I heard you were working for him. Playing detective."

Well, she had me there, but that was okay. I was just trying to get her to talk.

"We all were, Jake. One way or another." Leona looked away from me, out toward the back of the darkened showroom. After a moment she turned back to me and asked, "What is it you're trying to get at? You can't still be working for him."

"No, I'm not," I told her. "But he paid me for two days. Let's just say I'm trying to give him his money's worth. Tie up a few loose ends."

"Guilt money."

"Maybe." I glanced at my watch. Time was running out. "Look, Leona. The cops grilled me pretty good last night, and I've got a nasty feeling I haven't seen the last of them. On the one day that I did in fact work for Valentine, I came up with a couple of things that didn't sit right. Unfortunately, you were one of them."

Her mouth opened slightly, but nothing came out.

"Yesterday," I continued cautiously, "out at Sam's Town. You met with Christian."

"How did —"

"I saw the note in your dressing room. It made me uneasy. For you mostly. When I saw you leave, I followed."

"You had no right!" she protested.

"I think I had every right," I assured her. "Valentine offered to pay me to look into a series of threats he was being sent. I took the job reluctantly, but I took it. In any case, Sam's Town is a public place. I didn't interrupt. I was simply observing."

Leona crossed her ankles, then her arms. Body language shouted out.

"Damn!" she snapped, trying unsuccessfully to keep it under her breath. "Nobody was supposed to know about us . . ."

I said to her, "Nobody has to. It's just that he's dead, and I happened to be working for him when I found him facedown in his Jacuzzi. I just want to know what your meeting was about. Why the two of you had to go all the way out to Sam's to chat when you could have talked here."

She sat there, chewing on her lower lip, not responding.

"Look, Leona, as far as I know, I'm the only one connected with Christian Valentine who I am certain didn't kill him. Unfortunately, at least for me, I'm probably the one the police —"

That got a reaction. She stopped chewing. "The police," she repeated slowly. "You didn't say anything to them about Christian and me, did you?"

"Not yet. But that's the point, Leona. I'm getting all the heat and attention. And I'm not crazy about it. If the cops find out I held out on them, they'll probably really pour it on. But I was giving you the benefit of the doubt. For now. I can always go back and tell them that in all the excitement I simply forgot about your little powwow with Christian . . ."

Jeezus! Now *I* was using Valentine's stupid euphemisms.

"I'm pregnant."

"Yeah, I know," I said, slightly irritated, not sure if it was directed at her or at me. "We all know."

She turned to me. Tears were forming in both eyes.

"Christian," she said, biting at the words, "was the father."

Now *that* I didn't know.

"Jake, Christian was a lot of things, and not all of them good. I know that. In and out of the dressing room, I had heard all the stories, the wise-cracks, the jokes. I realize it's hard to imagine, but he was very good to me. He gave me my first big break, got me promoted right up to where I was. And he took care of me, set me up in an apartment, provided me with clothes, gave me cash when I needed it."

Leona wiped the towel briefly over her eyes. "Look, Jake, I'm not pretending to be naïve or anything, but I'm sure I'm not the only girl who's slept with someone and got ahead because of it."

Her tone was bitter, filled with spite. The revelation brought on thoughts in my mind of Rachel and her promotion. I shook the unpleasant thoughts aside. For now.

"I was trying to make our relationship different. Make it work. And so was he. Everyone knew he was fooling around, he always had, but he was going to get divorced."

I'd heard that story before, too. Earlier, with Murray. It was old news.

She seemed to sense my skepticism. "Oh, sure," she laughed accusingly. "I know what you're thinking. Another dumb broad falling for some jerk's line of BS. But this time it was supposed to be different. I know it was. He had talked to his lawyers."

The recollection of the legal letter in Valentine's safe danced through my mind. I kept the memory to myself.

"When I watched you two at Sam's, it looked anything but amicable."

"I know, I know," she said, nodding her head. "About a month ago, everything started to change. We hardly ever got together anymore. He always had something else going on. It was one excuse after another."

"Right about the time you announced your pregnancy . . ."

"Exactly."

"Out at Sam's," I said, "what was the big deal with the envelope?"

"It was payoff time," she sighed. "The big buyout. He told me we were through. That there wasn't going to be any divorce. That we'd had some good times, but they were over. In the end, Jake, it wasn't any different. And sure, I got taken in, but I wasn't the first, and I'm sure I won't be the last."

I thought about telling her she was the last for Christian Valentine, but I didn't.

"There was five thousand dollars in the envelope," she said.

"You know, Leona, there were measures you could have taken. People you could have talked to."

She gave out a tight laugh. "Sure, that's what I told him. And do you know what he said?"

I shook my head, but I figured I already knew the answer.

Leona held herself protectively. "He told me if I made any waves, said anything at all, he'd make trouble for me — and the baby. He said he wasn't going to lose any big money, or any sleep, over some stupid whore. He said he didn't have to. Not with his connections."

"Yeah, but five thousand bucks, Leona. That won't go very far. Especially in this town. That was a lousy settlement."

"That wasn't all of it, Jake. He said if I kept up my end of the bargain, he'd take care of the apartment, maybe toss me a few bucks once in a while. If I was good, and if I stayed out of the way."

"Sounds just like our boy," I added.

"In the end," she said firmly, "he really was a bastard. But I don't think I have to worry too much about the cops. Sure, I was bitter — I still am — but why would I kill off my 'meal ticket,' as you so aptly put it?"

She had a point and I told her so. I also told her I wouldn't be saying anything to Lieutenant Oakley, or anyone else for that matter, about her relationship with Christian Valentine. That was her business. Hers to deal with.

The one thing I didn't tell her was that I thought the cops would probably find out on their own anyway. But I'd gotten what I wanted from Leona Carter. She might've had it out for Valentine for her own good reasons, but it didn't have anything to do with Rachel. As far as I was concerned, my end of the case was now officially closed.

On my way back, I stopped and left a note with Security, telling Rachel to page me when she was finished. I also stopped to check the results of the sixth at Del Mar.

Morgan's Dancer had won in a cakewalk. Wise Sage had finished out of the money and so had I. My eyes averted the payout.

Why rub salt in an open wound?

Chapter

I was back at my empty blackjack table, just passing time, counting the "eyes-in-the-sky" that monitored the casino from their perches high above.

An elegant, silver-haired, elderly Arab eased himself down in front of me. He gave me a curt smile, nodded, removed a black cigarette from a gold case and lit up. A friendly puff of smoke blew my way and he plopped a handful of yellow thousand-dollar chips on the green baize. I blew back lightly from my lower lip and automatically reached for my cards, which were fanned faceup across the tabletop. Show time.

My natural reaction was to call out "shuffle up" like I was supposed to, then I remembered and looked around for McClusky. I didn't have far to search. He was barreling down on me from deep back in the pit, eyes wide, shoulders hunched, pen poised.

"Mr. H.N.," McClusky beamed to my customer. "How are you? It's good to see you back again."

Mr. H.N. must have been someone really important. Vegas was normally a one-initial town. This guy had two.

The man smiled back and flicked a thin ash into a palm-tree-stenciled ashtray in front of him.

"I came back to give you a chance at your losses," he said, clacking his impressive pile of chips in an appetizing manner, solely for McClusky's benefit.

McClusky was visibly pleased. "You don't want nothin' to do with Jake here, Mr. H.N." He shook his head and put a thick arm around my shoulder to reinforce his point. "No, sirree. Not Jake." He leaned across the table, pulling me with him, and whispered conspiratorially to the man with two initials. "Jake's hotter than a sailor on shore leave. Unh-unh. Let me fix you up with someone who'll at least give you a chance."

Mr. H.N. eyed me suspiciously. "What about that Kellerman girl from the other day?" he asked. "I liked her."

McClusky, still stinging from his encounter with his female nemesis, shook his head sadly. "Nah, she didn't show up for her shift today," he grimaced sourly. "One of those girl things," he explained, as if that cleared up the matter. He excused himself and went over and pulled a dealer off another table.

"This here's Vinnie," McClusky smiled. "Mr. Contini's very own nephew. Just in from Atlantic City and still wet behind the ears."

I knew it wasn't true, but apparently Mr. H.N. was buying it. He nodded his approval. "Then shuffle up. Let the games begin!"

I wanted Michael Buffer, the boxing announcer, to appear. This match had the buildup of a main event, and I could just hear Buffer calling out: "Let's get ready to rummmmmble!"

It was the type of bout I loved to deal. Instead, McClusky wished him well, wrapped his arm around me again, and led me away.

"I could have taken care of him, Coach."

"I know, I know. But you still don't look so good, Jake. You had a rough night . . ." He surveyed the casino with a wary eye and glanced back nervously to Mr. H.N. "As a matter of fact, Ace, things are kinda slow. Why don't you call it a day, get yourself some rest? Take off. I'll see you tomorrow." He punched me out on a nearby computer terminal, then he shook a thick index finger in the direction of my nose. "Bright-eyed and bushy-tailed," he called out over his shoulder, hurrying back to check on Vinnie.

I never even had the chance to tell him this was supposed to be my last shift on BJ, and I don't know if he would have cared.

After changing clothes, I made my way to the showroom. One of the girls told me Rachel had left to do some shopping, but had planned to return later that evening. Security confirmed she had received my message. With a little time to kill, I decided there was one other matter I might as well check into.

One of the friendly ladies in Personnel gave me Franco's auxiliary telephone numbers. Hotel policy firmly stated that all employees were required to be on twenty-four-hour call — maître d's included. I went to the dealers' break room and began dialing.

His heavily accented voice advised me that he wasn't in right now, but if I left my number, he would be sure to call me back. I doubted it and hung up before the beep. A second number brought only endless rings. On the third, I had better luck.

A female voice advised me that I had reached Exxon. Thinking I might have misdialed, I hesitated and then asked if I might speak to Franco Moretti. The voice at the other end hesitated too. Maybe we were having some kind of absurd contest. She clicked what sounded like a wad of gum, then asked if I meant "Frank." I said that he would do.

She told me that Franco — Frank as I now knew him — was busy and couldn't come to the phone. I thanked her and asked for their address. I managed, after another round of clacking and hesitations and the occasional snicker, to also learn his title: "Petroleum Transfer Engineer."

Las Vegas is a city of staggered and short working hours, so most maître d's, musicians and kitchen staff held second jobs. I wasn't really surprised to hear Franco was moonlighting too. After all, how strenuous or time-consuming could maître d'ing be? You dressed in a spiffy penguin suit for a few hours, five nights a week, checked and crossed off names in a big velvet book, bowed now and again, remembered a few important names. Big deal. The worst that could happen was you might break a nail shoving twenty-dollar tips into your pocket. But an executive at Exxon? Now that was pretty heady stuff.

I retrieved my Chevy from the employee parking lot and made for the interstate. I didn't know the northwest end of the city all that well, didn't even know that end had much in the way of industrial or office complexes, but I felt the freeway would help circulate the scorching heat of the late-July afternoon.

I slipped onto I-15 amid light traffic. At route 95, I took the traffic circle west and kept my eyes peeled for the Decatur Boulevard exit. Fifteen minutes later I eased onto the appropriate ramp. At the light I decided on north and regretted my decision almost immediately. The area was heavy with suburban-type homes and busy retail strip malls. I pulled a quick U-turn and backtracked.

When I finally located a number I could read, and then one more, it was apparent the address the receptionist had given me was back where I had first been. Circling back, I cursed and retraced my original course. Eventually the sporadic numbers cooperated, and in due time I was homing in on my target.

A few minutes later, stopped at the corner of Decatur and Vegas Boulevards, I carefully scanned the area for an office tower or industrial building. There was none.

Two small apartment buildings, a service station/convenience mart and a real estate office occupied the four corners of the intersection. The remainder of the area, for as far as I could see, seemed to be made up of more of the same.

The Chevy started making funny noises. The gas gauge hadn't worked for months, so I had learned to fill up every three or four days. In all the excitement, I couldn't remember the last time I'd filled my tank.

I cursed the gum-clacking switchboard operator with a few choice epithets and pulled into the gas bar behind a green, out-of-state, Dodge minivan just pulling away. Two brats stuck out their tongues and made ugly faces at me from the rear window. I waved them the finger in return.

After turning off the ignition and letting the engine run on to its eventual chugging demise, I heard the gas cap being turned and a nozzle start pouring. The attendant, complete with greasy coveralls, leaned down to my window wiping his oily hands on an even oilier rag.

"Fill it up?" he asked in a bored voice.

I hadn't recognized the accent because there wasn't any, but when I glanced up Franco's mug was staring at mine.

"Franco?"

He studied me for a second. First his eyes, then his face, gave way to a reluctant recollection.

"Oh," he said bitterly, "it's you." He gave the rusty and litter-strewn Chevy the once-over. "Nice car. You don't see many eight-track tape players these days."

I could have told him "Nice suit" but didn't. Besides, I hadn't driven all this way for nothing. I decided to try to stay on his good side. If he had one.

"No, I guess you don't," I agreed, playing along. "JC Penney had 'em on sale. Picked up a Betamax at the same time."

Franco grunted, measuring my sincerity. When he didn't add anything further, I decided to prod.

"Tough break," I said solemnly, wiping an old paper towel across my open neck. He fixed me with an icy glare.

Not wanting him to think I was talking about his being a gas jockey, I added, "About Valentine, I mean."

He nodded frugally, but it didn't look as if he was going to break down and blubber all over my elbow.

The heat was practically unbearable inside the car. Franco's hulking figure allowed a margin of shade I was grateful for. I swallowed some saliva and tried to clear my dry throat.

"You see him last night?" I asked.

He kept his black-eyed stare fixed, then shook his head with the bare minimum of exertion.

My skills as an interrogator were more than adequate. But in all fairness, talking with Franco was like arresting a mime and telling him he had the right to remain silent.

I decided to forge ahead. "I heard the two of you played gin between shows. Did you happen to play last night?"

Franco's body tensed at the question. An artery on his sweaty neck thumped erratically. "What the fuck's it to you?"

Finally, a reaction. I noticed, with great satisfaction, that his phony Euro-accent and well-heeled demeanor turned off and on with his job at the Oasis.

"Hey," I said pleasantly, "take it easy. I was just making conversation."

"It's none of your business what I do, or what I did," he sneered. "You might've been playing detective for Christian, but you're not anymore." He snorted at the recollection. "You're such a jerk. You don't know the half of it. You don't even know why —"

He caught himself before saying more on the subject and instead allowed a vicious smile to form on his perspiring face. "I already told what I had to, to the cops. I don't have to tell you squat."

The nozzle clunked. Franco squeezed the handle of the hose until another half gallon or so poured down the side of the car and puddled on the hot pavement.

"Hey, Franco," I called out amiably. "Be careful, buddy! We don't want any explosions, now, do we?"

The words affected him more than I could have imagined. He gazed off into the distance for a moment, as if in deep thought, then he swore mildly under his breath. "Oh, shit. The boat . . ."

His words obviously meant more to him than they did to me. I didn't have a clue what the hell he was talking about. Maybe he'd been sniffing too many fumes.

"Look," I tried to explain politely on his return, "Valentine asked me to help him. I was just doing what I was supposed to do. Gimme a break. I thought maybe you felt as bad about what happened as I do."

"Shit happens," he shrugged. "That's eighteen bucks."

I reached in my pocket and passed him a twenty.

"I understand you and Valentine had some pretty heavy action going," I said casually. "Word has it you were in pretty deep. Looks as if you're off the hook now, though." I allowed myself a small chuckle, trying to gain his confidence. "Ever hear that saying? 'Every cloud has a silver lining?'"

Franco grabbed the twenty and didn't bother to give me change. "Yeah," he sneered. "Ever hear the one: 'Fuck you and the shitbox you drove here in?'" He turned abruptly and walked away, headed for the cool confines of the convenience store.

I noticed a teenage girl inside, behind the counter. She was blowing bubbles with a wad of gum in her mouth, holding a phone to an ear with one hand and twirling curls into her hair with the other.

"Hey, Mr. Petroleum Transfer Engineer!" I called out when he'd reached the door. "What about my coupons?"

Chapter

I headed back to the Oasis in an attempt to catch up with Rachel, hardly noticing the heat still permeating the car. My thoughts were still on Franco. I couldn't shake the ugly feeling that there might be more to his involvement than met the eye.

Along with Leona and Murray, Franco apparently had his own motive. If he owed Valentine money, he was sure to benefit from the entertainer's death. However, my sole concern had been for Rachel's safety, and now that I'd talked to the three of them, there didn't really appear to be any need to worry.

After all, what more could I do? I'd exhausted my abilities at detection. And if somehow Christian Valentine was watching from that big showroom in the sky, I was confident he'd be pleased with my investigative performance. I had talked to the people he would have wanted me to talk to, and shaken the trees he had mentioned to see what fell out.

"Then why the hell am I carrying on?" I asked myself aloud.

As far as I was concerned, any one of them could have done it, including the Asian sex toy. But if I was a betting man, which I was, I'd slap my entire bankroll directly on the nose of his wife, Yolanda.

Besides, who had more to gain?

Murray Gladstone might feel that he had somehow avenged his daughter's slow, spiraling end. But did he have it in him to actually take another's life? Maybe, maybe not. But what would be the point? It most certainly wouldn't bring back Sherry.

As I drove leisurely along the interstate, bombarded by billboards advertising $4.99 buffets, I couldn't help wonder if anyone in town had a betting line on who had killed the illustrious showman. Knowing the town as I affectionately did, I wouldn't bet against it. If I was handicapping, I'd pencil in Murray as the logical long shot.

And what about Leona Carter? A promising career nipped in the bud and a wombful of problems procreated by the unscrupulous, dearly departed. Not that I didn't feel for Leona — I did. But from what I had seen and heard, she carried an inner strength and a will to survive that would do her well — with or without Christian Valentine. She too sat on the outside rail, somewhere between twenty- and thirty-to-one.

And then there was Franco Moretti. Deep down, I was hoping that if it was any of them, it was him. If I was called in for further questioning, I was going to let slip what I knew about those games of gin rummy and to what extent I felt Franco was in debt.

Lieutenant Oakley might not consider me the Sherlock of Glitter Gulch, but I hadn't forgotten about Valentine's notebook that showed the mysterious "F" owing more than eight thousand smackers.

Coincidence? I didn't think so.

Motive? Yeah, maybe.

Turning off the freeway, easing onto Flamingo, I mentally handicapped Franco Moretti at somewhere around four-to-one.

Which brought me to Yolanda Valentine. I didn't have any rationale or motivation at hand, other than an assumption of a rather healthy inheritance, but I had my instincts and gut intuition. I pegged the widowed missus as the odds-on favorite. Abruptly, a little voice inside reminded me I'd been wrong before.

The palm-tree-and-pond logo of the Oasis Hotel beckoned ahead. I drove on determinedly, shaking off bugaboo voices and trying to put the whole damn Valentine affair behind me.

The casino was packed with the sounds of winning and losing — bells, whistles, laughter and lamenting. Just another Saturday night in the middle of a Las Vegas weekend. People trying desperately to win back what they'd lost the night before, a last-ditch attempt to save face, a chance to right the wrongs. One final effort to return home a winner.

Rachel wasn't anywhere backstage and, I admit, my heart sagged. She hadn't been seen since she'd left earlier. I borrowed a dressing room phone and had her paged. I waited, wondering what it would be like hearing my own name called throughout the entire hotel and casino.

"Paging Mr. Morgan . . . Mr. Jake Morgan . . ." It certainly had a nice ring to it.

In many of the larger establishments, hearing celebrities paged was a common occurrence. In some cases, the pages were fabricated by hotel management to thrill the patrons, a shrewd marketing ploy designed so the excited visitors might remember and stay there on their next trip to the Mecca of Madness. They also provided guests with impressive stories to tell the folks back home.

During my tenure at the Oasis, I had heard a potpourri of well-known names called out over the intercom: Madonna, Shania, Eastwood, Jagger, Rodman, Leno, Ali — always a nice mixture of races, ages and tastes. Once, Mikhail Gorbachev had been paged, but no one could verify his presence. The comedian Yakov Smirnoff was booked into the Dromedary Lounge that week, and I presumed he must have had something to do with it.

"Mr. Morgan . . . Mr. Morgan . . ."

For a moment I thought I was being paged, then a finger tapped me gently on the shoulder. It was one of the stagehands.

"Mr. Morgan," he said politely, pointing to the phone at my ear. "The girls . . . they'll be arriving soon for makeup . . ."

"I'll be right out," I apologized.

With no response to Rachel's page, I dialed her home. She answered on the first ring.

"I'm so glad you called, Jake. It's been a horrible day."

"I know what you mean. Mine's been a bit of a horror show too."

"Care to talk about it?"

"Well, I would, but right now they're trying to get me out of the dressing room area."

"How about dinner?" she asked.

"Dinner sounds good. But I really do have to get home and change. I've been driving around most of the day and it's been hot as hell."

Just then I spotted Yolanda Valentine walking past one of the doors.

"There goes Mrs. Valentine," I remarked.

"What is she doing there?" Rachel said. "I would have thought she'd be home, mourning."

Something had been eating at me for a while and I suddenly realized what it was that was stopping me from putting the Valentine affair behind me.

"I really wanted to talk to her," I said. "What time were you thinking of going out, Rachel?"

"To tell you the truth, I want to get out of the house as soon as I can. Christian's murder still has me messed up." Her voice was a little shaky. "Look, Jake. Go talk with Yolanda. Give me your address and I'll meet you there."

Nothing could have made me happier than to give her my address.

"Great," she said. "I know the complex. I can be there in fifteen minutes."

"Okay, and if you get there before me, there's a key taped to the bottom of the flowerpot outside my door."

"Some cop," she said and hung up.

I rushed out of the dressing room, but Yolanda was nowhere in sight. The security guard at the entrance pointed to the Ali Baba Deli when I asked if he'd seen where she'd gone. By the time I caught up with her, she was just ordering a café au lait from the waitress.

"Mr. Morgan." She looked around as if she had been expecting someone else. "Uh, would you like to sit down for a minute?" She glanced around again. "Coffee?"

"No, thank you. I'll only be a minute." I did, however, take a seat in the booth.

Yolanda moved a large red bag to make more room. "I came by to pick up one of Christian's favorite suits." She sniffled and searched for a tissue in her purse. "I couldn't sit around the house any longer today. What with the police and all the phone calls," she said, "I just had to get out."

Her drink came and she started dabbing at her eyes. "So what can I do for you?"

"Well," I began, "first of all, I wanted to tell you how sorry I am for what happened to your husband." I searched around in my head for something nice to say about him, but it took longer than I thought. "He was a great entertainer," I finally told her.

"One of the best," she acknowledged, wiping at the corner of an eye with a tissue. "Thank you."

I nodded. "The other thing is, I don't know if he told you, but I was helping him on a couple of things."

"Yes, I heard you were trying to find out who was sending the hate mail and threats. Franco told me."

"Franco?" I asked, surprised. "I didn't realize the two of you were close."

She studied me for a moment, still dabbing, then she said, "It wasn't close like that. It was platonic. Franco spent a lot of time with my husband, and Christian confided in him. Sometimes more than he did me. In a way, I suppose Christian was trying to protect me from the business." She started to weep openly and dabbed even harder. "Bless his heart."

Watching people cry always makes me uncomfortable. "Uh, what I really wanted to do was return something." I reached into my pocket and handed her three crumpled hundred-dollar bills.

She looked at me strangely. "What's that for?"

"It's the balance of the retainer he gave me. I didn't have the opportunity to earn it."

Yolanda took the bills and stuffed them in my shirt pocket. "Don't worry," she told me with a small smile. "I insist."

"But —"

"*Ssshh*," she whispered, pressing a finger to my lips. "It's all right."

Her finger, as warm and nice as it was, remained on my mouth a little longer than necessary and now that she was talking so close, I detected the hint of gin and vermouth on her breath. I didn't like the direction the conversation was going. Especially considering her husband wasn't even buried yet.

"Uh, I really didn't earn it," I insisted.

Yolanda removed her hand and let her arm fall lazily to the back of the booth. "It's only a few hundred bucks. It'll make me feel so much better if you keep it." She lifted her hand and brushed lightly at my shoulder. "You were extremely brave to take on something so dangerous. I admire that in a man."

Her eyes were back to being dry.

I laughed nervously, trying to break the spell.

"Just how brave are you, Jake Morgan?" she asked seductively.

"Who, me?" I swallowed. "The bravest thing I've ever done was fry bacon in the nude." I knew it was the wrong thing to say as soon as I had said it.

She smiled widely at that. "I'd like to see that sometime."

I wasn't sure if she meant seeing me naked or dodging hot lard, but I wasn't going to take any chances. I changed the subject, made some small talk, excused myself and got the hell out of there.

As I passed the cashier, I heard my name being paged throughout the casino. It really *did* sound cool. I walked over to a courtesy phone and picked it up — the operator put me through.

"Jake." Rachel was breathing hard. "I just got to your place, but . . ."

"But what?"

"I hope you're coming over right away."

"What's wrong?" I asked.

After a moment she said, "I think you've been robbed, too."

Chapter

I asked Rachel to lock my apartment and wait outside. The coincidence gave me an eerie feeling, especially if there was any connection with the break-in at her place and the murder of Christian Valentine.

The apartment was a modest one-bedroom on the top floor of a three-story building. I'd been living there comfortably for a year now. When I first moved to Las Vegas, I'd stayed at a sleazy motel off the main strip. At the time, I was enrolled in a six-week course at the Las Vegas School for Dealers. I moved out right after landing the job at the Oasis.

I pushed the Chevy to her limit, and she responded with a certain amount of reluctance. It was just before six and the traffic was working in my favor. The apartment was located off Sahara Avenue, on a quiet street named Spencer, a ten- to fifteen-minute drive from the Oasis. I did it in eight.

Rachel was waiting outside. I stopped in a no-parking zone in front of the building. After making sure she was okay, we went into the building and took the stairs two at a time.

When we entered the apartment, Rachel exclaimed, "See!"

Letting out a deep breath, I went into the living room and started picking up stray shirts, pants, underwear, socks. Once retrieved, I tossed the pile around the bedroom door. I came back and sheepishly began collecting empty beer cans, dirty dishes, CD and cassette cases, crumpled bags of potato chips and two weeks' worth of newspapers, magazines and *Racing Forms*.

"Uh, Rachel," I stammered. "There wasn't any break-in . . ."

Judging by the state of her home, Rachel was meticulously neat and clean by nature. She surveyed the room and measured me for a moment, standing wide-eyed as I tidied up around her.

"You need a cleaning lady, Jake," she said, shaking her head.

"I, uh, have one," I confessed. "She comes twice a month. Every other Monday." I picked up two cushions from the floor and repositioned them on the sofa, motioning for her to sit.

"Today's Saturday," I explained weakly.

Rachel stepped gingerly around a package of Oreo cookies. She sat reluctantly, shaking her head some more. From the look of resignation on her face, I expected either "*Jake!*" or "*Oh, God!*" or "*Men!*" to be forthcoming.

She chose "*Men!*"

I went over and sat beside her. "I'm sorry if I gave you a scare, Rachel, but it just slipped my mind." She eyed me suspiciously. I smiled back and gave her my best Groucho Marx imitation, holding an imaginary cigar in my mouth and wiggling my fingers as I told her, "Why don't I make it up to you, sweetheart!"

"Don't get your libido in a knot, Hot Lips. There's no way in the world you're getting me in *that* bedroom." She gave me a saucy smile. "At least not until Tuesday."

I cursed myself for not springing for the weekly maid service. The vision I'd had of Rachel and me frolicking in clean satin sheets slowly dissipated out the window.

"Touché," I laughed, standing up and collecting myself as best I could.

"How about a drink?" she asked with a caustic smile, apparently amused by my physical discomfort.

"A drink. Right . . ." I picked up a handful of mail that lay strewn across the coffee table. "Stay right there," I said, not wanting her to follow. If the thought of my bedroom had turned her off, the kitchen would send her running to a convent.

"White wine if you've got it," she called out to me in the kitchen. "And a *clean* glass!"

We sipped wine, from clean crystal glasses, and went over how we had each spent the day. Rachel was sympathetic, and concerned for both Murray and Leona. By the time I told her of my encounter with Franco at the Exxon station she was back to her old self.

I offered her a refill. She accepted gratefully and recapped her day, most of which had been spent in lengthy, intensive interviews with the police. The rest had been spent in cast meetings trying to revamp the show around Johnny Ventura. She allowed herself a large smile and announced with great relief that she was still up for the major dance-and-song routines with the new star.

And that's when it hit me.

I had completely forgotten about Johnny Ventura, the young, rising talent-in-waiting. The morning papers had speculated that he'd be taking over for Valentine full-time. There was "motive" written in capital letters all across his capped pearly whites, not to mention his fat new contract. I ran this by Rachel.

"Oh, come on, Jake!" she scolded lightly. "You hardly know the man. Okay, he's a bit aggressive with the girls, but his bark is bigger than his bite. And he's been doing fine with the parts he's had. I've known him for years. Johnny Ventura wouldn't hurt a fly."

She had thought Christian Valentine was a stand-up guy, too, but I didn't remind her of that. Instead, I finished my drink, collected the glasses and made a point of taking them, as well as the bottle, to the kitchen.

"Maybe you're right," I called out. "But he's sure in one helluva better position now than he was a week ago." I came back into the room looking at my watch. It read 6:35.

"You hungry?" I asked her. "I could whip something up . . ."

Rachel eyed my hasty attempt at cleaning. "As a matter of fact, I am," she said, reading her watch as well. "But I have to be back by eight. The director's blocking out routines for next week. We're lucky. The Sultan's Tent is dark Sunday and Monday, so they're hoping to work me in by Tuesday." She gave the kitchen area a skeptical glance. "What say we grab a bite out? My treat."

Apparently, that reminded her of something important. She jumped up from the sofa, wiping a few scattered crumbs from her clothes, smiling radiantly. "Jake! With everything that's been going on, I almost forgot! You're not going to believe this. I don't know if I told you, but I really don't like gambling. Well, the craziest thing happened while we were waiting our turns with the police today. Jenny Tesio was flipping through one of the *Racing Forms* — you know how they're always laying around backstage — well, all of a sudden Jenny gives out this shriek and calls us over. She points at the form and gets all excited. She says, "It's an omen of some kind," that we *have to* take advantage of it, and she starts asking us girls to ante up."

I had an uneasy feeling of what was coming. I led her to the door. She was bubbling almost to the point of bursting.

"Jake, this is the crazy part," she continued, barely containing herself. "The girls have been talking about you a bit — you know how girls are — and I guess Jenny remembered your last name. You see, the horse's name Jenny was pointing at was *Morgan's Dancer*! — you know, sort of like you and me. Well, we managed to put together three hundred dollars and the silly little bugger went out and won!" She let out a tiny shriek. "We picked up around nine thousand dollars. Six hundred of that was mine!"

"Hey, that's great, Rachel!" I responded with what I felt was real enthusiasm. "That's a really great system, too. I'll have to remember it."

With that, I locked up and we left.

Chapter

Las Vegas is not a forgiving city. I had seen all kinds of wide-eyed schmucks who had arrived with high hopes, big dreams and fat bankrolls backed by surefire systems. Most of them left town wide-eyed, too — with their wallets empty and their tails tucked tightly between their legs.

Nor is Las Vegas a grieving city. I had heard that in '63 President John F. Kennedy received a paltry minute of silence when word of his assassination hit town. Bobby and Dr. King never even got that.

So it was no small wonder that, over the next three days following Christian Valentine's untimely demise, the status quo ante was restored.

Not that the media had let it go — they hadn't. The murder was still front-page news in most of the local and national newspapers. And it remained the opening item on almost every radio and television broadcast. They reported that the police investigation was in full swing, intensive and stepping up, but at this point no one had been arrested.

But life went on. After all, there were cards to be dealt, dice to be rolled, and lives to be gambled with.

I had finally finished my stint as blackjack dealer and decided to take the week holiday I had coming before moving into my new career as a poker dealer. I hadn't seen Rachel since Saturday, but we'd talked a few times over the telephone, discussing the Valentine situation. She had been working hard, preparing for her opening-night performance this evening.

For the first time in a long time, I had a good feeling about where my life was heading. My outlook was positive, I was sleeping much better and I hadn't had "the dream" in almost a week. The relationship with Rachel hadn't been consummated, but neither had it hit any bumps in the road. We had agreed to get together tonight and celebrate her debut. And the cleaning lady had come and gone.

These happy thoughts were wafting through my head, despite the fact I was standing in the middle of a cemetery attending Christian Valentine's funeral. It was just after ten, a fiery hot and cloudless Tuesday morning. Another start to an endless string of torrid temperatures. The kind of day snickering locals would explain to unhinged tourists with "At least it's a *dry* heat."

I tugged a wrinkled white handkerchief from the pocket of my rumpled jacket and wiped "dry" beads of perspiration from under my chin. A squadron of jet fighters from Nellis Air Force Base flew with majestic grace high above, their silver skins reflecting the dazzling yellow sun. The fragrance from hundreds of bouquets and thousands of sweet-smelling flowers drifted my way.

Not that I was anywhere near the hub of activity surrounding Christian Valentine's final performance. That was a couple hundred feet away. Instead, I was leaning against a tall gray monument dedicated to a fellow named Jerome Ferguson, gathering what little shade it offered, and glancing now and again at a crumpled *Racing Form*.

Christian Valentine, being the ultimate entertainer, had reportedly requested his remains be scattered throughout the Sultan's Tent showroom. But since he hadn't stipulated cremation, hotel management wisely declined. It was just as well, I thought. Who'd want to end up in the dusty bowels of some Hoover vacuum?

His funeral at Bunkers Memorial was well attended, despite being closed to the public. Entry was restricted to those with specially printed passes or those with employee cards from one of the better hotels. I'd noticed on my way in, however, a young guy scalping tickets he had somehow acquired. He was right next to the old woman selling T-shirts and glossy photographs of Christian Valentine.

The elite of the entertainment world strolled in a leisurely fashion under the hot desert sun, resplendent in designer threads and fashion sunglasses — the women protecting their face-lifted features with colorful parasols, the men trying vainly to keep mousse and gel from bubbling on their transplanted hair. Heat waves shimmered from the lid of the shiny mahogany casket. If Valentine wasn't somehow destined for an eternity in hell, he was certainly getting a good taste of it today.

The paparazzi were having a field day. It was comparable to big-game hunters having free rein in the San Diego Zoo. They knelt, aimed, focused, shot, reloaded and shot again, just to make sure. Then they sped off in search of other quarry.

And in order that inquiring minds be kept up-to-date, reporters from the grocery store tabloids mingled amongst themselves, apparently unfazed that they were being treated like lepers by the stars.

And the stars were everywhere. The music world was amply represented by the likes of Englebert and Tom, Reba and Garth, Barbra and James, Ozzy and Sharon, and Cher with some skinny kid from a heavy-metal band.

Tinseltown was out in force too. I could see Warren and Jack, Brad and Jennifer, Arnold and Maria and Liz and what'shisname.

The ubiquitous Mr. Blackwell, wearing a peach-colored Lord West tuxedo fixed with a mauve boutonniere, scribbled feverishly in a poppy-red spiral notebook.

It was insanity at its finest.

The cemetery had a festive air. A fifteen-foot banner with a photo of

Valentine performing hung high above the casket. Tables were loaded with hors d'oeuvres, Camembert, rock lobster, prawns and fat red snapper. Attentive waiters armed with thin bamboo fans stood nearby, chasing away flies and pesky desert gnats. A bar had been set off to the side, offering Grolsch beer, Bolla wine, Remy Martin cognac, Glenfiddich scotch, Dom Perignon champagne, and Evian water. It was lavish, but it was damned un-American.

A choir, bigger than the one at the Mormon Tabernacle and dressed in flowing white robes like gospel singers from the Deep South, stood precariously on hastily constructed, temporary bleachers. Led by a heavyset energetic black woman, the choir sang songs from Valentine's repertoire. At the moment, they were in the middle of a lively rendition of Rod Stewart's "Da Ya Think I'm Sexy?"

And to cap it all, Siegfried and Roy, the popular magicians, were walking around wearing sly smiles, suggesting they might be producing a white tiger from the coffin, or at least would enjoy doing so.

Like I said, the whole thing was nuts.

Rumor had it Barbara Walters was on the prowl for in-depth, behind-the-scenes interviews and after my local TV debut, I was hell-bent on keeping a low profile.

I spotted Rachel off to the left of the gathering. Most of the cast and crew from the show and the hierarchy from the Oasis were also present.

Murray Gladstone was looking terribly uncomfortable, but it might have been the heat. Leona Carter appeared quite forlorn and rejected. Johnny Ventura was waving and signing autographs. A tuxedoed Franco was chatting up a young female dealer and not getting anywhere. A perspiring Julius Contini was talking animatedly with McClusky.

A thought suddenly struck me. I had totally forgotten Contini on my odds list. News reports over the past forty-eight hours had mentioned that

Christian Valentine had three years remaining on a five-year contract. At a cool million a month for ten months a year, that added up to thirty big ones. And that didn't even take the hotel's insurance policy into consideration. Seemed like enough motive to me.

I took out my handkerchief and wiped again. In the great scheme of things, what did it really matter anyway? I wasn't working on the case any longer. At least I kept telling myself that.

With the large crowd, cars weren't allowed into this part of the cemetery. The lone exception was a white Ford minivan with tinted windows perched between two rows of tombstones, its engine working overtime to keep its occupants cool. If my guess was correct, the cops were videotaping the occasion.

Suddenly, heads turned. Yolanda Valentine was coming down a path in a black umbrella-topped golf cart chauffeured by a solemn-looking funeral director. A nervous priest sat facing backwards, a Bible in one hand and a rail grasped firmly in the other. The crowd hushed. The choir leader quickened the tempo to the last chorus of Paul Simon's "Fifty Ways to Leave Your Lover."

The golf cart squeaked to a stop, and Yolanda was helped out. She was wearing a black knee-length mourning dress with matching shoes, hat and veil. The priest, happier now that he had his feet planted on God's own earth, escorted her through the now-silent throng. As the huge crowd parted to let her pass, Yolanda stopped occasionally to dab at her eyes or to hug a sympathetic friend.

The death of her husband had taken its toll. She appeared frail and lost, devoid of the energy and self-assertiveness I'd seen when we met. She had to be helped to and from her seat during the ceremony.

A stream of guests took the podium to praise the great Christian Valentine. I wondered how many of the speakers were truly his friends.

What did they really know about him? My own experience suggested he loved himself more than anyone else — he was the supreme egoist.

As the proceedings drew to a close and they prepared to lower the casket into the ground, I heard a distant rumbling overhead. Suddenly, the jets I had seen earlier did a flyby in the classic "missing man" formation.

Now *that* was impressive. I wondered what it cost to get the Air Force to stage that little number? Had Valentine performed with Bob Hope overseas? Maybe he was a buddy of the President. More than likely, Christian had left instructions with his lawyers to pay for the show.

As the casket disappeared, Yolanda shrieked and fainted and almost fell into the grave. An alert funeral director caught her on the way down. Contini helped carry her to a nearby seat. A concerned crowd parted again as the golf cart revved into gear.

I slipped away, eager to beat the horde to the parking lot. As I left, the choir stood, ready to sing. I shuddered, but the tune turned out to be an appropriate gospel song.

Relieved, I picked up my pace. Elvis Presley's "Are You Lonesome Tonight?" had been one of Christian Valentine's biggest numbers.

Chapter

It was an hour before Rachel's premiere in the Oasis' new extravaganza and she was as nervous as a nun at a Chippendale show. The backstage area was crowded with cast and crew, abuzz with anticipation, alterations, and last-minute instructions.

Rachel stretched her lithe body, contorted into positions I could only hope to participate in, did a few meaningful knee bends and finished with a flurry of fine pirouettes. With her warm-up completed, she toweled off. After what I had just witnessed, I could have used a toweling off myself.

"God, Jake," she sighed. "I'm so excited, my body's trembling."

"Mine, too."

She took a sip of mineral water from a bottle nearby. "I can't believe this is really happening. It's absolutely fantastic! I've wanted this for as long as I can remember. And tonight . . . tonight it's all coming true."

"I hope so," I agreed, watching new beads of perspiration run down her slender neck and into the tight confines of her leotard.

"Rachel?" a pleasant voice called out. "We're ready for makeup."

Rachel let out a nervous breath. "I gotta run. Wish me luck."

"Break a leg, kiddo." I gave her a hug and a good-luck kiss.

She kissed me back, thanked me, then turned and left.

"Hell, break *both* of them!" I shouted affably.

For a Tuesday night the casino was jammed. The opening of the new show might have had something to do with it. The reason for having the expensive extravaganzas in the first place was to steer showgoers to the gaming tables either before or after the entertainment.

I had already laid down my bets for the day and was waiting patiently for the score of the ballgame back in Boston. Martinez was up again and I couldn't remember him ever losing two in a row at Fenway.

My luck was definitely changing. I had even picked a winner at Del Mar earlier in the day. The correlation of a horse's name, Cupid's Arrow, and that of Valentine hadn't been lost on me. The arrow reference had been a pleasant bonus, too, and although I'd used Rachel's system — silly as it was — I had not mentioned my win to her. She probably wouldn't understand my good fortune at Valentine's expense. In a way, I didn't understand it myself.

I trotted off to the Camel's Hump for a celebratory drink.

⊡

"Hey, Lieutenant. Mind if I join you?"

Oakley didn't come right out and say, "Oh, shit!", but he might as well have, judging by the expression on his face. He glanced around the busy bar as if he were searching for another table I could take. Then again, he might have been trying to see if he had any friends around who might spot us together. Finding neither, he stretched out one long leg and slid a chair my way.

He looked haggard, as if he'd had a long day or maybe two. His blue-eyed crispness had faded, his suit had wilted and a light growth of blond beard poked from his sturdy chin. In a way I felt sorry for him, because I knew the media could be relentless in their hounding. And there was probably all kinds of pressure coming down from the powers that be.

"Rough day, huh?"

He picked absently at a spot on a bottle of Perrier. "Yeah, you could say that."

An attractive black waitress, fully veiled and wearing a colorful harem-type outfit, glided up to our table. "How may I serve you?" she asked.

I ordered a Beck's. Oakley held up his water by the neck of the bottle, asking for another.

She smiled from behind her thin veil. "Your wish is my command." She bowed her head slightly, twirled a hand from forehead to waist and scampered off.

It was that kind of place.

"How's the investigation going, Lieutenant?"

He let out a deep sigh and thought about it for a moment. Then, as if he'd resigned himself to the fact that he was stuck with me, he said, "It's going. But it's going slow."

"Any leads?"

"None that I want to share with you."

"You missed a helluva funeral this morning."

A corner of his mouth turned up slightly. "Not really. I caught it on videotape." He shook his head, remembering. "And by the way, that little fortune cookie Valentine had hidden away has been cleared. She's a Keno runner here, and the tapes show she was working."

The waitress returned with our drinks. Although they were only a buck a piece, Oakley made no move to pay. I passed her a five, smiled, and told her to keep the change. She did the waving thing again and left.

Oakley saluted his thanks to me with his bottle. "Last of the big-time spenders, eh, Morgan?"

I returned the salute with my Beck's and drank straight from the cold bottle. "I had a great day today, Lieutenant, and I'm looking forward to an even better evening. By the way, if you want some free handicapping advice," I told him in a low voice, "you might want to put a few bucks on Martinez and the Bosox tonight."

He gave me a shake of his head. "I work too hard for my money, Morgan. Besides, word has it you're not the best of handicappers. Not by a long shot."

"Well," I said brightly. "I'm on a roll right now. I've got a real good feeling things are about to change. As a matter of fact, Lieutenant, I'm pretty sure I can peg the chief suspect in your case, if you're interested . . ."

"Not really, Morgan." He gave me an icy stare. "Unless you're going to confess . . ."

"*Moi?*" I said, pointing at my chest. "Come on, don't tell me I'm still on your hit list?"

"No. Unfortunately, I've moved you farther down." He paused for a second. "For now."

"So, who's your chief suspect?" I asked, pulling closer to the table. "It's the wife, right?"

Oakley gave me a condescending look for his reply.

"Well. Isn't it usually?"

"What do you expect me to say? You should know better."

"Really, Lieutenant," I chided. "You can't tell me you and the boys haven't investigated Yolanda Valentine inside and out and top to bottom. Come on! It would have been your first avenue. It's obvious she had the most to gain. That's the way I'd look at it at least."

"You know, Morgan," he said in a slow drawl, "for a cop with your record . . ."

"No, it's not that," I argued with an icy stare of my own. "It's just that —"

"What do you take me for? Look, I've checked you out six ways to

Sunday. And don't forget Morgan, you were my most likely suspect at the start. The first thing I did was get a hold of your police file from back east. You got an honorable discharge from the Boston PD. Big deal. And now you're going to tell me who the chief suspect is — or should be — in my investigation. Well, thank you very much, Detective Morgan, but yours wasn't exactly the most impressive duty sheet I've ever read."

He gave me a lazy glare, then he asked in a confidential manner, "You want to tell me why you didn't stay on?"

He was digging. Good cop/bad cop — all rolled into one. And he was doing a damn fine job of it, too.

My time spent in the Boston PD wasn't something I enjoyed talking about. Especially to cops. A distant memory flashed fast-forward from the deepest recess of my mind, and I fought it back to its proper hiding place.

"Look, Lieutenant, I'm not your adversary. Far from it. The job really wasn't that bad. It just wasn't for me. I gave it my best shot, tried to roll with the punches and put up with all the bureaucracy. Let's just say things didn't work out and leave it at that." I finished my beer in one long pull, perturbed at the resignation in my voice and the slight tremble in both hands.

"I gotta give you credit," he said affably. "A lot more than you give me."

It suddenly dawned on me: the bastard *knew*. He really *knew*! The gleam in his eye gave it away. I made motions to leave.

Oakley summoned our waitress. He slid back the sleeve of his rumpled suit jacket and glanced at his watch. It was one of those monstrous, complex jobs that I could never handle.

"Two of those," he told her, pointing at my Beck's.

When she'd left, Oakley sighed and sank back into the seat. He flicked open the top button of his wrinkled shirt, casually loosened the Windsor knot in his tie. His body language read "off duty," but I could tell his mind was working overtime.

"You know, Morgan, I shouldn't even be talking to you. As a matter of fact, I wouldn't be if it wasn't for what I read in your police file."

"Well," I said, summoning up all the good nature I could muster. "As you said, it really wasn't much of a report."

The beginning of a smile dripped slowly down Oakley's face.

I didn't like it.

"No, not that one," he shucked off with a wave of his beefy hand. "I mean the report that *wasn't* brought forward at your hearing. You know, the 'unofficial' account. The IA report. You remember the boys from Internal Affairs, don't you?"

Sure I did. And he knew damn well. A thin film of perspiration broke out all over my body. I was happy when the beers arrived.

"Is this some kind of formal interrogation?" I asked him. "Because if it is —"

"Come on!" he said with feigned shock. "This is just two guys sucking back a couple of brewskies, reminiscing about our good old days on the force. Isn't that what you wanted?"

I slumped back in my seat. "Right . . ."

"You want to tell me about it?"

"Not really," I mumbled. "Why don't you tell me."

There was a lull in the conversation, an impasse which I wasn't about to break. We sat like that for a full minute, Oakley sizing me up.

"Look, Morgan," he finally said. "I meant what I said earlier. About giving you credit. Whatever happened back in Beantown happened. It's water under the bridge. The fact is, you were ranked first or second in every course at the academy. To tell you the truth, I didn't believe it at first. You had the highest cumulative scores in the history of the Boston PD. And what about all the citations you received?" He paused and shook his head. "You turned down all kinds of promotions . . . and you threw it all away over some stupid gambling habit?"

I drank slowly from my bottle. "There was more to it than what was in the IA report."

"Usually is," Oakley nodded. "Tell me about it, Jake."

That was the only time he'd ever called me by my first name, and it took me by surprise. I had never told the complete story of what had happened and I wasn't sure I wanted to now. But there was something about Oakley's concern that appeared to be more than official interest. I believed his curiosity was genuine and didn't have anything to do with this case.

"I'd been working Traffic for about eight years," I began, "when a spot opened up in Vice. The thought of getting away from all the bureaucracy was really inviting, so I jumped at it. I started out busting strip joints and massage parlors. Then they put me on sting operations — everything from stolen cars to prostitution. I enjoyed it. I don't know if it was some kind of natural acting ability or what, but I fell into roles easily and had no problems ad-libbing bullshit."

"I can believe that," Oakley replied. "Go on."

"It was around that time the East was experiencing a rapid growth in underground gambling joints. Between Atlantic City and Foxwoods there are no legal casinos, and there were a lot of new players who had gotten their feet wet at these places. Underground card rooms started springing up all over the place, offering mostly Texas Hold 'Em poker, a lot of stud and even some craps. My lieutenant wanted somebody to go undercover and I jumped at it." I took a long drink from my bottle, staring off into the casino.

"You went too deep, huh?"

I turned my head back to him. "Yeah, you could say that. I was building a list on twenty or so joints. Was supposed to gather names of players, license plates, the hours of operation, and who was running the house. I must have been playing the part well, because we busted at least fifteen of them. Most of them opened up again in a week or two at a new location, but we started to make some inroads. And nobody got wise to me. We used the confiscated cash for my seed money and I just kept going." I paused and even managed a small smile. "I actually started doing well and was making money more often than not. I recorded most of my wins and losses truthfully on my reports, but not always. Then I started to play on my days off."

Oakley nodded.

"I don't know what came over me. These weren't even people I would associate with outside of a card room. Most of them were degenerates, didn't even hold a steady job, but they always seemed to have cash. Unfortunately my good luck started to turn. The more I pushed, the deeper I got stuck. I started really cheating on my reports, but it wasn't enough to cover what I was losing on my own time. By the end, I had tapped out my bank account and credit cards. I was on the sheets for more than ten grand and was starting to get squeezed for it. And that's when the shit hit the fan."

"You got winged in the shoulder," Oakley said. "How did that happen?"

"I was in a $40–$80 game and was running all over the table. It was the rush of a lifetime for me. I was up almost eighteen thousand and ready to pack it in. Literally. I had enough to pay off everybody and get my shit back together. I had decided to play one more round and call it a night.

"The next thing I know, there's four guys in ski masks pointing guns at the table and telling us to hug the floor. As three of them started scooping cash off the table, all I could think was how my world was going to sink even further than it had. Then they started to take wallets and jewelry. When this elderly player wouldn't give up his diamond wedding ring, he was whacked on the side of the head with a pistol butt. They tried like hell to get it off. When they couldn't, one of them cut the finger right off his hand.

"It was the proverbial final straw. I snapped. And to tell you the truth, at that point I don't really know if I cared if I lived or died. I knew losing the cash in front of me, and what I had in my pockets, would put me in a hole I would never get out of. Seeing this poor bastard lying next to me holding his bloody hand just put me over the edge.

"They had one of the guys who was running the house up against a wall and were demanding to know where he kept the house money. He'd already given them what he had in his belly belt, but they wanted more and had a gun to his head. I knew he'd given them everything he had, as most of us had been playing for two days and had run up a lot of credit on the sheet. They told the other house guy they'd shoot his partner if they didn't get what they wanted. The one against the wall was shaking and crying and the other was pleading and swearing on his mother's grave that they had given everything there was. He got shot in the knee and fell to the floor.

"The attention was all at that side of the room, so I reached down to my ankle holster and yelled out 'Police!' The shooter turned and aimed at me, and I put one round through his chest. He was dead before he hit the ground. The other, with the gun on the house guy, managed to hit me in the shoulder, but I got off two more rounds and caught him in the thigh. The remaining two grabbed him and ran for the door. I rolled over, blacked out and that was that."

"So much for your cover," said Oakley.

"Yeah, not to mention my career. Internal Affairs had a field day. Officially it was written up as an 'on-duty' shooting because of my under-cover status, but my superiors had dug deep enough to find out the real story. They wanted me out but didn't want any negative coverage in the media."

"So they gave you a discharge," Oakley stated.

"Yup, then I got the hell out of Dodge."

"Your first one, right?"

I swallowed hard. "Yeah, and my last. Turned out to be some kind of gang initiation. The kid was eighteen."

"You still see it?"

"Uh-huh . . . most nights. But it's getting better."

Oakley studied me hard, then he slapped both hands on his thighs. "Okay, I was razzing you earlier to find out what makes you tick. I guess maybe I owe you. You get one question to ask on the Valentine case. Fire away."

His candor caught me off guard momentarily, but then I asked him: "Did you ever find the photograph of Christian Valentine and Rachel?"

"Unh-unh. We searched high and low. His suite, his home, even his dressing room. Not a thing."

"I suppose whoever whacked him could have taken it."

He nodded his agreement. "I suppose . . ."

"The wife," I pointed out. "For some reason I can't help but keep turning back to her."

"Maybe you've been reading too many whodunits. Or watching too much TV."

"Nah, it's more than that. It's something here," I said, pointing to my gut.

Oakley afforded an off-duty smile. "Women's intuition?"

"Yeah, maybe," I smiled in return. "I might be trying to show my feminine side."

A small beep permeated the air. Oakley glanced at his watch. He fumbled with various buttons on the gadget. Finally, he managed to silence the thing. "Look, I gotta be going soon. I've got a wife, two kids and a golden retriever who haven't seen me for almost three days." He gulped the remainder of his beer, then he looked at me in an almost fatherly fashion. "Forget Yolanda, okay? You were right about one thing, though. We did check her inside and out. Up and down. Zilch."

"Her alibi was that clean?"

"The cleanest. She was spotted heading across Lake Mead that very evening."

"Lake Mead? What the hell was she doing out there?"

He shrugged his massive shoulders. "Apparently she spends her week-ends out on their yacht — hates the chichi crowds that roll in from California. She takes off on Fridays between eight and nine, just before dark, and hauls over to Hamblin Bay. She drops anchor and spends her nights on board and days up in the hills. It's deserted out there, nothing but dirt, cactus and rocks, but she likes to spend time getting in touch with nature. Hasn't missed a weekend in four months."

"She could have doubled back."

"Come on, Morgan," he said dryly. "Give us some credit. This baby of hers has every navigational option and gadget possible. Boat's worth about a half mil. We checked the mileage — or whatever you call it on a boat — and everything matched. We even had the logs from her fuel purchases cross-checked. The dockmaster fills her up every Friday afternoon. They matched bang on."

I thought about that, getting discouraged, then I suggested, "Maybe she doubled back by land."

"Not unless she flew. There's no roads. Besides, it would be a four- or five-hour drive even if she had transportation. She never would have made it back in time."

"I don't know," I mused. "It sounds too pat."

Oakley turned up his palms. "That's the way it is."

"Still, she had one helluva motive. Valentine must have been loaded. There are no kids, so I guess everything's hers."

"Yeah, I know. That's what I thought, too. But Christian Valentine wasn't near as loaded as everyone thinks. He had a lot of bad investments. And he's been losing at the baccarat tables. Not here, over at Caesars."

"Must have pissed off Contini — Valentine losing so much at another casino and not his," I said, wondering about that for a moment.

"I guess. But seriously, forget about Yolanda Valentine. Forget the whole case. You may not think we're as sharp as the Boston PD, but believe me, the good citizens of Clark County are getting their tax money's worth."

The skepticism must have shown on my face.

"Morgan, mull this around in your head for a second. Why do you think you're off my top-ten list of suspects?"

I thought about it but nothing came to mind.

"Well, it's not because I like you. Come on, show me what they taught you back east."

I thought about it even more, but still nothing came to mind.

"Okay, here's a hint. It's for the same reason Yolanda Valentine isn't on it."

He had me there. "Somebody spotted me on Lake Mead, too?"

"Very funny." He knocked back the few remaining drops of beer. "But no. We picked up an excellent set of prints in three different places in the suite. They're all from the same person. And guess what? They weren't Christian Valentine's. They also weren't yours, or Yolanda's. Hers were easy to check; we just called and she offered. Yours we got from the Oasis. Luckily, every hotel and casino in the state has their own file on their staff for security reasons. It's just a matter of time. The computers are working twenty-four hours a day. But it's a big job."

He was right. The Oasis alone had six thousand employees.

Oakley's wrist beeped again. "Damn thing," he said with an air of frustration and poking frantically at his expensive toy. "Look, I gotta run."

I glanced at my easy-to-read, fifteen-dollar Timex. It was 7:50. Rachel was due on in ten minutes. I was looking forward to the show, but even more so to the celebration I hoped to have with her later.

"I'll be running too," I said. "Thanks, I enjoyed our chat."

"Let's not make a habit of it," he stated firmly. "And by the way, keep what I told you under your hat. You do, and I'll keep Boston under mine." He reached across the table, extending an open hand.

I took it, surprised at his congeniality but not half as surprised as I was at the strength in his grip. Maybe he was making a point.

An even louder beep broke the air. Oakley reached into his jacket pocket, came out with a slim cellular telephone. He put it to his left ear.

"Oakley here. Yeah . . . Unh-huh . . . Unh-huh . . . Okay, I'm on my way." He slipped the phone back in his jacket, looking grim. He studied my face for a moment, took in and let out a large breath. He eased himself from the seat and stood, towering over me.

"Is there a break in the case?" I asked him.

"Yeah, you could say that." He did up the top button of his shirt, pulled and straightened his tie. He was back on duty.

"We're about to make an arrest in the murder of Christian Valentine."

"Who is it?" I asked, filled with anticipation.

Oakley's face filled with a foreboding, dark look. "It's your girlfriend, Rachel Sinclair."

Chapter

Two hundred years before the Flamingo Hotel was a glint in Bugsy Siegel's eye, early Spanish explorers dubbed this sparse part of the Mojave Desert *Las Vegas*, which meant "the Meadows." Beats me why. Maybe their vocabulary didn't have a word for "Sagebrush Valley." The land was hot, dry and rugged, supporting little else than scrubby plant life and an occasional Joshua tree.

Vegas is surrounded by numerous craggy mountain ranges: the Pintwater, Spotted, Sheep, and Desert from the north; Sunrise and Frenchman's to the east; and the McCullough Mountains to the south. The city is enclosed from the west by Red Rock Canyon and the Spring Mountains. That's where I was.

Everyone needs a place of refuge, somewhere to escape to, to clear one's mind. And mine needed a thorough clearing. Normally I'm a pretty upbeat guy. When I did find myself in a funk, though, I would drive the fifteen to twenty miles and park on a secluded side road just off Highway 160, savoring the solitude, collecting my thoughts, gazing out over the neon backwash of the city below me. I had been out here only two or three times in the past year, but I needed it now more than ever.

It was just before midnight. I was lying on the hood of my car, back against the windshield, digesting the blockbuster news of Rachel's arrest.

As surprisingly open and congenial as Lieutenant Oakley had been, he wasn't about to let me see Rachel. She had been arrested backstage minutes after Oakley left me, sitting dumbfounded, in the Camel's Hump. My attempts to talk with her were thwarted by hotel security and stern-faced cops.

In the short time I had been backstage, I stumbled from one bewildered emotion to another. Gentle, disbelieving words of sympathy and understanding from Leona, Murray, and friends in the crowd confused me all the more. Shushed whisperings and severe stares from Franco, Contini and Johnny Ventura did little to help.

I unwrapped the cellophane from the package of Marlboro Lights I'd bought at the hotel gift shop and lit up. The last cigarette I'd had was back in Boston, under the scrutiny of my superiors and Internal Affairs. At least then I had my own convictions and wits to contend with the situation. Now Rachel was in trouble, and I felt powerless to help.

I inhaled deeply, then let the expended smoke drift lazily toward the dark, star-studded sky. The desert air was cool yet comforting, the still quiet broken by intermittent eighteen-wheelers gearing down in the distance or the occasional foraging of an unseen night creature closer to the car.

Something was wrong. I couldn't believe Rachel had anything to do with Valentine's murder. I realized I didn't know her all that well, still I was sure she couldn't be involved. I just hoped I wasn't letting my feelings, or my hopes of getting closer to her, affect my intuitions. No matter how I looked at the facts, or her, it just didn't make sense.

I spent the next half hour lost in thought, chain-smoking to relieve the tension. Obviously, Rachel needed my help. If she was taking the fall for someone, I was fairly certain it was someone I'd already talked to. And no matter what I did, I was determined to get Lieutenant Oakley alone again. There were too many questions left unanswered.

The night air had grown colder. I flicked the half-finished butt into the darkness, confident Smokey the Bear didn't work these parts. Out here, it would likely be Leo the Lizard on patrol. I didn't want to surprise any creatures of the night that might have wandered near, so I banged the fender of the Chevy loudly before I eased myself off the hood.

Once inside, I patted the dash for good luck. This was not the place to be with a car that wouldn't start. The engine fired on the first try. I slipped into reverse and made my way through the soft, sandy soil. The eventual feel of pavement did wonders for my confidence.

Driving back to town, I decided to talk again to everyone I had spoken to since Christian Valentine hired me and maybe a few others for good measure. It wasn't a great plan, but it was somewhere to start. Feeling much better, I tossed the pack of smokes out the window.

⊡

Julius Contini's hotel suite/office was luxurious beyond belief. Located on the northwest corner of the penthouse floor, facing the flashing gaudiness of the Strip, the complex consisted of three thousand square feet of imported Italian marble, Indian rugs, Old English sofas and chaises, Oriental artifacts and an art collection rivaling most galleries.

It was 2:30 Wednesday morning and Big Julie was incredibly pissed off with the person he was talking to on the telephone. He sat behind a mammoth mahogany desk with his side to me. His feet were propped up on a matching antique credenza, his portly frame resting in a tall black leather swivel chair. The air around him was filled with thick gray smoke, and the back of his neck was wet with perspiration.

I was in one of three matching visitor chairs positioned directly in front of the desk. As Big Julie wrapped up his heated, one-way conversation, I debated my approach in talking with him. When I had stopped by the Oasis after my trek to the canyon, a grim-faced McClusky had mentioned that Contini was looking for me. That was fine with me. Big Julie was one of the people I wanted to talk to.

After speaking with McClusky, my first impression was that I was being fired for my involvement with Rachel and her connection with the Valentine mess. But during the ride on Contini's private elevator, it dawned on me that he wouldn't bother himself with a nobody like me. After all, that was McClusky's specialty.

"That's what I pay you shysters for. Just take care of it!" Big Julie slammed the receiver down and spun around to face me. "Fuckin' lawyers . . ."

He stubbed the remainder of his thick cigar into a large marble ashtray. The air conditioning worked quickly and the gray cloud evaporated like magic. He slipped a pair of gold wire reading glasses over his ears and dug around on the desktop. Finally, he found what he was looking for. He took a minute to read from a sheet of fancy hotel stationery.

"Too bad about your squeeze," he said, replacing the paper and glasses on the desk. "Tough break."

"Actually, Mr. Contini, Rachel's not really my girlfriend," I told him. "It's a relationship in progress, I think. At least I hope so. But I have to be frank with you, sir, I don't believe Rachel had anything to do with it."

Big Julie pulled a pale blue handkerchief from his pocket. He studied me as he mopped his brow. "Neither do I."

I didn't bother hiding my surprise.

"Morgan, that's why I called you up."

"What do you mean?"

"Look, obviously I'm aware you were helping Valentine out last week."

"Yeah, apparently everybody was."

"Supposedly, he was being blackmailed, wasn't he?"

When I answered with a nod, he continued. "Well, this Rachel Sinclair doesn't seem to have any motive. Not from what I can see at least. And she'd just landed a pretty juicy part. It doesn't make a whole lotta sense."

I agreed with him, but I also remembered his disdain for me when we first met in Valentine's suite. "That's my thinking too, Mr. Contini. But frankly, if you don't mind me saying, I'm surprised you'd be this concerned."

"Sure I'm concerned. What kind of owner wouldn't be?"

Apparently he cared as much about Rachel's welfare as I did. So much for my thinking he and the hotel corporation might have had something to do with the murder.

"Well, I'm glad to have you on Rachel's side. Especially with all those rumors floating around town . . ."

Big Julie raised an eyebrow. His neck, what there was of it, seemed to tighten. "Like what?"

There was no sense getting him agitated. "Well, you know," I chuckled good naturedly. "About the insurance and all. Ventura packing them in. The hotel saving money . . ."

"That's bullshit." Contini fired up a fresh cigar. When he got it going to his satisfaction, he pointed it in my direction. "Sure, I'm probably saving a million a month with Valentine gone, maybe more. And, yes, there was a nice disability and death package on him. But that's not unusual. Every hotel does it. What can really hurt, in the long run, is if your friend is found guilty. Then it's not so good that another employee of this fine establishment is hung with the rap. It would definitely be bad for business."

So much for corporate compassion.

"Look," he went on, glancing at his big Rolex, "I'm not sure what you dug up while you were working for Valentine, but what I want you to do is keep poking around. See what else you can find out." He let out a large sigh. "Take some time off and dig a little deeper. Preferably outside the Oasis, if you get my drift."

Frankly, I didn't care where I looked. My only concern was to get Rachel off the hook. Oasis or no Oasis, it didn't matter much to me.

"I was planning to dig deeper," I told him. "But I can't take time off work. I've got rent to pay. I'll snoop around on my own time. If it's all the same —"

He held up his hand, stopping me, and picked up the letterhead he had been reading earlier. "McClusky knows what's best. That's why he's down there — looking after my best interests. This here paper says you're one of the top shooters I've got downstairs, have been for the last five or six months. That's good work and I appreciate it."

He flashed his capped pearly whites in a show of gratitude. I would have preferred a raise.

"Tell you what I'm going to do," he continued. "You'll draw your salary, same as if you were still dealing. How's that?"

It didn't sound all that bad. Considering I was taking off some time before starting in the poker room, this would be like a paid vacation.

"What about tokes?" I asked. Tips made up a good portion of a dealer's take-home pay. I'd be losing almost thirty percent of my gross.

"Nothing I can do about that," answered Big Julie, shaking his head. He hoisted his bulk from the chair and, with a great amount of effort, made his way to an elaborate bar. He poured a glass of water from a crystal carafe and pulled two tiny pink tablets from a silver pillbox. "What I'll do, though, is comp you meals."

I gave him a perfunctory hesitation before responding to his offer. "Okay, Mr. Contini. You've got yourself a deal."

What the hell, I was pretty sure I could eat thirty percent's worth. On top of being a stress-smoker, I was a stress-eater, too.

"Oh, one more thing, Morgan." Contini popped the pills into his mouth and washed them down. "Stay away from those television interviews."

The first thing I did when I left Big Julie's office was head down to the hotel's twenty-four-hour deli. Besides not having eaten since lunch, I had a lot more to think about. I flashed my comp card to the hostess. She led me to what she told me was her best table. It felt good.

I worked my way through a toasted ham-and-cheese sandwich and a few cups of coffee. Contini's reflections weighed heavily on my mind. What bothered me most was the possibility of him being on the right track. What if it *was* someone outside the hotel? Christ, if it was, what were my chances of finding them? I had to be honest with myself and accept the fact that my resources were somewhat limited. However, I still felt my initial footwork had raised some interesting questions.

For starters, there was the altercation at Sam's Town between Leona Carter and Christian Valentine. Leona had woven a good, if not sympathetic, story. Some of it may even have been true. Obviously she was pregnant, she was leaving the show. Knowing Valentine, he was probably the father. But what if the payoff envelope hadn't contained cash? There was still the matter of the missing photograph of Christian and Rachel that Lieutenant Oakley was unable to find. Maybe Leona had had something to do with that.

And although I liked him, Murray Gladstone was somebody who needed closer attention. I didn't care what he had told me, the loss of his daughter might have festered all these years and just finally erupted. Deep down though, I couldn't see him doing Rachel for the fall. Mind you, that depended on what the cops had on her.

Even Franco might've had enough motive to have blackmailed Valentine — to help pay down what he owed him. But somehow murder seemed pretty severe for Franco. The one big thing he had going for him was his attitude. That, and the fact he just pissed me off.

I washed down the crumbs of my blueberry pie with the last of my coffee, regretting I hadn't ordered it à la mode.

Johnny Ventura was a large question mark, too. I didn't know all that much about him, but I would try to get a line on him as soon as I could. The new kid seemed to be relishing his new role. Could he have been that stupid? Especially with the way he was carrying on. I reminded myself I would have to be careful with Johnny. Contini would have my nuts served up on a craps table if he found out I was even talking with him.

The meal and the hour were working against my mental state. In the past year I was used to working with my hands, not my brain. I decided to get some sleep, then take another crack at Lieutenant Oakley.

Just before I got up to leave, another thought entered my weary mind. This one didn't go down as well as the blueberry pie. I actually shook my head to help ward it off, but the damn thing kept coming back to haunt me.

What if Rachel Sinclair *was* involved?

Chapter

If I slept like a baby, it must have been Rosemary's baby. My entire body was damp with perspiration. The bedsheets were crumpled and heaped in a far corner of the room. The pillows were nowhere to be seen. I stumbled out of bed in a stupor, fumbled through a steaming shower and a dull-razor shave, and stuffed toast and coffee down my throat.

Stopped at a light on my way downtown, I glanced toward the curb. An uneasy sensation stung my chest. Rachel's downcast face stared back at me bleakly from a *Review-Journal* newspaper box. "SHOWGIRL ARRESTED" screamed the banner headline.

I slammed the Chevy into park, searching through my pockets for change and opening the door at the same time. I didn't bother acknowledging the angry blare of horns as I returned to the car and ran the yellow light.

I turned into a gas station, parked off to the side and began reading. The article didn't tell me much I didn't already know. The paper was a first edition and the details were sketchy. It stated Rachel had been arrested for the murder of Christian Valentine after an intensive investigation. Evidence was conclusive but not available for publication. Police statements from Lieutenant Oakley were vague, yet confident.

Police headquarters was located off Fremont, just down the street from the Clark County Courthouse. Oakley was in one building, Rachel in the other. She wasn't allowed visitors, so instead I waited in a stiff plastic chair outside Oakley's office, leafing through a tattered copy of *Police Product News*. A television crew from KVBC-TV was inside interviewing the lieutenant, their bright lights barely breaking the translucent windows and door.

It was 1:30, Wednesday afternoon. Midday, midweek — a tame time for Las Vegas and its police force. Uniformed and undercover cops mingled near the front desk, sipping from white Styrofoam cups and exchanging good-natured banter.

I was flipping through the magazine for the third time when the brightness inside Oakley's office dimmed. A moment later the door opened, and a two-man crew carted their equipment away. The lieutenant, smiling and ignoring my presence, escorted a pretty female reporter past me and down the hall toward the front door.

Oakley held the door open and shook hands good-bye. He appeared satisfied and pleased as he ambled to the front desk and checked with the sergeant for messages. He stood there for a few minutes, accepting accolades and handshakes from his colleagues. Contrary to my own feelings, a convivial air pervaded the foyer. He waved off congratulations with a thumbs-up salute and made his way to a coffeemaker behind the front desk. I returned the magazine to the seat beside me and walked over.

"Lieutenant? Can I speak with you for a moment?"

Oakley finished pouring and glanced over his shoulder. His spell of satisfaction dissipated instantly.

"Coffee?" he asked glumly.

I walked past the desk sergeant, who gave me the once-over. The lieutenant stirred two big helpings of sugar into a ceramic white mug labeled "World's Greatest Dad."

"Thanks," I told him. "Just cream."

Oakley tested his drink, added one more sugar, turned and walked back to his office. I took a Styrofoam cup from a stack and poured my own, adding powdered whitener until the dark black liquid turned beige.

The lieutenant was sipping at his drink, waiting inside his doorway. When I entered, he closed the door quietly, walked behind his desk and sat in a comfortable-looking leather chair. He pointed to a cloth-covered, steel-legged seat in front of me. I placed my cup on a cork coaster and sat as instructed.

Oakley's office was nicer than I expected. The furnishings were modest yet modern and, like the man, neat and masculine. An array of computer and electronic equipment monopolized his highly polished oak desk. Pictures of his wife and kids and a number of high school football trophies occupied the top of a bright blue file cabinet.

I sat back in my seat and sighed once, loudly. "What the hell do you have on Rachel that makes you so damn sure she's guilty?"

He gave a tight smile that was meant to comfort me. "Morgan, I can imagine how you feel. I really can. But there's nothing you can do for her now. You have to face the facts — the case is closed. There's so much evidence against her, hell, even Judge Judy could handle the trial."

I didn't appreciate his attempt at humor, and my silence told him so.

"Look," he explained, "I know the two of you were close. But you can't take this personally. You're not the one up on murder charges, she is. And she's the one who's going to take the responsibility for her actions. Not you."

"Bullshit," I said firmly. "Somebody wanted an arrest and the boys came up with one."

"Careful," Oakley said calmly, sipping from his mug. "You're on *my* turf here."

I breathed deeply, trying to relax. "I don't think she had anything to do with Valentine's murder."

"How long have you known her? A couple of weeks? A month? That's hardly a lifetime." He shook his head sadly. "She may be one of the most gorgeous showgirls in Vegas, Morgan, but start thinking with your big head, not your little one."

I stared at him, trying to collect my thoughts.

Oakley studied me without comment while I drank from my cup. He opened a thick manila file on his desk. The file was titled "Sinclair, R." in thick black marker.

"Where did the two of you meet, Morgan?"

"Well, the first time was at the Oasis. A staff party."

"And that was, what, a month ago?"

"Yeah, about that. Why?"

"And she was a dancer at the Oasis then, right?"

"Of course she was. She moved here a couple of years ago. She's been dancing in the Sultan's Tent since it opened. What are you getting at, Lieutenant?"

Oakley studied me again. "She moved here *three* years ago."

That's not what she'd told me during our last dinner, and it must have shown on my face.

"Ever hear of Hardbodies?" he asked.

"No."

Oakley nodded his head slowly. "I guess there's really no reason you should know it, seeing as you've only been out here a year. Anyways, we closed it down two years ago."

"So?"

"It's where your friend Rachel used to work."

I wasn't aware she had worked anywhere but at the Oasis and the Rio in Vegas. But she had told me she'd worked as an aerobics instructor back in Minnesota.

"It sounds like some kind of gym to me," I said. "Maybe she was running an aerobics class. What's the big deal?"

Oakley pulled at his left earlobe. "Hardbodies wasn't a gym." He cleared his throat twice. "It was an escort service."

I gave that little gem a moment to sink in, then I laughed out loud. "Yeah, right," I said when I'd finally collected myself.

The lieutenant wasn't sharing in my mirth. He slid a single sheet of paper across his desk toward me. There was a photograph of Rachel stapled to it. I knew a rap sheet when I saw one, so I wiped the stupid smile off my face and picked up the report.

It was just as Oakley had said. Rachel had been arrested, along with thirty-seven others, after the cops had raided an exclusive escort agency by the name of Hardbodies. The owner, Larry Levine, had been charged with living off the avails of prostitution and was serving five-to-ten in Carson City's state penitentiary. His stable of girls and boys were charged and released after paying a mandatory fine.

To Oakley's credit, he didn't rub it in. Instead, he browsed absently through his files until I slid the rap sheet back his way and sat back in my chair. I left my coffee where it was, getting cold.

Finally I told him, "It doesn't prove she killed Valentine."

"No, it doesn't," he agreed, making a steeple with his hands. "But it proves you didn't know her as well as you thought you did."

He had me there.

"Look, Morgan," he sighed. "You're right. This Hardbodies bust doesn't mean squat in the overall scheme of things. But there's a lot of concrete evidence that does."

"Such as?"

The steeple collapsed. "It's none of your business."

"Well, I'm going to make it my business, Lieutenant. Sooner or later they'll let me speak to Rachel. Or at least her lawyer. I'm going to find out one way or the other."

Oakley studied me intently. I studied him back. It was a battle of baby blues. He blinked first.

"Jesus Christ, Morgan. What is it with you? You never quit." Oakley flicked the edge of his file a few times with a fingernail. "I guess it's true."

"What's that?"

"Contini's got you playing detective now. Just like Valentine."

I was surprised he knew, but I didn't let it register. "It's got nothing to do with it. Contini wants someone from outside of the Oasis to be found guilty. Me, I don't give a shit. As long as I find 'em."

"Good luck," he said, shaking his head. "You've got your work cut out for you."

"Maybe, but you could make it a lot easier if you just told me what the hell you found that's so conclusive."

Oakley smiled by tightening his lips and fell into a deep rumination. I didn't know what was going through his head, but I sat there quietly, rolling with it.

"Okay," he said finally, slapping his desk. "I'll throw you a few bones. If you can prove otherwise, I'll eat my leather sap. Number one is the three-parter I told you about in the bar last night. There were three sets of prints in Valentine's suite that didn't fit in with the rest. We found the two clearest ones on the bottle of champagne and a glass. They were, without question, Rachel Sinclair's."

I tried to take that in without letting the impact show. "They worked together, Lieutenant," I chided. "They were going to be performing together. Big deal. Did you ever stop to think that maybe they were rehearsing?"

"In the bedroom? Are you forgetting where we found them? The prints weren't on the bar or in the music room, Morgan. They were right there beside the Jacuzzi. At the murder scene."

I was just about to tell him that anybody could have moved a glass and a bottle when he added, "The third set of her prints were found in the bedroom, also. On the light switch."

"Come on! That's circumstantial!"

"Oh! Now all of a sudden you're a lawyer too?"

"Gimme a break, Lieutenant. The prints don't mean she was there when he was killed. She could have been up there earlier. For any number of reasons."

"She also might have been up there trying to stop him from hitting on her . . ."

"What the hell are you talking about?" I asked. "He hit on all the girls. Ask any of them."

"We did. They all said the same thing. Christian Valentine was putting the squeeze on Rachel at her most vulnerable moment — just after she'd been promoted and was preparing for her new role. It'd be pretty hard for her to turn back at that point. It was advertised in all the papers and show magazines. They even had the promotional pieces printed on posters."

I knew that didn't mean a thing. The whole charge was based on conjecture. I leaned forward in my chair to make that exact point.

"Oh, yeah," Oakley said as an afterthought. "There's one other little item. When we searched your friend Rachel's house, we found a fifteen-thousand-dollar sequined jacket in her bedroom closet. Mrs. Valentine identified it as hers. So did the manager at Sak's."

I fell back in my chair and exhaled loudly. I remembered the jacket. When Yolanda Valentine had forgotten it in the Sultan's Tent after the show, I had picked it up and placed it in Christian Valentine's suite myself.

So much for conjecture.

"Look," the lieutenant said softly, closing his file. "These things happen. But as I said, it's over. There's nothing you can do. Be as smart as I'd like to think you are. Let it go."

I sat there for a moment, mulling over his words. Finally, I got up from my chair, walked toward the door and opened it. As I began to leave, I stopped and turned my head.

"I hate to disappoint you, Lieutenant," I said. "But maybe I'm just not that smart."

Chapter

Maybe Oakley had pulled a few strings. When I arrived at the Oasis there was a note for me on the dealers' room message board to call him at the Court House. The call had been taken at 2:15. It was now 2:28. The room was relatively empty, but still active. Some of the dealers present asked questions I couldn't answer, while others offered their opinions concerning both Valentine's and Rachel's plight.

"I guess Valentine called somebody Tonto one too many times," remarked a Native American dealer named Jerry.

"Nah," someone else stated. "They woulda used a long bow, not a crossbow!"

A couple of others laughed.

"Hey, Jake," somebody called out loudly. "They gonna let you have conjugal visits?"

Everybody wants to be a comedian.

I overheard two female dealers say, "You think she'd kill the guy just so she wouldn't have to sleep with him? What's the big deal? She wouldn't have been the first one Valentine bagged."

"Yeah," her companion agreed. "No biggie!"

A roulette dealer named Bianca entered the room waving a sheet of paper. "Got one!"

It was one of the promotional posters with Valentine and Rachel smiling brightly for the camera. Apparently they were now hot souvenir items.

Just like the one I'd seen in Valentine's safe . . .

Maybe it was my cop's instinct. Maybe it was my gambler's intuition. Maybe it was a little bit of both.

Or maybe it was just me wanting to feel those long dancer's legs wrapped around my back.

Whatever it was, the sight of that poster woke something inside me. The torn photograph had never turned up, and that bothered me. If Rachel had planned to murder Valentine, why would she threaten him with a photo of the two of them? It didn't make sense.

Oakley hadn't left a number, and somebody had walked off with the telephone directory a few weeks ago. I called Information and dialed the number given to me.

A receptionist advised me that Lieutenant Oakley had left the building moments earlier. My frustration must have been evident, because she jumped in to tell me he had left a message. After a few moments filled with the sounds of rustling paper, I was told that visiting privileges had been granted to me between three and three-thirty that afternoon. I glanced at my watch. It read 2:44. I thanked her profusely and hung up.

Although the Strip was the most direct route downtown, it was not necessarily the quickest. I raced westward on Flamingo, caught Interstate 15, just past Caesars Palace and headed north. As expected, traffic was light. Ten minutes later, now eastbound on Route 95 and making excellent time, I managed to keep all four tires on the pavement as I swung the car down the Stewart Avenue exit ramp. I backtracked smartly along Stewart and turned down Main, driving slowly as I searched up and down side streets for a parking spot.

Casino Center Boulevard was directly behind the Court House. The majority of vehicles there were police cruisers and motorcycles. I spotted a white Honda Civic easing out from a meter. The Chevy responded to the tap of my foot and shot forward. I arrived just as the Honda nosed out, slapping my right turn signal as I prepared to parallel park.

Glancing over my shoulder, I noticed a police squad car barreling down three car lengths back. His signal was on too. I whipped the transmission into reverse and hit the accelerator, tucking the Chevy in as neatly as you please on the first attempt. The cop car screeched to a stop beside me, blocking my driver-side door.

I got out from the passenger side and locked up. A horn blasted once. I turned my head toward the sound. A heavyset cop was leaning across the front seat of his car.

"Hey, smart-ass!" he yelled out.

"No *speaky Eengly*," I shrugged, dropping two quarters in the meter.

·

The visitation room was plain, cold, unadorned in any way. A female guard led me to one of the six vacant glass-partitioned cubicles.

"Wait here," she said in a weary voice before leaving.

I slid the plastic chair out from the small counter and sat. It was a few minutes past three. Outside of my pounding heart, the room was still, deathly quiet. Only once did a noise break the solitude; a video camera hummed as it panned the room and settled on where I sat. It whizzed and whirred for a moment as it focused, then fell silent. A tiny red light flashed off and on beneath its lens. I passed the time wondering what exactly I was going to say to Rachel.

Finally, around 3:10, a door opened on the other side. The same tired guard escorted Rachel into the room, and then left.

Rachel stood there, glancing at the closed door, then at me. A tan-colored shift hung loosely on her body. She wore thin paper slippers on her feet. Her blond hair was askew, combed haphazardly.

A thick lump formed high in my throat. I motioned for her to join me.

"Jake," she cried out softly through the telephone on her side of the partition. "What's going on?"

"Don't worry, Rachel. Everything's going to work out."

Tears welled in her eyes. Both hands trembled as they worked their grasp on the receiver.

"Have you talked to a lawyer?" I asked her.

"Yes," she nodded. "A Mr. Baxter. He was sent by Mr. Contini early this morning."

"Good. I'm glad the Oasis is behind you."

Rachel shook her head gently. "It isn't. I think he's Mr. Contini's personal lawyer."

"I see," I said, not seeing anything at all. There may have been too many political ramifications for the corporation to get involved at this time. I decided to keep that to myself and not discourage Rachel any further. "That's nice of Big Julie," I told her.

The glass between us was smudged with greasy fingerprints and the faint remains of old lipstick stains. Our eyes locked. I tried to encourage her with a smile.

"When's bail being arranged?" I asked.

Rachel's face darkened. "Mr. Baxter says the bail hearing won't be for a few more days. At the very least." A solitary teardrop ran down her cheek. "He says there might be a problem making bail. It could be hundreds of thousands . . ."

"Don't worry," I said, trying to console her. "I'll talk to Big Julie, see what he can do."

Julius Contini might be helping out with legal counsel, but something told me he wouldn't come up with that kind of dough. Not out of his own pocket.

"Rachel, I'm going to do everything I can to get you out of here. But we don't have much time. You've got to answer some questions for me. Are you up to it?"

She wiped her bare wrist along her wet cheek, sniffled, and nodded.

"Good girl," I told her. "Okay, first things first. Were you rehearsing with Valentine, up in his suite, the night he was murdered?"

She shook her head, still sniffling.

"Rachel," I prodded gently. "The police say they found your finger-prints in the suite."

"Jake," she cried out in astonishment. "That's impossible! I've never been to his suite. Not that night or any night!"

That wasn't the answer I'd expected. I mulled that around in my head for a moment, then I asked her if there was any truth to the rumor that Valentine had been making passes at her.

She lowered her head, running the fingers of her free hand through her hair. "Yeah, I guess. But it wasn't anything to worry about. Christian was like that. He made passes at all the girls." She raised her head in a show of strength, looked me directly in the eye. "I've been around, Jake. I know how to handle guys like that."

I didn't bother to tell her that was what the cops thought, too. Instead, I said, "Okay, can you tell me anything about the jacket they found in your closet? The one they say was Yolanda Valentine's."

"No. When they showed it to me and asked me about it, I told them I'd seen her wearing it when she joined us for drinks, during Christian's performance. That's the first and last time I ever saw it."

None of this was making any sense to me. It must have shown on my face.

"Jake? You have to believe me! You're all I've got . . ." The tears started up again. "You *do* believe me, don't you?"

I felt terrible for even thinking what was on my mind. "Of course. But Rachel, there's something I need to know." I searched her hazel eyes deeper than ever before.

"Jake! What is it? You're scaring me."

Holding my gaze, I said, "Tell me about Hardbodies."

She flung her head back. "Damn it!"

I gave her a moment, then prompted her gently, "Rachel . . ."

"All right." She had collected herself. An inner strength seemed to have taken over. She sat upright, her shoulders back, and began her story.

"I moved out here about three years ago, with stars in my eyes and a tiny bankroll that I thought would get me through to my first dance part here. I was going to show everyone back home how I could take Vegas by the balls and shake it till I got what I wanted. What a joke! Two months later, I was flat broke. And it wasn't from any lack of trying. I must have hit every hotel at least three times, talked to each and every musical director, practically begged for work. Nothing.

"Oh, sure," she scoffed. "Some of the guys promised me work if I'd 'put out' for them, but that wasn't the way it was going to be for me. And I wasn't going to call home for money. I just wouldn't do it, Jake."

I raised an eyebrow. "Yeah, but . . ."

"What do you think I did? Took a job as a hooker? An escort? Is that what you —" She shook her head dejectedly and said, more to herself than to me, "Just when you think you really know someone . . . Jake. How could you?"

I felt even worse than I did before, but I still wasn't any clearer.

Rachel continued, "Okay, I can see how it might look to you. But there wasn't enough money for me to even enrol in a dealer school, and I couldn't have supported myself for the six weeks it would have taken. I didn't even have a place to stay.

"I had three choices while I waited for a dancing job to open up. I could serve drinks as a cocktail waitress at one of the downtown casinos. Nice work, if I wanted guys with names like Clem and Otis peeking down my top while they pinched my ass. Or I could sling hash in a hotel restaurant, serving pissed-off losers and bad drunks. That would've been terrific. In my off hours, I could watch my varicose veins sprout while I waited for one of the directors to call."

The door on Rachel's side clicked open. The female guard closed the door, leaned against it, and held up two fingers in our direction.

Rachel caught the guard's signal and immediately returned to her original, nervous state. Her eyes widened and became moist again.

"Jake, I *did* take a job at Hardbodies. But it wasn't what you or the police think. I was a receptionist! The owner of the place thought I sounded like Kathleen Turner. He was a weasel but he was nuts about my voice. All I had to do was answer the phone and pass them names and telephone numbers. They'd take care of the rest.

"It seemed harmless, Jake. The calls were going to come in whether or not I was there. And since I worked nights, it left me the whole day to follow up on my interviews at the showrooms. That's all I did! But it didn't seem to make much difference to the cops who raided the place. I was there and I got arrested."

The guard cleared her throat. "Time's up."

Rachel gave me a beseeching look. "I wasn't proud of what I was doing. That's why I didn't tell you about it. You believe me, don't you, Jake?"

My face brightened. I gave her my most inspiring smile. "I do believe you, Rachel. You just hang tough. I'm going to get you out of here myself. I promise."

The guard strolled over, hung up the receiver and led Rachel out of the room. I sat there, all alone with my thoughts.

I *did* believe Rachel. And to top it all off, I was absolutely certain of her innocence. The only thing that bothered me was my promise of getting her out.

Just how the hell was I going to do that?

Chapter

I drove back to the Oasis after my visit with Rachel. It was around 5:00 p.m. and all the hotel restaurants were packed. Lines of waiting people snaked from the restaurant doorways and through the casino.

The Casbah was the fanciest eatery the Oasis Hotel had to offer. I walked up to the VIP line and flashed my comp card to the hostess. She gave me a private booth. There's no need to go into the list of what I ordered. I was under a lot of stress, and the meal was in the grand tradition of a Henry VIII feast.

I waddled out of the Casbah around six-thirty and decided it was time to have a little chat with Johnny Ventura. Providing, of course, Julius Contini wasn't nearby.

The first performance in the Sultan's Tent was scheduled for eight o'clock. Most of the cast usually arrived around seven. I went to the showroom on the off chance that Johnny Ventura might be early. I was right. Security called the new headliner in his dressing room, and Johnny told them he would meet me outside his door in five minutes.

The backstage area was deserted. I was waiting in a long, dim hallway filled with odds and ends from previous productions. The steady whirring sounds of a hair dryer could be heard coming from his room. On his door was a large silver star with a peephole in the middle. I tried peeking through, but everything was blurred.

The sounds of the hair dryer continued. Johnny had a good head of hair, and I suddenly realized I could be out here longer than I thought. I leaned wearily against a plywood wall filled with peepholes to see backstage, crossed my arms and dug in for a battle of determination versus vanity.

While I waited, I heard the sounds of activity through the wall behind me. A piece of wood landed on the floor and someone cursed. I could hear tools and equipment being jostled. A light tapping vibrated in the thin wood at my back.

I glanced down at my feet for something to do. The floor was scattered with a combination of cigarette butts, candy wrappers, bobby pins and makeup-smeared facial tissues. One of the butts caught my attention. Two thin silver bands encircled it, right above the filter — the same as the ones I'd seen in Rachel's house after the break-in.

As I pushed away from the wall and bent over to retrieve the butt, a tremendous bang filled the air. I fell flat on my face. The smell of dirt and concrete and gunpowder filled my nostrils. My ears were ringing slightly, but I could hear something being dropped on the other side of the wall. The sounds of fleeing footsteps followed.

The hallway was still empty. Glancing to where I had been standing moments before, I saw a jagged hole in the wall, right where my head had been. I felt the back of my skull, but nothing was leaking. I couldn't say the same, for sure, about another part of my anatomy.

I rolled on my side and banged on Johnny's door. The hair dryer whirred on. I got to my knees, reached up and tried the doorknob. It was locked. I started knocking even harder, then I noticed something long and silver stuck in the door. I looked around once more and stood.

Wedged into Johnny's door, at eye level, was a nail with a small washer fastened to the head. I twisted the nail out. It was warm to the touch. Footfalls sounded down the hall and I froze. A security guard yelled, "Hold it right there, pal!"

"Somebody just took a shot at me!" I shouted, showing him the nail.

He gave me a confused, bewildered look, and considering the evidence I held in my hand, I couldn't really blame him.

Before I could explain, the sound of the hair dryer stopped. "Mr. Ventura?" the guard called out, rapping on the door. "You okay in there?"

The door swung open inward. Johnny Ventura stepped out into the hall. "Hi, Sam," he said cheerfully, his hair thick and dry. "What's up?" He turned in my direction, holding out his hand. "You must be Morgan."

I transferred the nail to my left hand, and shook his. With the introductions now over, I explained what had just happened. Johnny snuck a glance at Sam. The uniformed guard shrugged his shoulders.

"Look," I said seriously, in an attempt to prove my sanity. "I know this sounds crazy, but if you come backstage with me, I bet we'll find a nail gun on the other side of this wall."

I was about to tell them how Murray had warned me about the tool, then I thought better of it. I wanted to talk to Murray alone.

Johnny Ventura raised an eyebrow to Sam and, as if to humor me, said, "Why don't you take him over there, Sam. I'll talk to him when he gets back."

Sam nodded his head and smiled, going along with him. "Sure thing, Mr. Ventura. Maybe you should call 911. The number's in the book somewhere." He turned and motioned for me to follow.

It was just as I had told them. The nail gun was lying on the floor directly behind where I had been standing. I could see the silver star on Johnny's door as I peeked through the hole in the wall.

"See for yourself," I said to the guard, leaning over and lifting up the heavy power tool. I knew it would look stupid, but I sniffed the barrel anyway.

The security guard sighed loudly and peered through the hole. I held out the nail gun when he was finished. "Smell this."

He bent over, stuck out his nose, and inhaled deeply. "Come on," he said, standing straight again. "This don't prove somebody was shooting at you. Someone was probably working back here. It was an accident, that's all."

I gave him a look of exasperation. He turned and started to walk away. "I got more important things to do," he said, waving a hand in disgust.

"Try not moving your lips while you're reading the comics," I told him.

⊡

Johnny was busily working his fingernails over a long black emery board when I entered his dressing room.

"Well?" he asked as I closed the door. "Any luck?"

"If it wasn't for bad luck, I'd have no luck at all. The gun was there, but the place was empty."

He nodded and went back to his filing. "Probably an accident," he explained. "So what can I do for you?"

Before I could answer, there was a light knocking from the far side of the room. Another door opened. One of the casino cocktail waitresses stuck her head through the partial opening. "You ready for a little relax —" She suddenly spotted me standing there. "Oops, sorry," she giggled.

"Gimme five, Domino," Johnny said to her, glancing at his watch.

"Sure, Johnny," she giggled again and closed the door.

"Domino?" I quizzed.

"Yeah, it's my pet name for her," he laughed. "She delivers it hot in under thirty minutes — or it's free." He tossed the emery board onto his dressing table and examined his nails with a discerning look. Apparently satisfied with his work, he asked, "So what's up?"

"I guess you didn't hear the gunshot, huh? Or my knocking on your door?"

"Hey," he said, returning a stray curl back behind his ear. "I was dryin' my hair. I couldn't hear a thing."

Glancing toward the far wall and the other door, I wondered exactly where it led. "And you were here the whole time . . ."

He leaned back heavily in his chair. "No, I always leave my hair dryer on while I go for a walk. Of course I was here. Where the hell else would I be?"

I didn't offer a suggestion just then, but I kept one in the back of my head. "Mind if I sit down?" I asked.

"Sure," he replied, peeking at his watch. "You can stand on your head for all I care. But you only got four minutes left."

"Okay," I said, choosing a soft blue leather settee and ignoring his caustic tone. "I'll get right to the point. What do you know about Christian Valentine and his murder?"

"I know what I read and hear," he smiled.

"Meaning what?"

"Meaning it was Rachel that offed him. What else?"

"Rachel didn't have anything to do with it, Ventura. She was set up. She didn't have anything to gain."

"And I did, I suppose?"

"Yeah, well, now that you mention it, I guess you did. You had a lot more to gain than Rachel. You're a big shot now. The headliner. And you're pulling in more bucks in a week than you were pulling in a year before Valentine bought it."

Johnny's face went livid. "I'm headlining because I worked my ass off, numbnuts! I'm good at what I do. I deserve everything I'm getting. And more!"

He certainly had taken over for Valentine — he sounded just like him.

"I guess you were just at the right place at the right time?"

"Yeah, something like that. Everyone gets what they deserve, and now

I'm getting mine. If Rachel's guilty, the way the cops say she is, she'll be getting hers, too."

"So you think she did it?"

He squared his jaw in my direction and added, "Hey! If it looks like a dog and barks like a dog — it probably is a dog."

I fought back a knee-jerk reaction to punch his pretty face in. Big Julie would go apeshit if I marked up his rising star.

"I don't know why you're so hot and bothered," he continued. "It's not like the two of you were really going out or anything. You never stood a chance from the get-go!"

"I'm helping out Contini," I explained, taking a deep breath to help restrain my fury. "He wants me to see if anybody knows anything they don't want to tell the cops about."

"Is that all? Hey, look, I got nothin' against Rachel. But what's the big deal? These broads are a dime a dozen. Tell Big Julie not to worry. I'm going to be a bigger star and draw in more people than Valentine ever could. The fluff that fills in around me doesn't matter! As long as they got legs that go up to their necks and a nice rack, that's what counts. Know what I mean?"

"I know one thing for sure," I eased myself out of the settee. "Valentine was an arrogant asshole, Ventura, but you're an even bigger one."

"Oh, is that right?" he countered. "Well, Valentine's star burned out and died. That's show biz! It's *my* turn now! And if the broad takes the rap — well, so be it. One way or the other, I'll be heating up the Sultan Tent stage while she's frying in the Carson City electric chair."

I was now standing next to him. I picked up a plastic bottle of baby powder, unscrewed the cap, and emptied the contents over his head. I scooped up a big handful of cold cream and smeared it on his powdery locks, wiping my hand on his silky white shirt when I had finished.

"What the hell —"

There was a tap from the far door. "Ohhhh, Johnnyyy . . ."

I threw a towel into his face. "You better get cleaned up," I told him. "Your pizza's getting cold."

Chapter

I was leaning against a proscenium arch on the apron of the stage, studying the cigarette butt I'd picked up on my way from Johnny Ventura's dressing room. It *was* a Gauloises, just like the ones found in Rachel's kitchen after the robbery. I suppose anyone could have dropped it in the backstage hallway, but it was a rare imported brand, and most interesting was the fact it was found outside Johnny's door.

I took out a stick of chewing gum from my pocket, unwrapped the silver foil, stuck the gum in my mouth and rolled the wrapping around the butt. I put it in my pocket for safekeeping, along with the nail I still insisted was aimed at me.

Murray Gladstone arrived about seven-fifteen. He began arranging a row of spots that lit the backstage. I ambled over, stuck out my hand and said hello.

A terrific frown filled his face. "Sorry to hear about Rachel," he said, taking my hand and shaking it. He let go immediately. "What the hell's that?"

"Oh, this thing," I said, balancing the nail on my palm. "I found it in the hallway. In Johnny Ventura's door, actually." I waited for a reaction, but didn't get one.

"Huh," he responded indifferently. "Strange to find one out there."

"Yeah, that's what I thought, too. Looked as if it came right through one of the panels back there."

"Really? We usually monitor these. Had an elephant step on one last year. Nearly ran through the friggin' curtain and out into the audience."

"Is that right? This one nearly ran through *my* friggin' head!"

"How's that?"

"I was standing outside Ventura's door when this baby came flying through the wall. Missed me by a pubic hair."

"What the hell you talkin' 'bout, Jake? Like it was shot at you?"

"Exactly, Murray. Were you or anyone else using it fifteen or twenty minutes ago?"

"Christ no! I'm the only one who's supposed to use the gun. Let me see it for a minute, will ya?"

I tossed him the silver spike.

"It's one of ours all right," he mused. "Wonder how the hell it ended up out there?"

"Yeah, me too . . ."

He handed me back the nail. "Hey, Jake! I don't think I like what you're getting at." He looked genuinely hurt.

"I'm not saying you had anything to do with it, Murray. I'm just hoping you might be able to enlighten me, that's all."

"Okay," he said softly. "I don't know who could have fired the damn thing. I just pulled into the parking lot five minutes ago and came straight here. I didn't see or hear nothing."

I made a mental note to check it out with Billy later.

"Okay, but tell me, you know that door in the back of Ventura's dressing room?"

Murray nodded.

"Where does it lead?" I asked him.

"Nowhere, really," he shrugged, taking out a soft pack of Marlboros and offering me one. I resisted the temptation.

"It's just a storage area," he continued, after lighting his smoke. "Joins a walkway from some of the other dressing rooms."

"Could someone make it from, say, here," I asked, pointing to the floor, "to that door in his dressing room in under a minute?"

"Yeah, no problem. What are you getting at, Jake?"

"I'm not really sure. But tell me, does Johnny smoke?"

"Are you kiddin'?" he answered caustically, blowing a gray cloud into the air. "He won't allow us to smoke anywhere near him. Says it might damage his valuable vocal chords." He glanced around the area and, satisfied Johnny was nowhere near, added, "Arrogant prick."

"Yeah, I know what you mean."

"What's him smoking got to do with the nail gun, Jake?"

"Nothing really. I noticed some Gauloises butts outside his door and just wondered."

"Jesus Christ! Not those French weeds!"

"You know them?" I asked with renewed interest.

"Yeah," he said with a disgusted face. "I was out of butts a couple of weeks ago. Bummed one of 'em. Smelled like burning camel shit. Tasted like it too."

"From who?" I asked trying to contain myself.

"I don't know," he said with a shake of his head.

"What do you mean you don't know, Murray? You mean you don't remember?"

"No, I mean I don't know. Like I said, I was out of butts and there was no one else around. I couldn't leave to go to the gift shop because of the equipment being out in the open and all. So I went up to the front doors there," he said, pointing to the back of the showroom. "You know that podium where they keep the reservation book for the shows? Well, the doormen don't want to have their cigarette packs get in the way of their tips, so they stash their smokes in there. I peeked in there and that was all there was. Yechhh."

I thanked Murray with a slap on his back and told him I'd see him later, then I raced to the back of the auditorium. I went directly to the cherrywood podium and slowly opened the lid.

There was a collection of tiny flashlights, a few pens, some coins and a bunch of showroom maps with numbered tables on them. And one other item: a crumpled pack of Gauloises cigarettes, just like Murray had said.

I lifted the pack out and tapped out a cigarette. The two silver bands brought a smile to my face. I replaced the cigarette and slipped the pack into my pocket.

Any one of the doormen could have owned them, but I had my money riding on a maître d' by the name of Franco Moretti.

Finally, I was getting somewhere.

A key sounded in the door a few feet away. It clicked and the doors swung open. There, in all his tuxedoed splendor, was Franco.

He gave me a cold stare, then cracked his face in an awkward kind of smile. "Hey, Charlie Chan, you okay? I just heard what happened from Sam."

"Really?" I smiled back. "What did you hear?"

I already knew what was coming.

He could barely contain himself. "I heard you almost got *nailed!*"

"Well, Number-One Son," I replied affably when he had settled down, "as you can see, I wasn't. On the other hand . . ." I could feel the pack of cigarettes in my shirt pocket and knew it was Franco who was really nailed. "Uhhh, never mind."

I started whistling that old Queen tune, "Another One Bites the Dust," as I turned and left.

Chapter

I wasn't exactly sure what I was on to, but I wanted to share my new find-ings with Lieutenant Oakley. He was the only link I had who might help me clear Rachel. Unfortunately, when I called him, he wasn't available and couldn't be reached until after midnight.

Not being the kind of guy who can go home and read a book just to kill time, I resorted to what I usually did when I didn't know what else to do. I went to the casino to gamble.

As an employee of the Oasis, I'm not allowed to play at the gaming tables or on the slot machines in the casino. Management feared collusion between a staff player and a dealer, or a slot mechanic on the take. I thought about going to the poker room to play some Hold 'Em but knew I had too much on my mind to concentrate on cards. Both my nerves and legs were still wobbly, so I headed for the quiet and more refined setting of the Sports Book. The hotel wasn't crazy about the staff hanging around the Book either, but since there was no real advantage to the player they usually looked the other way.

I sat back in the soft confines of a sofa chair and wiggled my fingers at a passing cocktail waitress. I didn't even have to flash her my comp card. All anyone had to do to get free drinks in the Sports Book was bet. If there was a better life to be had, I couldn't imagine what, or where, it could possibly be.

After relishing my surroundings for the next few minutes, I studied the odds board closely, then I walked up to the counter and put a C-note on the Dodgers and another on the Giants. Satisfied with my selections, I returned to my seat, picking up a *Racing Form* and a pencil on the way. The monstrous dark wall in front was lined with ten huge screens televising baseball and horse racing from all around the country. It was heavenly. I sat back, relaxed and nursed numerous Miller Lites over the next four hours.

Both teams won as I thought they would, and I had parlayed my baseball winnings into an even larger win on the ponies on a racetrack in Japan. By the time midnight rolled around, and the Sports Book was shutting down for the night, I was up a nifty 1200 bucks. Even more if I counted all the free beer.

Not only had the night been beneficial monetarily, but I had also had time between races to come up with a few scenarios that might help Rachel. Granted, these scenarios were only seeds germinating in my brain, but with a little bit of luck, I thought I might be able to bring them to fruition.

I finally reached Lieutenant Oakley at a quarter to one in the morning. After some prodding and gentle persuasion, he reluctantly agreed to see me.

All in all, I was feeling pretty good. Except for almost being killed earlier in the evening, things seemed to be going my way for a change. Or so I thought.

Metro headquarters was a mess, and it wasn't even a weekend. Uniformed and plainclothes cops were scurrying everywhere with charges in tow. Pimps, hookers, bikers, drunks and even a couple of middle-aged guys in suits walked by in cuffs. And there was no discrimination. I saw young, old, black, white, and a woman in a sari with a male escort donned in a bright red turban. It looked like an international affair uniting under one roof.

"Quite a night, Lieutenant," I said to Oakley as he led me into his office.

"Yeah," he sighed, closing the door. "There's a chartered accountants convention in town. I guess these guys go nuts after looking at numbers all year long."

I nodded. "Maybe that's why they're called 'certified,'" I offered.

"Maybe," he mused. "I never thought of it like that."

Oakley took his seat and I took mine.

"So what's up?" he asked in a tired voice.

"Well, I think somebody tried to kill me earlier tonight." I dug in my pocket and brought out the cigarettes, placing them on his desk.

The lieutenant eyed my collection. "Somebody's making you smoke yourself to death?"

"Come on, I'm being serious." I tossed him the nail. "Take a look at this."

Oakley studied both the spike and me suspiciously. "I thought you said you were being serious." He dropped the nail on his desk.

"I am," I insisted. "Somebody tried to put it through my head."

"Hmm," he smiled. "Did you happen to get a good look at the carpenter . . . I mean, perpetrator?"

"Come on, Lieutenant. It missed my head by this much." I held my thumb and forefinger out, an inch apart.

"Okay, okay," he said, putting on a sincere face again. He selected a gold pen from his pocket, clicked the end once emphatically, and held it poised over a yellow pad of paper. "All right, let's take it from the beginning."

I sighed with a great amount of relief. "Thanks, Lieutenant. I appreciate that."

"No problem. Okay, let's see . . ." He cleared his throat a few times. "Uh, did you, umm, get a good look at the hammer?"

I rolled my eyes to the ceiling. "Jesus Christ."

"No, it's important," he said facetiously. "Could you tell if it was a ballpeen or the kind with the claw at the end?"

"I thought you said you had no sense of humor?" I crossed my arms across my chest. "Go ahead, get it out of your system."

He did.

"Ahh, I'm sorry," he apologized after he had finished. "You know, when I first met you, I thought you were a real jerk. A royal pain in the ass, actually. But when I have nights like I've had tonight," he said, making a fist and pointing his thumb in the direction of the lobby, "well, let's just say listening to you eases the frustrations of the job."

"That's great, Lieutenant. I'm glad I could help. But now, if you've really got it all out of your system, can we get on with it, please?"

"Sure, Morgan. Go ahead."

And I did.

I recounted the events of the evening, expressing my concern that there might be a connection between the cigarettes, Franco and the attempt on my life. The lieutenant must have been taking me more seriously, because he quietly jotted notes on his pad and never laughed once.

"And you think the break-in at your friend's house is related somehow? That the evidence was planted to set her up?"

"That's what I think. It's just too much of a coincidence."

"I agree it's an unusual brand," Oakley said, "but you might be overreacting. Hell, twenty-four hours ago you were positive Yolanda Valentine was guilty. And now it's Franco. Who's next? Contini? Ventura? One of the dishwashers? . . . Me?"

He studied my passive face while I studied the crease in my slacks, then he let out a long breath and continued. "I know it's hard for you to understand and accept the work we've done on this case. I know you don't think I've been sympathetic to Rachel's situation, and you haven't got a leg to stand on with what you've brought me, *but* . . . that doesn't mean I don't think any of it holds merit. It might, it might not. But there's too much hard evidence against her for the district attorney and the department not to proceed in the direction we're going. I might even cut you some slack here and there, let you sort things out for yourself, but you'd better keep it between you and me."

I nodded my gratitude.

"But listen very carefully to what I'm going to say," he said in an official tone. "In the meantime, it's all systems go. I will continue, in my capacity as the officer in charge, to forge ahead with this case as it stands. You won't like it, but you're going to live with it. Get in the way with any bullshit, or falsified information, and I'll be on your ass faster than a vulture on roadkill. *Comprende?*"

"*Comprende.*"

"Good. Now back to this," he went on, pointing his pen at his pad. "It might be just that — a coincidence. As for the nail through the wall, well, that could have been an accident."

We sat in silence for a few moments. I watched him doodle absently on his pad of paper until he finally stopped and looked at me as if he were trying to read my mind.

He swiveled his chair to face his computer. "How do you spell 'Moretti'?"

He used two fingers to punch in the letters on the keyboard as I spelled it out for him. I couldn't see the screen from my vantage point, but whatever was printed there caught his interest.

"Humph," he said, pulling at his lower lip.

"What is it?" I asked, craning my neck trying to read the monitor.

"Oh, it's probably nothing, especially for Las Vegas, but this Franco character is floating a lot of markers around town. He doesn't owe you, does he?"

I raised an eyebrow. "A couple of gas coupons maybe . . ."

Oakley gave me a puzzled look.

I said, "It's a long story."

The intercom on his desk beeped. "Sergeant Turner's on the line Lieutenant," a raspy male voice announced. "She says it's urgent."

Oakley picked up the receiver and punched a button on the terminal. "Hi, Laura. What's up?" He was watching me intently as he listened.

"Okay," he said, glancing at his watch. "I'll meet you out there in an hour or so." He replaced the receiver and studied me for a few seconds.

"You got a car here?" he asked.

"Yeah, sort of. Why?"

"Let's go for a drive," he said in a friendly voice.

Not being totally stupid, I knew there had to be more to it than that.

"Sure, I guess so," I told him. "Where we going?"

"Been out to Hoover Dam recently?" he asked nonchalantly.

"Not for a couple of months." I looked at my watch. It was 2:33 in the morning. "A little late for sightseeing, isn't it?"

"That's what makes Vegas so interesting. It's a twenty-four-hour town." He got up out of his chair. "Come on, Morgan. Let's go visit your friend Franco."

Now I was really confused. "I thought you just said we were going to Hoover Dam?"

"We are," he said, slipping on his jacket.

"Franco's touring the dam?"

"Well, not exactly," he said, straightening his tie. "But seeing as you're here and you're so intent at playing detective, I figured you might as well come along and identify his body."

Chapter

If it wasn't for Hoover Dam, Las Vegas might not exist. The dam supplies enough electricity to power half a million homes and all the neon in Nevada. The magnificent, Pantagruelian, wedge-shaped structure is a skateboarder's wet dream come true. Built into the craggy walls of Black Canyon during the 1930s — about forty miles east of downtown Vegas — it took more than 5000 men working around the clock more than four years to complete, bottom to top. You can be sure it took Franco less than that, top to bottom.

Lieutenant Oakley and I were in an elevator being whisked down fifty-three floors to the bottom of the dam. I'm not very good with heights, or fast downward elevators for that matter, and I was grateful my dinner had been well digested beforehand.

We exited the warm elevator after a one-minute ride. A man in dark green coveralls greeted us, and we followed him through a series of tunnels and a monolithic room housing the dam's massive turbines. The air here was cool and much appreciated.

We were met by a young, uniformed cop who led us to a group of more uniforms and suits. Everyone was standing around staring at a lumpy yellow blanket. Oakley nodded his hellos to them, then turned to me.

"This isn't going to be a pretty sight," he advised gloomily.

I told him not to worry; I'd seen my share of bodies.

Oakley shrugged and tossed back the blanket.

A few seconds later, I tossed too. All over my shoes. Franco Moretti's once-sturdy husky frame had been reduced to a tangle of twisted limbs and limp skin. The back of his skull was flattened into the bloodied concrete.

"You all right, Morgan?"

"Yeah," I answered, wiping spittle from my lips. "I'm okay."

A couple of the cops in the group snickered. "Maybe it was that elevator ride," one of them offered.

"Can it," Oakley told the witling. He crouched down beside the body, examining it, then glanced up. "Well?"

"Yeah, it's him," I nodded.

The lieutenant turned back to the body. I forced myself to hold my gaze. Franco was wearing sneakers, jeans and a checkered short-sleeved shirt. Oakley pulled a pencil from his pocket and probed around Franco's once-muscular arms, searching, I gathered, for needle marks or some such thing. There were no track marks that I could see, but there was a brightly colored anchor-and-rope tattoo on the inside of his thick forearm. The rope dangled from the anchor and eventually became a vicious-looking serpent that snaked its way to a pair of dice about two inches lower.

There was something oddly familiar about the tattoo, but I couldn't place it.

Oakley stepped over the body and checked the other arm, where another tattoo professed Franco's love for someone named Tina.

"Any suicide note?"

"None that we found yet, Lieutenant."

"Have somebody get an address, check for it there. What about a vehicle?"

"Sergeant Turner's upstairs checking, sir. By the way, Lieutenant, there was something strange that we found."

"What's that?"

The cop opened a briefcase. Inside was a plastic bag filled with hundred-dollar bills.

"This was on the victim's person?"

"Not exactly, sir. It was spread out all over the bottom of the dam here. Like somebody threw it in the air from above. We don't even know if we got it all."

The trace of a siren wailing could be heard from high above. We all glanced up. I could make out the quick flash of red and blue lights through the bright spotlights shining down from the top of the dam.

"Meat wagon's here," somebody called out.

"All right," Oakley told his charges. "Wrap it up."

He motioned for me to follow. We walked to the base of the dam, and I watched him slowly unwrap a stick of gum. He didn't offer, so I pulled out my own. The gum helped soothe the bitter taste in my mouth. The two of us stood there chewing for a minute, alone with our thoughts.

"You ever figure the guy for a jumper?"

"No," I answered. "Just the opposite."

"How's that?"

"I'd picture him more as a 'pusher.'"

Oakley nodded his head, chewing thoughtfully. "Yeah, but he owed a lot of money around town. Maybe he couldn't take it any longer. Took the easy way out."

"Nah, I don't think so. He never struck me as the kind who'd run from his troubles. He'd tackle them head on."

"Maybe, maybe not. Don't forget, this is a hard town. Somebody might have decided to collect the only way they could — make an example of him."

I shook my head. "I don't think so. And what about all that money? There could be more behind this."

"Ah, come on, Morgan. You don't still think he had something to do with Valentine's murder after this, do you?"

Something still bothered me about seeing Franco. "I wouldn't be too quick to write it off as a suicide just yet, Lieutenant. Maybe someone was making sure he'd stay quiet."

Oakley spat his gum into the foil wrapper, rolled it up and placed it in his jacket pocket. "I hate to break it to you, but you're grasping at straws."

"We'll see."

He stood there shaking his head. "Good luck," he said with a rueful face. "You'll need it."

"I'll make my own luck," I told him. "You going to want a lift back downtown?"

"Nah, I'm gonna have to stay here for a while." He made an attempt to clear his throat. "Besides, I don't think I could take another ride in that Mad Max vehicle of yours. Thanks anyway."

I waited patiently for two paramedics to push their gurney off the elevator before getting on. An elderly security guard held the door for me, then we started up.

"You look a little pale, son."

"Yeah, well, it wasn't a pretty sight."

"Nope," he agreed. "They never are, Off'cer."

Okay, so he thought I was a cop. I could live with that. It might help me get the answers to some questions I wanted to ask. Besides, he was just an old security guard. He couldn't charge me with impersonating a police officer. At least I didn't think so.

"These things happen often?" I asked officially.

"Often enough, I s'pose. New York's got all them subways and Frisco's got that big bridge, and since most of the hotels in Las Vegas got them windows that don't open — not to mention that shatterproof glass —

well, outside of the big slide at the Wet 'n' Wild park, this here dam is about all we got for jumpers. I think this one's number seven this year."

He thought about that for a moment. "Of course, it's only July . . ."

"Anybody see him jump?"

"Nah, like I told that cute little Sergeant Turner up top, it was pretty late. The only traffic was light, comin' over from Arizona. Fred and I — Fred's my partner — we was playin' cribbage up in the office and I was kickin' his ass real —"

A bell sounded and the car slowed. "Ladies' Lingerie and Housewares," the old man joked as we came to a stop.

The doors opened and we stepped out. The early morning air was cool, helped by a light breeze blowing through the opening of the Black Canyon gorge on its way over to Lake Mead.

I was wondering if Franco had come by himself or if he had been driven out here. "Was there a car found up here?" I asked.

"Don't think so. People ain't supposed to park here, even though they do stop to snap a few pictures. Prob'ly parked over at one of the lookout lots. There's a bunch of your buddies over there checkin' them out, I know that."

"So you didn't see anyone walking around up here, nothing that looked out of place or suspicious?"

The old man made a puzzled face. "Nothin' strange about people walkin' around out here, Off'cer. That's what they come out here to do. You know, walk around, take pictures. Sure, there was a few people here, I guess." He scratched at the stubble on his chin. "I saw a few couples strollin' around while we were playin' crib. Then Charlie from downstairs called up to say we had another one down. But nobody saw nothin'."

The sounds of hurried footfalls coming from the Arizona side of the dam broke my line of questioning.

"Well," smiled the guard, hiking up his belt. "Here comes that pretty sergeant lady. Maybe she's found something."

"Mr. Leach," she called from thirty feet away. "Can I speak with you a moment?"

"Why sure, darlin'. I was just talkin' to the off'cer here . . ."

I had already turned and walked the other way.

The drive back to town gave me lots of time to think. I knew Franco wasn't the kind to do himself in, but at the same time I didn't believe Franco would have let himself be shoved off the top of Hoover by a bunch of loan sharks. He was just too big and powerful — and probably not stupid enough. He'd know something was up if three or four guys were taking him for a walk. Even if he *was* that stupid, he would have put up a hell of a struggle. And besides, if somebody was "taking him out," why not just shoot him and bury him out in the desert like everybody else did?

No. It was more likely that somebody had caught him off guard.

I was tossing ideas around as the darkness of Boulder Highway gave way to the neon flash of Sam's Town Casino and Hotel. The huge, computerized billboard out front advertised cheap meals and thrifty rooms, as well as all the games of chance offered inside. A cowboy popped up on the screen and immediately dealt me a blackjack. He smiled widely and shoved a pile of chips in my direction. As I slowed for the turn onto Flamingo, a pair of dice rattled and rolled in brightly lit colors, and I passed by before seeing if I had won. I took the corner, turning left on a red light, moved to the shoulder of the road and stopped.

Something in the dice roll had caught my eye. I pulled a U-turn and made my way back onto Boulder. I turned left into the parking lot of Sam's, parked facing the sign, and waited for the computerized sequence to begin all over again.

The cowboy smiled, dealt me the same blackjack and paid me off, then the screen lit up with the tossing and turning dice that rolled to a rest. The dots that made up the numbers on the cubes flashed alternately in bright blues and reds.

And that's when it hit me. The dice tattoo on Franco's arm had the same coloration as the "snake eyes" doodle I had seen in the notebook and on the nautical charts stashed in Christian Valentine's safe.

I sat through the computerized sequence twice more while I thought about the connection.

A few minutes later, I was back on Flamingo and on my way home. A tinge of pink shone above the top of the Black Mountain range to the east. I decided to get a couple hours of sleep. The offices at the Oasis would be open at nine, and there were a few things I wanted to check in the hotel's employee files.

I stopped to pick up a couple of jelly doughnuts and a Sanka decaffinated from a coffee shop on the way home. As I munched and sipped and drove, I couldn't help wonder what Rachel would be having for breakfast in her cell.

Chapter

I strolled into the Oasis just after ten. The morning crowd of gamblers was sparse but energetic. It was Thursday, and many of the guests who came in for the weekend charters were storing their luggage with a bell captain and waiting for their rooms to be cleaned. Waiting for your room had become a favorite pastime for the heavy-duty gamblers. It gave them an excuse to get right to the tables and machines. The casino loved it too. There was nothing better than a gambler with a full bankroll cramped up from a six-hour drive or suffering jet lag.

I stopped in at the poker room but things were quiet. Kenny came by and I promised him I would be at his card game this weekend.

As I passed the crap tables on my way to the executive offices, a big Texan wearing a white Stetson yahooed until his face turned crimson and the arteries bulged out on his neck. He had one thick arm around the bare midriff of a slinky young thing in a Dallas Cowboys halter top. I slowed down to watch. She giggled and turned to the side. He rubbed the dice vigorously on the bright red silky short-shorts that barely covered her butt. Normally the pit bosses didn't allow the dice to leave the table, but Tex was betting a pile of thousand-dollar chips, so I guess that made it okay. He finished rubbing and flung the dice to the far end of the table, praying with his eyes to the chandeliered ceiling and bellowing "Yo, 'leven!" at the top of his lungs.

Miss Dallas Cowboy giggled and gave me a wink before turning her attention back to the action. I gave her a friendly smile and a wink back. I didn't bother giggling.

"Eleven a winner," droned the stickman. "Pay the line."

I left to the sounds of "Yyyeeeeehahhhhh!" ringing in the background.

Julius Contini wasn't in yet. His young and curvy secretary knew of my deal with Big Julie. She called downstairs, providing me with the credentials needed to access the employees' files. After explaining that I wanted to surprise her boss, I asked that she not mention my visit. I didn't want Contini getting wind of me going against his direction to stay away from anybody working at the hotel.

The same friendly woman who had supplied me with Franco's telephone numbers earlier in the week was more than happy to help me again. She pointed out the cabinets that held the files on the employees and cleared off a desk for me. I was told the same information was loaded into the computers, but I declined. I knew computer files could be easily accessed and altered, and that the paper files were harder to get to. I signed in on a clipboard and accepted her offer of coffee.

No mention had been made of Franco's demise since I had entered the hotel. The event had not occurred all that long ago, so I assumed the police were keeping it quiet for their own good reasons. I figured I'd go along with them and keep it to myself as well.

I decided to carry out my investigation systematically. For me, that meant alphabetically. I took out a pen and a new notebook and began to read.

First on my list was Leona Carter. Leona had been born Cindy Mansworth and raised in Los Angeles. Her parents had moved there from Buffalo when she was three. She was the end product of two failed marriages and one dead husband — and all before she was thirty. She had been working off and on in Vegas since 1992, after winning a Star Search competition. Most of the rest of the information was drab and uninteresting, except for her appointment to the '88 U.S. Olympic team. Because of her eventual move into dancing, I had presumed her specialty would be something athletic: track, gymnastics, or maybe even swimming. Surprisingly, her claim to fame had been in archery of all things, where she had placed out of the medals but a notable seventh overall.

I jotted down the gist of Leona's information and pulled out the file on Murray Gladstone. I read through it but learned nothing new. Everything Murray had told me checked out with his file: his residing in New Jersey, his working for Contini at the Rosemount Hotel back east, and the deaths of both his wife, Clare, and his daughter, Sherry. All in all, Murray didn't seem to have any skeletons in his closet worth mentioning. Except that he'd had a run-in with Christian Valentine just after joining the Oasis. He had been reprimanded but was able to save his job because of Big Julie's intervention. Interesting. I scribbled some more notes, replaced the folder and skimmed to Franco Moretti's file.

He'd been born in 1953, in Turin, Italy. His parents had immigrated to the U.S. when Franco was a child. He hadn't graduated high school, and had turned to boxing at the age of seventeen. His pugilistic record was a dismal three and twelve, and by the time the bells stopped ringing in his head, he had switched careers and joined the Navy. Within a year he was promoted to the Seals. His forte had been explosives, and he had just missed out on Nam.

Later, he bounced all over the country, working in various restaurants, hotels and catering firms. He eventually landed in Nevada, and after a stint as a maître d' in Tahoe he found work at the newly constructed Oasis Hotel and Casino here in Vegas. The file confirmed his affection for gambling and his friendly relationship with Christian Valentine.

I perused the file one more time to make sure I hadn't missed anything and replaced the folder in the cabinet. I thought about having a look at Rachel's file but decided to go with what she had told me. I knew I'd never get credit for it, but it was a show of trust I felt I owed her. I flipped to the V's.

Christian Valentine's file wasn't there. Either the police had removed it during the investigation, or the hotel had decided to pull it after his death.

There wasn't much to report on Johnny Ventura. He had kicked around the continent for most of his adult life, playing in clubs from Toronto to Tucson. He ended up at the Oasis after a couple of years of singing in lounges around town. He had been waiting in the wings ever since.

Leaning back in my chair, I glanced at my notes, not knowing if I had anything that would help Rachel or not. The one thing that stuck out like a sore thumb was Leona's experience with the bow and arrow. But would she have been so obvious? The cops would be all over that gem. And the more I thought about it, the more I would like to get my hands on a copy of the hotel's insurance policy on Christian Valentine.

Before leaving, I peeked at my own file and was pleased to learn that I had made a good impression with the powers-that-be since joining the Oasis. There were a few recommendations from McClusky and various pit bosses on my prowess as a dealer. My run-ins and drink-related problems with players had been recorded and written off as "customer temperaments." Most of the other stuff they said was true, too, except for the part about me possibly having a gambling problem.

It was time to sign out. The friendly lady who had let me into the files was busy on the phone. The office was abuzz with activity. The running of such a huge hotel was filled with complications. I sat down at a desk facing her while she tried to soothe someone on the other end of the line.

"Yes, Pierre," she explained patiently, "I'm sure we ordered the lobsters yesterday. Yes, I know you're almost out. No, no, of course you can't use chicken. Hang on and let me check." She held her hand over the mouthpiece of the telephone and looked in my direction. "Can you do me a big favor?"

"Sure," I told her.

"Thanks. The kitchen's going bonkers. Would you mind hitting the report button on that fax machine in front of you?"

The machine was one of those new ones, with more bells and whistles than a clown costume. I didn't have a clue where the report button was. I looked to her for help.

"Up near the top," she explained, wiggling a finger. "Just above the numeric pad."

I found the button and pressed it. In a few seconds the machine started feeding out a sheet of paper, which eventually fell into a basket attached to the front. Printed on it was a list of numbers with the dates and times of each call placed. I took out the sheet and handed it to her.

The secretary smiled her thanks. "Let me see if the fax went out, Pierre." She scanned down the sheet. "Yes, here it is. It was ordered first thing yesterday morning. It should be on the plane and here this afternoon. Uh-huh. That's right. You're welcome."

I was impressed. "Email may be taking over the world, but there's still something to say about old-fashioned technology," I said when she replaced the receiver.

She passed me the clipboard and smiled again. "You've got that right. We must have ten of them around the hotel. And so many people still use them in their homes. I even know a few who have mobile faxes."

"My Chevy would have a hissy fit." I initialed the time on the clipboard and thanked her again.

Once outside, I took a shortcut on my way to the parking lot by cutting across the swimming pool area. It was almost noon, the sky clear, and the temperature hovering somewhere in the high nineties. Hundreds of greased-up bodies were sprawled lazily on pink chaises longues, basking in the searing sun. And except for a few kids splashing each other near the miniature island, the pool was vacant.

Much of the near nakedness was of the female persuasion. Lucky me. Many of the hotel's dancers and cocktail waitresses — and yes, hookers, too — worked avidly at their tans off-hours. And because tan lines are frowned upon, most of the girls' swimsuits looked like Band-Aids held together with dental floss.

Seeing all that skin was driving me crazy. I couldn't help wonder what I would do if Rachel didn't get out soon. I picked up my pace. One of the things I *wouldn't* be doing in the near future was going anywhere near the damn pool again.

On my way out of the parking lot, I stopped to speak with Billy. He confirmed what Murray had told me last night. I was also able to learn that Franco had left around midnight — alone, but in a real hurry. Billy hadn't heard about his death, and I didn't bother to fill him in.

Chapter

It was a lot easier getting in to see Rachel this time. We were sitting in the same room, at the same cubicle, being watched by the same bored female guard. After filling her in on Franco's death, I told her why I thought he'd had something to do with Valentine being knocked off. She was quiet and sullen, but seemed to be taking everything in.

"Tell me about the flowers and champagne you got at home."

She gave me a quizzical look. "You mean the ones you sent?"

I just knew that little white lie was going to catch up with me in the end. "Uh, yeah," I said. "Those ones."

"I don't understand. *You* sent them."

Admitting I wasn't her secret admirer wouldn't help things right now. "Of course I did. But can you remember anything about the delivery?"

Rachel was still confused and I couldn't really blame her. "God, Jake. What difference does it make? A guy came with them. He knocked at the door, said he had a delivery for me. I didn't ask him where he was from. Don't you remember where you ordered them?"

"Of course I do," I lied. "But did he have a uniform? Was there a truck outside?"

She thought about it for a moment. "He wasn't wearing a uniform. He was just a young guy, dressed casual, like you'd see anywhere. He had long hair — blond, I think — and a skull-shaped earring . . . Wait a minute! There *was* a truck out there. A van. Yes, I remember seeing a van parked in the driveway when I looked out the window. A yellow one, I think. With a big pink bow on the roof."

"Was there a name on the van?"

"I couldn't really tell. It was parked facing the door. But I'm sure it was yellow."

"That's good, Rachel. What about the card?"

"It was just a card. One of those small ones they give out at flower shops. Didn't you pick it out?"

"No," I lied once more. "I phoned it in."

"I don't understand. You think the florist had something to do with it?"

"No, but I think the bottle had something to do with your being charged. The Gauloises cigarettes, too."

"The ones we found in the kitchen?"

I nodded and told her about my adventure outside Johnny Ventura's dressing room.

Rachel bit lightly at her lip. "Maybe you shouldn't get mixed up in this anymore. I'd feel terrible if anything happened to you, too."

"It's okay," I reassured her. "That was before Hoover Dam. I don't think there's much chance of anything else happening."

She looked at me with moist eyes. "I hope you're right."

Las Vegas never ceased to amaze me. I knew from flipping through the Yellow Pages during breaks that there were more than fifty wedding chapels and forty escort services in town. That didn't surprise me. But 217 florist shops? Who would have guessed?

Most of early Friday afternoon was spent on the telephone trying to discover which one of the 217 had a yellow van with a pink bow on the roof and a young guy with long hair as its driver. I eased the load by concentrating on the ones south of downtown, and on or near the Strip, as well as those that would also purchase and bill for Dom Perignon. That cut it down to between thirty and forty, but it was still a big job.

I kept my questions general, told the person answering that I had missed the delivery to my home last week and had not been able to give the driver the large tip he had coming. A lot of them had drivers with long hair and earrings, but only one had a yellow van with a pink ribbon that had been out on delivery at Rachel's address the week before. My veiled request for the purchaser's name was met with an apologetic explanation that they didn't disclose that kind of information. I noted the address and told the female clerk I would be out there within the hour. I gave her a false name, just in case.

·

The Sweet Memories Flower and Gift Shop was two or three miles west of my apartment, a block or two from the Oasis Hotel. It was located near the end of a strip mall, appropriately sandwiched between Linda's Love, Lace and Lingerie and Larry's Liquor Outlet.

As I entered the florist shop, a bell announced my arrival. A young woman in tight jeans and baggy T-shirt greeted me as the door closed.

"Hi," I said in a friendly manner. "I called a little while ago . . ."

She thought about that for a moment. "Oh, right! The big tipper." She slung a large orange purse over her shoulder and brushed by me. "Look, I'm just on my way out. I told Bruce you were coming by. He's out back, sorting through deliveries. He'll take care of you in a minute."

The bell over the door sounded again and she was gone.

Great, I thought. Rachel's in jail, my sex life is nil and here I am alone in a florist shop with some guy named Bruce.

The store was small, crowded with floral arrangements of all sizes and colors. The heady scents were overwhelming. Two playful kittens jumped out from behind a fiftieth-anniversary wreath and stopped their frolicking to study me. One of them spotted a bunched-up piece of red ribbon and swatted it smartly across the floor. The other gained traction after a couple of false starts, and the chase was on.

There was noise and movement from the back of the store. A few moments later, the rear doorway filled with boxes stacked one on top of the other. The pile was tall, and the person carrying them had to squat to get the top box clear of the doorframe. As the boxes were placed on the floor, the top one slipped and fell.

"Damn!" cried a voice from behind the boxes.

I had a feeling this was Bruce.

The kittens scurried for cover. A body followed the voice out from behind the pile, and the eyes focused on me. "Oh, excuse my French. I didn't know anybody was here."

Bruce was no Brucey, or if he was, I was in trouble. He was about six-four, 260 pounds, and he carried the weight in all the right places. He wore a blue, sleeveless, Gold's Gym T-shirt and burgundy track pants, and his long black hair was tied neatly in back with a yellow sweatband.

"Can I help you?" he said in a raspy, bass tenor voice.

"Would you mind holding up my Chevy while I rotate the tires?"

"Huh?"

"Never mind. I called earlier. About a delivery last week. The girl that just left —"

"Oh, right." He snapped his fingers and the kittens scurried off again. "Clare mentioned somebody was looking for one of our drivers." He crossed his thick arms as best he could across his massive chest and scowled. "Is there a problem?"

"No, no," I explained, shaking my head. "It's just that a driver made a delivery to a friend of mine and my friend forgot to give him a gratuity."

Although the excuse for coming by had sounded good over the telephone, it was now sounding weak judging by Bruce's reaction. He flexed his pecs a couple of times for effect, then scrunched up his brow and asked, "You're not one of those . . . fairies, are you?"

"Who, me?" I gasped. "Are you kidding! I can name you every starting quarterback in the NFL last season."

Bruce considered that for a moment. "Okay, so what's up?"

"Here's the way it is," I explained, noticing my voice had dropped an octave. "Last week, a friend of mine — a *girlfriend*, I might add — received a delivery from one of your drivers. I guess she was so excited with the gift, she forgot to tip him. She feels real bad about it, too. I'd like to take care of it if I could."

Bruce unfolded his arms. "Do you know his name?"

"No," I told him. "The lady that answered the phone said you had a driver matching his description. Tall, skinny kid with long hair. Has an earring in the shape of a skull."

"Sounds like Damien." He walked slowly toward the counter and opened a register book. "What was the date and address?"

I gave him the information and he flipped through the pages.

"Here it is. Oh, yeah, I remember this one. Not many orders go out with Dom Perignon. They usually just settle for a bottle of wine. I arranged this one myself. Grenada Drive, afternoon of the seventh. Delivered by Damien to the home of Rachel Sinclair."

"That's the one." I reached into my pocket and pulled out a twenty-dollar bill. "I'd appreciate it if you'd give him this for me."

Bruce took the bill. He stuck a yellow Post-It sticker to it and wrote down Damien's name. "Sure, I'll give it to him next time he's in." He tucked the money under the counter and began to walk back to his work.

"By the way," I said amiably. "Would you mind telling me who phoned in the order?"

Bruce took out a pair of scissors from his back pocket. "No can do," he said, snipping away at a carnation arrangement.

I reached into my pocket again. "There's another twenty in it for you . . ."

"Oh, yeah?" he scowled.

"Okay, take it easy . . . I'll make it forty."

He studied his creation, frowned, then fluffed the flowers until he was satisfied. "I'm afraid it's policy," he finally said.

"What's the big deal?" I asked.

He picked up his clippings and dropped them into a pail by the counter. "We can't go giving out that kind of information. This is Las Vegas! We have to protect our clients. Who knows? You could be a disgruntled boyfriend, or a stalker." He eyed me up and down. "Or something."

"Oh, come on," I smiled widely. "Do I look disgruntled?"

He chose a thank-you card from a rack and began writing.

"Okay," I apologized. "You're probably right. I can see how it might compromise you in that kind of situation."

Bruce finished writing and took the time to draw little hearts above all the i's. "I'm glad you understand. The person who ordered them is a regular."

"So they just phone in, place the order, and you fill out the cards for them and bill them later. Is that how it works?"

"That's about it." He selected a ribbon from a spool and slipped it through the card, then walked over to the arrangement and tied the card to the wicker handle. "Believe me, you don't have anything to worry about with this customer and your girlfriend. They must fax in seven or eight orders a month. It's one of our best accounts."

A buzzer sounded loudly from the back of the store.

"I've got a truck to unload. I'll tell Damien you came by." The buzzer rang again. "Okay! Hold your water. I'm coming!"

A few moments later, the sound of an electric door being rolled up echoed from the deepest recess of the store. I peeked around at the front door. Satisfied that no one else was about to enter the premises, I snuck behind the counter.

The fax machine was on a shelf behind an elaborate funeral wreath. The activity report button wasn't in the same location as the one I had used in the Oasis, but I found it farther down the function panel. As I stuck out my finger to press the button, the machine beeped twice and lit up. The display window flashed the word *Receiving* and began to slowly spit out a sheet of paper.

From the rear of the store came sounds of a truck's ignition catching. I knew the electric door would be next. I knew too, that if Bruce caught me behind his counter, he'd snap me in half like a stale breadstick.

A horn tooted and gears meshed, then the electric door began its descent. The fax machine continued outputting. Just as I had decided the paper would continue forever, the machine beeped once and went dark. The sheet fell silently into a tray marked "In."

I jabbed at my target button. Bruce was whistling "Eye of the Tiger" in the back room. The display lit up again and told me it was reporting. I smiled to myself. A sheet of paper fell out of the machine and I quickly scanned it. I stopped smiling. The report told me only the last ten or so faxes.

The sounds of rummaging and whistling got noticeably louder. I scanned the function panel more thoroughly and found a button marked "Expanded Report." I almost punched my finger through the console in my exuberance. The machine kicked back into action.

In less than a minute, I had the monthly report listing the numbers with corresponding dates and times. I folded the sheet of paper and stuffed it down the front of my shirt. Bruce reentered the store just as I sounded the bell above the door to leave.

"You still here?" he asked in a wary voice.

"Uh, no," I lied, closing the door as if I'd just walked in. "You see, I got to the car and realized maybe I did need something. A small bouquet, nothing too expensive."

He crossed his arms as if he didn't totally believe me. "And what's the occasion?"

"It's for my kid sister," I explained casually. "She just had a baby."

Ten minutes and a couple of lies later, I was out another thirty-five bucks.

Bruce sprayed the arrangement with a coat of water. "Was it a boy or a girl?"

"Uh, a boy, I guess . . ."

He reached under the counter and came up with a silver-and-blue balloon that announced "It's a Boy!" and tied it to the arrangement in a neat little bow.

I thanked him and left. Before getting in the car, I untied the balloon and watched it float above the parking lot until an updraft caught and carried it straight up. It hung there for a while, went one way and then the other, dropped and then lifted again. It reminded me of my life.

Eventually, I lost it in the high afternoon sun.

Chapter

The Oasis offices were still active. I placed the floral arrangement on the friendly secretary's desk and she gave me a quizzical look.

"For me?"

"Sure," I told her. "I appreciate your helping me out earlier today."

"Why, thank you," she blushed, holding the vase high in the air for the other ladies to see. They all smiled and cooed accordingly. She cleared a space on her cluttered desk and set the vase down. "You know, Mr. Morgan, it really wasn't necessary. I was happy to help."

I told her to call me Jake. "Look, Ms. . . ?"

She gave me a light laugh and said I could call her Betty, and told me I was more than welcome to her assistance.

"Okay, *Betty*," I smiled brightly. "As a matter of fact, there was one other little thing I was wondering if you could help me with." I explained about the fax sheet, told her what I wanted to find out.

"Well, Jake. There's a directory of fax numbers, just like the telephone book. Unfortunately, the numbers are listed by the customers' names. Unless you know who you're looking for . . ."

"Hmm," I murmured, studying the sheet from the florist. "Can I see a sample of one of the faxes you get here?"

She sifted through a pile of papers on her desk and finally found what she was searching for. "Sure, here's one." She handed me the page. "You see, if you could get a peek at the originals from your sheet, you'd easily be able to find out who sent them. There's usually a cover sheet showing who sent them, or the company's logo."

Remembering Bruce, I told her, "I don't think that'll be possible. I had a hard enough time getting this."

Betty sensed my dejection. "I don't know what else to say."

I searched the fax she'd given me carefully. "What's this?" I asked, pointing to some fine type at the top of the sheet.

She leaned over the desk. "Oh, that's the originating number of the fax. Most machines are preprogrammed to list their number across the top. It gives the receiving end the date and the time sent, and the number of pages sent too. Does that help?"

After thinking about that for a few moments, I said, "Yeah, it might, if you can lend me a couple of things."

Betty was eager to help. Twenty minutes later I was all set. She'd loaned me a desk, some blank paper and a word processor. I was also given access to one of their fax machines. After a few minutes with the machine's manual, I figured out how to erase the preset program and set my own.

I read over the phony letterhead I had typed up. It stated simply that I was an insurance salesman who was going to be in their area tomorrow calling on their neighbors, and if it was convenient, I'd be dropping in on them too. Should they not be interested, I told them, all they had to do was check off the "Not Interested" box at the bottom and return my fax. To capture the desired effect, I had named the company Harry Grabbit Insurance. I gave the hotel machine's number as mine.

Next, I took the florist fax and began crossing off the few names of companies listed and the calls that had come in from out of town. Then I began sending my fax, one at a time. I'd kept the letter short and sweet, but it still took me half an hour to complete the task.

It was 2:27 when I finally finished, and I realized I still hadn't eaten anything.

Betty liked the idea, but she seemed skeptical. "Do you think anyone will answer, Jake?"

"Would you?" I smiled.

She thought about that for a split second. "You're damn right," she shuddered. "I hate insurance salesmen."

I laughed and told Betty I'd be back shortly. She explained she was off soon, but that somebody would be there all night. She thanked me again for the flowers.

Downstairs, I grabbed a couple of chili dogs and an order of nachos and found a seat in the Sports Book. Del Mar still had a few races left on their card, and I intended to make the most of it. I reached over to an empty table and relieved it of its *Daily Racing Form*. A waitress dropped off a big plastic cup of cold draft beer without comment. They seemed to know me around here.

By 3:10 I was down to my last nacho and realized my mind wasn't really on the horses. I kept thinking of Rachel. Then of Rachel and me.

I made a circuit of the casino on my way upstairs. I stopped to chat with a few dealers standing at empty BJ tables. The word was out on Franco — they all mentioned his suicide. I passed the baccarat pit. As usual, it was practically deserted. This never failed to amaze me, since baccarat has the lowest house advantage of any game in town — just over one percent. And the player doesn't have to do anything except bet. The bettor could choose "Player" or "Bank" to put his money on and then get two cards. The rules of the game govern whether you stand or draw with the cards you're dealt. Whoever got closer to nine would win, and the casino collected five percent of any bets on "Bank." That was it! Still, tourists preferred to pump their purses and wallets into the greedy slots that held back up to twenty percent of everything put in. *Most* of the tourists, but not all.

You would hardly ever see the Asians wasting their money on the slots. They are practical people. They preferred baccarat, where they could go head to head with the house at a hundred grand a hand. When I stopped to think about it, maybe that's why they had so many of our American dollars to play with.

Betty had already left by the time I returned to the office. I hadn't been sure what to expect from my little exercise with the fax, but judging from the pile of paper sitting on my borrowed desk, it had been a whopping success. And the fax was still spitting out sheets.

I smiled to myself, settled into a chair, and began reading. As expected, a few were from local firms and businesses, but as Betty had pointed out to me earlier, a large number came from personal residences.

There was one in particular that caught my attention. And it was a beauty. The originating information at the top of this fax listed the sender as "C & Y Valentine."

Bingo!

Chapter

I sat there for a full three minutes, allowing the impact of this little treasure to sink in. It could be a coincidence, but somehow I didn't think so. If I was on the right track, one of the Valentines had sent the flowers and champagne to Rachel, and may have had something to do with Rachel being set up for murder. I read the rest of the faxes to see if any of the other names were familiar. None was.

My first instinct was to call Lieutenant Oakley and let him know what I found, but where would that get me? What if the Valentines had sent the gifts as a simple goodwill gesture? Oakley would probably make some wisecracks, like he had about the hammer and nail, and tell me to stop wasting my time. No, I didn't need more of that.

There was only one thing to do. I packed my pile of papers and exited the office, leaving the machine on in case anyone else responded.

The late-afternoon sun was edging toward the Spring Mountain range to the west. I was coasting south along Boulder Highway for the second time in twenty-four hours, sorting through my thoughts and the questions that had to be asked.

Boulder Highway runs almost perfectly straight for seventy or eighty miles, from downtown Las Vegas, through Henderson and out to Boulder City. And unless you're traveling in from Arizona, visiting Lake Mead, or driving out to Hoover Dam to identify a body, there's really no reason to be out here. There are no real sights or attractions, except for a few sawdust joints in Henderson. The land is bleached brown, flat and scrubby, like most places off the Vegas strip, and it is home only to the occasional RV park, service station and warehouse outlet. Gun shops were the big thing out here. Perhaps I should have taken that as an omen.

Most everyone who lived in Las Vegas knew the Valentines had a mansion out near Boulder City, and from what I had heard it was immense: twenty-seven rooms spread out over 30,000 square feet, built in the foothills of River Mountain. Knowing Christian Valentine, it shouldn't have been that difficult to find. The egomaniac probably had klieg lights installed out on his front lawn.

After about forty minutes, I passed through Henderson and picked up Interstate 93, now heading east. The craggy mountains in the distance cast a surreal effect. Their chiseled ridges and layers of multicolored sandstone sculptures would leave a *National Geographic* photographer breathless.

Up ahead, on a slight barren rise, four or five large homes loomed in stark contrast to the natural beauty of the land. The structures were similar in construction, stucco-and-brick and red Spanish tiles, but one in particular stood out from the rest. This one dwarfed the others by half, its configuration intimidating, brazen and bold, yet magnificent all the same. The estate sat far back from the others, elevated higher as if to oversee its brood.

I turned off onto a dusty dirt side road and navigated the Chevy through a twisting course, around polished boulders, cactus groves and thick stands of Joshua trees.

As I passed the smaller homes, I noted they each had patches of imported grass out front. Beside one of them, an elderly gentleman was busy watering a bed of flowers bordering his property and the next. I stopped to ask directions to the Valentine residence. As expected, he pointed toward the mammoth dwelling at the far end of the road.

The Valentine property was encircled by a short brick wall. An elaborate iron gate, more decoration than anything else, stood invitingly open. I parked in the circular gravel driveway and made my way to a double set of solid-looking oak doors. Instead of a bell, each door wore a heavy brass knocker in the shape of a treble clef.

I was about to rap when the door suddenly opened. A startled Hispanic woman clasped a hand to her chest and almost dropped the picnic basket she was carrying. I apologized for the scare, introduced myself by showing her my hotel identification, and politely asked if I could speak with Mrs. Valentine.

"Señora Vee not at home," she told me in a heavy accent. "I am sorry."

"When is she expected back?" I asked, trying to hide the urgency I felt inside.

"The señora will be gone for all weekend." She handed me the basket and closed the door. "She is on boat. I take food to her."

Of course. This was Friday. Oakley had told me she went away each weekend by herself, but with the recent death of her husband, one would have thought she'd be too distressed. One, perhaps, but not me.

Explaining in a solemn tone that I'd worked for the late Mr. Valentine, I told her it was important that I speak to his wife. I offered to take the picnic basket for her. She thought for a moment, then asked me to wait outside while she called her employer.

It was easy to understand why the Valentines had chosen this site for their home. They had a magnificent view, facing west, where the sun would set over the McCullough Mountains, and a partial view of the Colorado River to the south. I jealously drank in the scenery. My apartment overlooked a golden arches and a billboard advertising tune-ups for $59.95.

The maid returned while I was taking it all in.

"The señora says 'Yes,' it is okay." She gave me directions to the marina and told me where I would find the yacht.

I arrived at the Lake Mead Marina fifteen minutes later. Locals were hitching small fishing boats back onto the trailers behind their cars as I pulled into the lot. The harbor was filled with daytime boating enthusiasts returning from their afternoon of fun and sun. Out on the dock, kids tossed handfuls of bread out onto the water, laughing and shouting as hundreds of carp battled each other for position.

Seven or eight wooden docks branched off from the main one. I stopped at the dockmaster's station and was directed to the far end of the marina. I was told the Valentine yacht was easy to find — it would be the largest one on the water.

With the heavy picnic basket in hand, I negotiated my way carefully down the crowded narrow dock. The Valentine boat was at the very end and, like the house, dwarfed everything else nearby. It was a sleek cabin cruiser forty to fifty feet in length, and it wore the name *Mine — All Mine* in large, fire-engine-red lettering on its white stern.

"Permission to come aboard, Mr. Morgan," a pleasant voice called out.

I peered up at the pilothouse, shading my eyes with a hand.

Yolanda Valentine stepped through the doorway. She wore a yellow two-piece swimsuit, a matching scarf and a pair of dark tortoiseshell sunglasses. The woman may have had ten years on me, but she still looked damned appealing. Her legs were long and lean, her stomach taut and tanned, and she carried herself with an air of quiet confidence.

Yolanda glided up to the edge of the cockpit and smiled warmly. She lifted a bare leg and placed one foot on a short railing, straining the bikini bottom's thin material against the natural folds of her body. Out of sheer modesty, I dropped the hand that was shading the sun and let the rays blind my view.

"Well?" she asked.

"I come bearing gifts."

"I've heard that one before," she laughed saucily. She stood back and opened a gate built into the railing. I walked up a short wooden gangplank, stepped on board and handed her the basket.

"Let me put this downstairs. With all this heat, I don't want anything to spoil." She turned and went down a short flight of steps, calling out over her shoulder, "Can I get you a drink? A beer? Some wine maybe?"

"A beer would be great."

I glanced around the boat while the sounds of closing cupboards and clinking glass came from inside. The cockpit had a set of controls similar to those in the wheelhouse above the cabin and the deck area was capable of entertaining a large number of guests. The seating was limited to cushioned benches built into the side and a couple of chaises. Retracted against the back of the wheelhouse was a red-and-blue-striped canopy. A propane barbecue was positioned on one of the rails.

Yolanda came back on deck and handed me a bottle of Coors. She had a clear tumbler of something else for herself. I held my beer out and toasted it in her direction. "To Christian Valentine. One of the greats."

She was sipping slowly at her drink, watching me carefully over the edge of her glass. After a moment, she eased into a chaise and lay back in a comfortable pose. "You know, that's really quite comforting, coming from the friend of the woman who murdered him."

I studied her right back as I drank from my bottle. "She didn't."

"The police seem to think so." Yolanda reached into a large handbag beside her chair. She removed a cigarette and lit it. "And that's good enough for me."

"Not as far as I'm concerned."

She blew a long stream of smoke skyward. "Don't tell me you're still playing detective."

"I'm not *playing* anything." I pointed to the cushioned bench to her right. "May I?"

"Go ahead, make yourself at home." She loosened the straps of her top, then adjusted her bra downward. "Take your shirt off, if you want. You look like you could use some sun."

Two could play at this game. I undid the buttons but left the shirt on.

"So what brings you out here?" she asked, flicking ash to the teak deck.

"Mrs. Valentine," I sighed. "Rachel Sinclair wasn't connected with your husband's death. She was set up. I'm not sure how, but I think you might be able to clear up a few things."

"Me?" She looked genuinely startled. "What the hell are you talking about?"

"The police have a lot of circumstantial evidence —"

"I know what they have!" she said acidly. "He was my husband, for Christ's sake!"

"They're wrong," I told her. "But if you help me, maybe — "

"Hold on a second! Are you saying I may have had something to do with . . . I don't believe this shit!" She spun and flung the cigarette far out into the water. "Get the hell off my boat!"

I stayed right where I was, collecting my thoughts, sorting through the possibilities. I knew I was better off with her on my side rather than against me, so I reached out a hand and patted her bare thigh.

"Yolanda," I said beseechingly, "I'm not accusing you. I need your help! Rachel's innocent and somebody is letting her take the fall. All I want is for you to straighten out some things for me. Help me find who did kill your husband." The pats to her thigh became slow circles. "You don't want to see the real murderer get away with this, do you?"

She fired up another butt. "What is it you want?"

"Look," I explained, "somebody went to a great deal of trouble to plant some heavy evidence on Rachel. But it's almost too good. Too perfect."

"Love sure is blind," she said, shaking her head slowly.

Ignoring her comment, I reached into my shirt pocket. "The cops found a bottle of Dom Perignon in your husband's suite with Rachel's fingerprints on it. She says she's never been up there. And there were only two times she had champagne recently. One was last week when you joined us in the Sultan's Tent. The other was at her home when the two of us celebrated her new part in the show. Rachel thinks I sent her that champagne, because it was signed 'From a Secret Admirer.'" I unfolded the fax sheets. "You see, the point is, I never sent anything to her. And apparently you have an account with the people who delivered them."

I showed her the printout from Sweet Memories, as well as the corresponding numbers from their sheet and the one I had received at the Oasis.

Yolanda Valentine shrugged her shoulders. "So, big deal. My husband and I have accounts all over the city! It's probably just a coincidence."

"Well, that's what got me thinking — about coincidences, that is. The really big one was somebody broke into Rachel's home the very next day. A few things were taken: some costume jewelry, a radio, nothing of real value. But no one bothered to check the garbage. Who would have thought to?"

Yolanda looked at me as if I'd lost my mind. "What the hell are you talking about? I don't see what any of this can possibly have to do with my husband's death."

"Well, actually, it may have everything to do with his death, and what's important to me is that it may also have something to do with Rachel's arrest. You see, I find it rather strange that a bottle with Rachel's prints on it just happens to wind up at a murder scene right after her home had been broken into. My thinking is that somebody sent her that bottle, then retrieved it and planted it as evidence."

"That doesn't explain the rest of the prints. What about the glass and the light switch? And my jacket, for God's sake!"

"Picking up somebody's glass is simple enough. Hell, I remember you leaving the table in the Sultan's Tent with a champagne glass in your hand. The table was filled with glassware. That glass could just as easily have been Rachel's."

"I don't think I like your insinuation," she said calmly.

"I'm not insinuating. I'm just explaining how easy it would have been. And the same thing with the light switch. Anyone with a basic knowledge of electricity can take out and replace a wall switch. Hell, I could probably do it! But my thinking is the same person who broke into her home for the champagne bottle swapped switches too."

I told her about the cigarette butts in Rachel's kitchen, and the ones found in the dressing room area and podium at the Oasis. She hadn't heard about Franco's cordless bungee jump off Hoover Dam, but the news didn't really seem to faze her.

"That's too bad, he was a nice man," she said softly. "But I understand he had a gambling problem. Maybe it was his only way out."

"I doubt it," I said casually. "But maybe he was involved with someone else in your husband's murder, and that someone was making sure he didn't talk."

"Like I said, you're really grasping at straws. You should hear yourself. It's pitiful!" She sipped at her drink. "What do the police say?"

"I only came up with most of this in the last twenty-four hours. I haven't had a chance to give them my theories, but I will as soon as I put a few more pieces of the puzzle together."

Yolanda didn't appear impressed. "Let me see the florist's fax again."

I did and she held it out at arm's length to read. "That's our number," she agreed. "But you know what Christian was like. He must have sent the roses and champagne to her. He was always doing things like that, trying to win over some starry-eyed dancer who might want to further her career."

I sipped the remains of my beer. "Those two assumptions are wrong, Mrs. Valentine."

She gave me a quizzical look. "What are you talking about?"

"Well, first of all, Rachel wasn't some starry-eyed dancer bedding down the star. I believe she got her promotion on merit."

Yolanda huffed and finished her drink.

"And secondly," I continued with a cold stare, "who said anything about roses being sent with the champagne?"

"You did . . ."

"No, I didn't. All I said was somebody delivered a bottle of Dom Perignon. How would you know about the roses if you didn't send them?"

She waved the fax sheet and tossed it in my direction. "It says right there that it came from a florist. I assume somebody's going to send flowers with champagne if they're ordering from a florist. Christian would have. Wouldn't you?"

"I don't have those resources," I told her.

Yolanda eased out of her chaise. "Look, if you don't believe me, call Sweet Memories and ask who sent them." She lifted the lid on a teak compartment, reached in, and handed me a cellular telephone.

"I already tried that," I explained. "It didn't do me any good. They wouldn't tell me a damn thing."

"Well, they'll tell me." She dialed information, was given the number, and dialed again. "This is Mrs. Valentine. Oh, hello, Bruce . . . Yes, I'm fine, thank you. Yes, Christian was a fine man. I appreciate that. Bruce, I need some information to clear up a bill I received from your store. Could you tell me if my husband ordered an arrangement and a bottle of champagne last week? . . . Yes, I can wait."

She stood and lit another cigarette. While waiting, she paced back and forth across the deck, surveying the dock area and the boats nearby. "He ordered *four* of them last week? . . . Hold on." She held the phone away from her and asked me, "Where's Rachel live?"

When I had given her the address, she walked over and parked herself beside me. She repeated the information into the receiver and then held the telephone to my ear. "Yes, Mrs. Valentine," Bruce's voice called out, "Mr. Valentine did order to that address last week. On the seventh. You know, it's funny," he added with a chuckle, "some goofy guy came by just a little while ago, asking the very same thing!"

I let that go. Now that my theory was shot full of holes, I was in no mood to argue. I handed the telephone back.

"Yes, thank you, Bruce," Yolanda said politely into the receiver. "I think that clears it up."

She replaced the cellular into the compartment. "Don't look so morose, Jake. At least now you know Christian was the one who sent them. Does that help?"

"Not a bit." I went to take a drink from my bottle and found it empty.

"Let me get you another beer."

I hadn't planned on staying much longer, but I still wanted to find out more about her and Christian's relationship. "Just a quick one, then I have to go."

Yolanda took my empty and proceeded carefully down the steep flight of stairs to the galley. The information from the florist was not what I had hoped for. I was totally discouraged and got up from my seat to pace.

The late-afternoon sun was sinking fast. The activity around the dock area and the other boats had subsided and things were quiet. Out on the water, a couple of skiers were getting in the last of their rides. A flock of roving seagulls descended on the picnic area next to the parking lot.

"Here you go, Jake." Yolanda placed the fresh bottle on the top step. "I'm going to bring up a fruit plate."

"Don't go to any bother," I told her.

She smiled brightly. "It's no bother, really."

I walked over to the passageway and got down on one knee to reach my beer. I smiled my thanks to Yolanda standing at the bottom of the stairs. She smiled back cheerfully.

As I leaned over to retrieve the bottle, a bolt of lightning shot through my skull, then shimmered crazily down my spine. My teeth cracked hard against each other. Both knees buckled. The sky blazed bright white, then faded to total black.

I felt myself falling in a bizarre, slow-motion spiral and, much to my dismay, there wasn't a damn thing I could do about it.

Chapter

Being knocked unconscious was nothing like what I had read about in detective novels. In a book, the private eye usually bounces right back and retaliates. In reality, that's impossible; plus it hurts a whole lot more.

This sleuth was crumpled in a fetal ball at the bottom of the stairs, face-down in a mixed pool of wetness. The vile stench that filled my nostrils was proof enough that it wasn't just blood I was lying in. My skull felt fractured, my shoulders numb, and every nerve in my neck and spine screamed out in pain.

When I tried to bring my arms around to check for cranial and facial damage, I realized — a moment too late — my wrists were tied securely behind my back. I fell face-forward, crushing my nose into the floor, and threw up again for my efforts.

Twin engines fired up. I rolled gingerly to my left and worked my way into a sitting position. Fortunately my feet were not bound. The boat began to move just as I tried to stand, and my equilibrium failed to make the adjustment to the craft's light planing. I crashed loudly into a cupboard and slid back down to the cabin floor.

"Well, well, well. How was your nap?" I turned my head slowly upward to the sound of the somewhat familiar voice. The sunlight shining down from the open passageway seared my eyes and I looked away. I went to vomit again, but my tank was empty. I dry-heaved once and coughed violently instead.

"Come on up where I can keep an eye on you."

It wasn't easy, but after a couple of minutes of pushing and prodding and pulverizing my face even more, I managed to work my way up the five or six steps and stagger to my feet.

"No standing yet, we're still in the harbor!" Yolanda took one hand off the wheel, pushed me to the deck. I rolled into, then past the chaise and eventually came to a stop at the end of the cockpit.

I lay back, resigned to the uncomfortable position, watching mast tips slowly pass as we chugged our way out of the harbor.

"We going for a ride?" I asked through clenched teeth.

"That's right," she said acidly. "Might go for a swim, too."

I didn't like the sound of that. I wasn't a bad swimmer, but I had never tried it with my hands tied behind my back.

It hurt like hell to talk, but I figured it would hurt a lot more to drown. Especially now, knowing Rachel was being held for a crime that only the murderer and I knew she hadn't committed.

"So tell me, does killing get easier as you go along?"

She didn't answer right away. Instead she gave a polite wave at what I assumed was another boat. "See you Monday!" she sang out brightly.

We had been traveling at a slow speed. Yolanda pushed the throttle forward and the craft responded instantly, settling into a smooth clip. She looked in all directions, and apparently satisfied with our situation, she turned toward me, shaking her head.

"You look like shit." She took a cigarette off the dash just as the lighter popped from the console.

I wiped at something warm running into my eye. "I think my nose is broken."

"Oh, no. Let me see." Yolanda scanned the water ahead and then hurried back to me. She knelt in front of me and gently probed the bridge of my nose, then she squeezed it savagely as she pressed down.

My eyeballs almost shot out of their sockets. I gasped so hard no scream would come out.

"Yep, you're right," she said, returning to the wheel. "It *is* broken."

When the pain finally subsided, I asked her for a smoke.

She studied the lake as the boat sped ahead. "It's bad for your health, sweetheart," she smiled back at me. "And you need to save what little you have left."

"Did I ever tell you I was a stress smoker?"

"Life's a real bitch, Jake."

I didn't remind her that death was too. I straightened my arms behind me and squirmed into a sitting position, the back of my battered head resting on the edge of the cushioned bench. From this vantage point, I had a good view of the fancy control panel and most of its instrumentation. We were doing either thirty miles an hour or thirty knots. I didn't know much about boats, so I wouldn't have known the difference. There was a large gauge that apparently gave the depth of the water, because it read 210 and was climbing steadily.

"You just couldn't leave well enough alone, could you, Jake?" she said bitterly. "Well, you pushed your luck too far this time. And you're supposed to be some hotshot gambler?" She laughed and shook her head. "A good gambler knows when to back off on a loser. You should have quit when Christian cashed in his chips."

"Yeah, likewise." The words were coming out funny, because my lips had started to swell. "Knocking off your husband was one thing, but killing me . . . I could start to take it personally." The glimpse of a thought entered what was left of my mind. "Is that what happened to Franco?"

She slid the throttle forward another inch. The boat planed higher and a broken beer bottle rolled my way. I tried to reach it with the tip of my shoe, but only managed to knock it farther away.

"Franco was a fool. And a lousy gambler. I gave him fifty grand, but it still wasn't enough. I caught him out here on the boat last week and he told me he'd changed his mind. He wanted more! He had a good thing going and he blew it."

"So you pushed him off Hoover Dam?"

"Everyone gets what they deserve . . ."

"That must have been a struggle. He wasn't exactly a small man."

"Not by any stretch!" she laughed loudly. "But you men are so easy. There's two things that turn your minds to mush: pussy and money." She looked at me as if for confirmation.

I didn't necessarily disagree with her, but I didn't let on. "Don't tell me the two of you were getting it on at the top of the dam?"

"No. We were standing at the railing, talking. I told him I'd give him one last payment, then I fanned through a thick wad of hundreds for effect and tossed it to him. When he reached out to catch it . . . oops!"

So that was what all the bills at the bottom of the dam were doing there.

"I wonder what was going through his head when he hit the bottom?" she asked.

"Probably his ass," I said.

"Now that's a pretty picture." She laughed again. "But really, you men are all the same. A bunch of greedy, overbearing, self-serving egomaniacs. Every single one of you!"

"I'm willing to try and change," I said.

She whipped her head around at my words. "You know, that's exactly what Christian said," she hissed.

"Yeah, but murder was a little drastic, wasn't it? There were other options available — like divorce."

"Oh, sure, I thought of that. Even threatened him with it. Ten minutes later he was using my head as a medicine ball, with the walls and furniture for partners! There was no way he would give up half of everything he owned, he said. Not a chance in hell."

She stopped suddenly, as if recollecting the scene. "I think his exact words were 'It'd be a lot cheaper if you just had a bad accident.'" The laughter that followed was filled with dark contempt. "Considering the people he knew, that would've been easy to arrange. Christ, if I hadn't acted first, I probably wouldn't be alive today!"

That was a pisser. If I'd been clairvoyant I might have tried to protect Valentine and not found myself in this state.

"So that's what gave you the idea?" I ventured.

"Exactly," she smiled devilishly. "Better him than me!"

We must have been well into open water, because she accelerated even more. A fine mist of Lake Mead water sprayed over my face. It was welcome and refreshing. I tried to stretch my neck so I could get more of it.

"I gave that son of a bitch the best years of my life!" Yolanda yelled, the wind whipping at her hair. "He wouldn't have gotten where he was without me. Christ, when I first met him, he was singing in some backwater joint in the Catskills — for nothing! Bed and board and a little bit of exposure. Big fucking deal! I was the one busting my ass, waiting on drooling slobs by day and washing dishes by night!" The memories seemed to come flooding back. "It took him ten years to become an overnight success. Then he shoves me aside, keeps me locked up in the house just so he can go play Hide the Salami whenever he wanted. He wanted to get fucked, so I fucked him! He got exactly what he deserved. And now I won't have to settle for half of anything. It'll all be mine. Including a rather nice insurance policy."

The boat began to slow. "Shit," she muttered, easing up on the throttle.

Yolanda was peering out over the bow. Whatever she was looking at wasn't making her happy. I stretched my legs, trying again to hook the broken bottle, but it skidded and rolled to the far side, banging into a railing post.

"You're really starting to piss me off, Jake." She slipped the throttle into neutral, walked to the back of the cockpit, picked up the bottle and held it firmly against my chin. "I'd slit your throat right here and now if I didn't think you'd squeal like a pig and worry those guys fishing up ahead." She dug the jagged glass into my skin to prove her point. "But you would, wouldn't you?"

As difficult as it was, I kept my mouth shut.

"Well, don't worry your pretty face, hon. As soon as I get rid of those bozos" — Yolanda tossed the bottle overboard — "being cut is going to be the least of your worries." She reached into a compartment and removed a small caliber pistol. "Just one peep," she said, aiming in the general direction of my groin, "and I'll blow your balls off."

We sat in silence for the next few minutes. She was smoking quietly, monitoring the lake ahead, while I lay there watching the drops of blood pool on my chest hairs. The sky was beginning to darken. It would only be light for another half hour or so. I had to try to distract her, keep her talking. And come up with a plan to save the Morgan family jewels.

"Why Rachel?" I asked.

After a moment, Yolanda turned her head my way. "Why not?" she grinned. "Rachel was perfect. The ideal mark. Beautiful, talented and on her way up. She represented everything I hated most in Christian and his fame." Her grin faded noticeably. "And everything was going according to plan. I hadn't expected any interference from you after I dealt with Christian. But there you were! I still can't believe you caught on to me." She studied me for a second. "And *if* you got involved because of Rachel,

I probably did you a favor by setting her up. She would have turned into a self-serving bitch and broken your heart."

Yolanda looked out over the bow again. "Do these guys plan on staying out there all night?" She flipped at a switch on the dash and the air was filled with the sounds of loud music. "Maybe that'll get them to move." She turned the twin speakers built into posts at both sides of the boat and aimed them forward. To make matters worse, she switched the music to a hip-hop tune.

"Invite them over," I said. "We could have a fish fry."

"Not tonight," she sneered. "The cops might still be keeping tabs on me. And I want to be on my best behavior. I have to be in Hamblin Bay by nightfall, just like I have every weekend for the last five months. I've planned this thing down to a tee."

As long as she was in a confiding mood, it was in my best interest to keep the conversation going. "You really fooled the cops," I told her. "How did you manage to be seen on your boat and still get back to the Oasis in time to get Christian? Did you have a car hidden somewhere in the hills?"

"I guess it doesn't really matter what I tell you now, does it?" Yolanda flicked her cigarette overboard. "No, a car would have been too easy to check. I had Franco buy a rubber dinghy and put it on board earlier in the week. When I went out last Friday, I waited around the other side of Burro Point until it got dark. Franco had a rental car parked at another marina. After I got back, I sunk the dinghy. I was fast asleep in Hamblin Bay when the cops showed up to tell me about poor Christian."

The thought brought a smirk to her face. "Just up ahead is the deepest part of the lake. I've got one more piece of unwanted baggage to deep-six, then I'll be on my way."

She opened a large compartment under the console and dug inside. When her arms finally came out, she was carrying a heavy load of rope.

She tossed the bundle in my direction. There was a loud clanging sound when it hit the deck. I realized, with far more regret than I'd care to admit, that the noise was caused by the weight of an anchor somewhere inside.

Yolanda returned her attention to the men fishing. She watched them for a few more moments, then cranked the volume of the music to its maximum. A minute later, she grinned. "Well, they finally got the message." She gave me a solemn smile.

"You a good swimmer, Jake?"

Assuming the question was rhetorical, I didn't bother to respond. The music subsided, then the sounds of an approaching engine drifted our way. Yolanda walked along the deck, blocking me from the other boat. The gun hung loosely at her side. An aggravated male voice shouted a few choice epithets in our direction. Yolanda waved and shrugged her shoulders.

I knew if I was to have any chance of drawing their attention, this was probably it. I quickly pushed off from the bench and struggled for an upright position, then I lifted my head, opened my mouth, and prepared to shout for all I was worth.

Yolanda turned immediately and kicked me square between the legs. The sky shimmered and flared briefly in bright tones of red and yellow, then turned dark. I remember sucking for air before I blacked out.

I couldn't have been unconscious long, because when I came to, the sky was still light. I also realized what had brought me around. My mouth had been gagged with an oily-smelling rag, and the stench from the fumes had made me nauseous again. To make matters worse, the boat was flying over the water, bouncing and bumping and tossing me around. The motion did nothing to help the pain still throbbing in my groin. To avoid passing out, I kept breathing through my nose, light and steady, and tried to focus my eyes.

Yolanda was standing stiffly at the wheel, staring straight ahead. I glanced down at my legs. The rope and anchor were not yet attached to me. I made an effort to sit up, but only groaned at my feeble attempt.

"You're awake," she announced with an evil grin. "And just in time, too. We're almost to the middle of the lake."

The fumes from the gag were mildly intoxicating. I lay where I was, training my eyes on the console. We really must have been closing in on the deepest part of Lake Mead — the depth gauge read 340 and was still climbing.

My mind began to jump from thoughts of Rachel and wondering if I'd ever see her again, to Lieutenant Oakley and then to my misadventures since signing on with Christian Valentine.

The entire process didn't take long. The thoughts — snippets, really — bounced crazily around in my head. Three or four of them stood out in particular. I glanced again to the console and focused as best I could.

And that's when it struck me. The gauge now read 365. I thought back to Valentine's hotel suite, centering my recollection on the navigational chart with the depth markings in the safe, and then to Franco's employee file. My guts tightened uncontrollably as I watched the depth pass 380. If I was right, once it hit 410 the yacht was going to explode.

I screamed through the oily cloth like a madman, trying to warn her.

"No one will hear you, so don't waste your breath," she yelled over her shoulder. "In a couple of minutes, you'll need every gasp you've got."

I shook my head crazily, still screaming, fighting the pain as I tried to stand. I made it to my feet and staggered toward her.

She must have sensed me coming, or caught my reflection in one of the dials on the dash, because as soon as I got near her, she spun and shoved me. I ended up flat on my back, lying across the side bench. I lifted my head. The gauge was at 395 and rising.

The predicament facing me seemed hopeless. I was convinced the two of us had only seconds to live, but if I did what I had to do, I'd surely drown. My love for the long shot won out.

Working myself into a sitting position, I took three or four deep breaths through my busted nose. The needle breaking the 400 mark was the deciding factor. I scrambled to the end of the boat, inhaling as I went, and flung my battered body overboard.

Throwing myself off a speeding boat while bound and gagged may not have been the smartest thing I'd ever done, but landing on my back made it worse. What little air I'd managed to conserve in my lungs came whooshing out upon impact.

The good news was the coolness of the water alerted every nerve still working in my body. The bad news was I started to sink. Maybe ten or twelve feet. I kicked for all I was worth.

I broke the surface and fought for air, remembering the gag when no oxygen entered my burning lungs. Before panic could take over, I thrust my head back and inhaled short bursts through my nose. When I had filled my lungs sufficiently, I straightened and tread water by kicking my legs. I got my bearings and spotted the boat. I searched frantically in every direction to no avail. It was just the two of us.

Yolanda was maybe fifty or sixty yards away. She was looking back over her shoulder, screaming incessantly as she spun the wheel hard to the left. It was obvious she hadn't let up much on the throttle, because the boat arched precariously, the side of the hull grazing the top of the waves.

Son of a bitch! She was going to run me down!

I began choking on the gag. I tried to shift it with my shoulder but the cloth was a sodden lump and wouldn't budge. Yolanda was completing the turn, so I got ready to dive before she could hit me. I snorted air, timing the action as I watched the boat approach.

My legs felt like jelly, but somehow I kept them moving. I even tried to dog-paddle with my hands behind my back. She was bearing down on me.

And then it happened. A giant fireball and a thunderous roar ripped across the water. I went deaf as I ducked below the waves, a nanosecond before splinters of wood, metal and fiberglass were hurled toward me.

I surfaced a moment later, elated at my good fortune. But the jubilation was short-lived when I realized I was miles from shore with no help in sight. I brought my knees to my chest and tried to bring my arms under me and out front. The effort cost me what little strength I had left.

It was no use — I could barely kick. My leg muscles started to cramp, and I began to sink. I was about to give up. To ease the spasms, I tried lying on my back in a dead-man's float. The irony made me laugh. Then I realized I must be hallucinating. I hated that I was checking out this way — losing my final bet.

Suddenly I realized I was underwater again. I kicked my legs into action and came up to the surface. How many was that? Two, or three? I vaguely remembered reading that people usually drowned after going under for the third time.

I must have been in the water for some time, because the sky was now completely dark. Occasionally pieces of flotsam would drift my way, but none was large enough to do me any good. I couldn't feel my arms or legs.

For a second, I thought about asking the Big Guy for a little help, but I had never been a religious man, and knew how hypocritical that would seem. I didn't want to go out like that. No, I finally admitted, the best thing might be to just lie back and swallow in Lake Mead. Besides, I had traced the faxes with their implicating numbers. And Oakley was a pretty good cop. I just hoped he was good at math. Once he found my body, and put two and two together, he should be able to come up with four.

These thoughts brought a certain amount of contentment. My body began to relax. My eyes closed involuntarily. Soft waves washed over me.

As I calmly drifted off, I sensed a beam of light shining down on me — just like in the movies.

That too, brought solace, because if there was a God, or a life hereafter — well, at least I was going in the right direction.

A man in a long white robe reached his arm out to me. I smiled inwardly, stretched out a leg, and let Him take me up.

Chapter

"Well, Morgan," the heavenly voice said sympathetically. "You really went and did it this time."

My surroundings were filled with muted light, soft tones and clean, bright whites. I was lying comfortably on my back, on a big fluffy cloud, trying to figure out why God sounded so much like Lieutenant Oakley. My eyes kept fluttering open and closing again.

"*Morgan?*" His Holiness sounded agitated. "Can you hear me? Come on, keep your eyes open, for Christ's sake!"

The sacrilegious statement stunned me. My eyes popped open and stayed that way. "Holy smoke," I croaked in surprise. "You even *look* like Oakley."

"What the hell are you talking about, Morgan? I *am* Oakley!"

I focused harder. He was absolutely right. He *was* Lieutenant Oakley.

"Lieutenant!" I yelped. "What are you doing up here?"

"What do you mean *up here?* We're on the ground floor!"

I rolled my head slowly to the side and frowned. This wasn't heaven at all. It was a hospital room, and the fluffy white cloud was a bed. The Lieutenant was leaning forward in his chair, next to an intravenous stand with a clear plastic tube trailing into my left wrist. My entire body ached, especially in the groin, and my face and head were swathed in bandages.

"What happened?" I asked groggily.

"I was going to ask you the same thing."

I let out a deep breath, remembered the oily gag, and then it all came back. I was happy to note that my arms had been untied and were lying comfortably at my side. I took a few more deep breaths of oxygen — just because I could.

"Oh, boy," I exhaled loudly. "Does that feel good."

"Well, you better watch it. You looked like you were going to hyperventilate a minute ago. And listen, keep your hands off your head. You've got a few stitches in there. Don't try to pick your nose, either. It's broken."

"It's good to see you again, Lieutenant." I tried to grin, but my whole face hurt. "What day is it?"

"It's still Friday. A little after midnight."

So I hadn't been out all that long. "You first, Lieutenant."

Oakley proceeded to tell his side of the story.

As it turned out, I had been dragged from the lake, unconscious and practically dead, by the fishermen Yolanda had sent on their way. The Lake Mead Marina dockmaster had seen the billowing smoke and called for help. I was transported by air ambulance to Desert Springs Hospital, and taken off life support when I had come around shortly after my arrival. Oakley told me I owed a lot of thanks to the paramedics on the helicopter. I agreed wholeheartedly. Deep inside though, I was disappointed I couldn't remember my one and only chopper ride.

The lieutenant pulled out his notebook. "Okay, your turn."

I reached for a plastic cup on the side table, happy to find it filled with orange juice.

"Where would you like me to start?"

"Let's try the beginning."

"Okay," I said, sipping slowly through one of those flexible straws. "First off, Yolanda Valentine murdered her husband."

I watched Oakley for a reaction but there wasn't one.

"Go on," was all he said.

So far, so good. I went on to explain that Yolanda had admitted hiring Franco to help make it look like a simple B&E at Rachel's house. Whether Franco knew he was becoming an accomplice to murder was something else, although the fact that he was being paid fifty thousand dollars probably would have made it a moot point. I outlined how the two of them had retrieved the champagne bottle from the garbage. When the investigating officer had asked for a list of missing items, neither of us had bothered checking the trash. Who would have? The break-in would also have allowed them to swap light switches and install the one from Rachel's place in Christian Valentine's hotel suite.

"What about the champagne glass?" Oakley asked.

I told him about our "chance" meeting with Yolanda in the Sultan's Tent showroom during her husband's performance.

"When she left our table, Lieutenant, she wrapped a napkin around a glass and took it with her. I'm sure it was Rachel's — the same one your boys found beside Valentine's body."

Oakley thought about that for a moment. "How do you figure Franco was involved?"

"I think he was playing both sides of the fence. Remember the notebooks in Valentine's safe? The one with all the numbers that looked like a gin rummy scoresheet?"

"Yeah, sure."

"Well," I continued, "for a while I thought the 'F' in there owing $8,400 was Franco. It was common knowledge the two of them played gin between shows to calm Valentine down. But the real big loser was somebody nicknamed 'Snake Eyes.'"

Oakley nodded in understanding. "Like the tattoo on Franco's arm."

"You got it, Lieutenant." I sipped at the juice. "Besides being up to his ass in debt all around town, Franco was into Valentine for almost forty thou. And it may not have been on the level."

"How's that?"

"Do you remember the card that fell out of Valentine's towel beside the Jacuzzi?"

"The one you caught."

"Yeah. Did you dust it?"

"That doesn't wash, Morgan. The only prints on it were Christian Valentine's."

"Exactly." I described how a gin cheat could palm a card out of a game. "Knowing what melds can't be made is a huge advantage. Practically insurmountable. That's why everyone in the book owed Valentine. He was cheating them blind. That six of spades in the towel proves Valentine wasn't alone. He had been playing gin with Franco when his wife walked in and shot him in the back with one of his own crossbows. The two of them must have missed the card in the towel when they cleaned things up to make it look as if he was having a whirlpool alone. I'll bet you dollars to donuts if you find a deck of cards in Valentine's suite, the six of spades will be missing."

Oakley jotted that in his notebook. "Okay, so let's say we agree Christian Valentine wasn't a stand-up guy. How does that tie Franco in with all this?"

I adjusted the pillows behind my head. "Christian Valentine was piling up big losses around town. It was you who told me he was being taken to the cleaners over at Caesars. I think he was losing more than he could afford to. And on top of that, he had his wife threatening him with a divorce."

"Yeah," said Oakley, slow and deliberate. "The letters from the law firm in his safe. Makes sense. He must have been trying to figure just how much it was going to cost him."

"Exactly," I agreed. "And that's where Franco comes in. I read in the hotel files he was an ex-Navy Seal. His specialty was demolitions. I think Valentine convinced Franco to blow up his yacht on the premise of collecting the insurance. In return, he'd wipe out the forty grand Franco owed him."

Oakley was scribbling like mad in his notebook.

"The thing was," I continued, "Valentine was going to kill three birds with one bomb: collect on the boat's insurance, get the wife's insurance, and not lose anything in a messy divorce."

"So what you're saying, Morgan, is that Franco may not have known what he was getting into at first." He mulled that over for a second, then he said, "You might be on to something."

Encouraged, I went on, telling of the run-in with Franco at the service station, how he had mumbled about an explosion and how he would have to remember to do "something." "It must have dawned on Franco that, with Christian dead, the boat was still set to explode. Yolanda told me she found Franco snooping around the boat after the funeral. The way I figure it, he went there to disconnect the bomb, but she interrupted him before he finished. Even Franco wasn't stupid enough to let the goose get killed while it was still laying golden eggs. And that's when he came up with the brainstorm to put the squeeze on her for more cash. She must have realized it wasn't going to stop, so she told him to meet her at Hoover Dam for the big payoff."

I went on to tell him how Yolanda had flipped him off the dam, and what all those bills were doing at the bottom.

Oakley nodded, so I continued. "Look, I hate to admit it, but Christian Valentine was playing me for a patsy. He knew I had the hots for Rachel. Hiring me was nothing but a red herring — so it would look like he was actually being threatened. It would certainly take away any suspicion from him when his wife was blown up on their yacht. I can see him now, crying his eyes out, explaining to the cops that it had really been meant for him."

"But if there was a bomb on board, why didn't it go off *last* Friday when Yolanda went out on it?"

I reminded Oakley of the nautical charts of Lake Mead in Valentine's safe. "That bomb was set to go off at a depth of 410 feet. Check the map you confiscated. It's been circled. There's only one spot in the entire lake where the water is deeper than 400 feet — and that's right in the middle where Yolanda had to pass to get to Hamblin Bay."

"But everything checked out," he interrupted. "You mean she never went that way last week?"

"No, she didn't." I told him how she admitted veering off to Burro Point and using the dinghy to get back to the marina. "She scuttled it somewhere near there when she got back. By doing so, she never crossed the deepest part of the lake."

"She must have known we'd check her mileage and fuel," he said. "I'll have a diver out first thing in the morning. But it makes sense."

I sat there quiet for a moment, mulling over a loose end.

"What's bugging you?" Oakley asked.

"I know this is a hell of a time to bring this up," I said. "But there's something wrong with my own theory. I can understand why the boat didn't blow up on the way to Hamblin Bay, since she made a pit stop near Burro Point, but why the hell didn't it explode on the way back? It had to cross the middle of Lake Mead!"

"Look, Morgan. You've been doing a good job, but maybe I can add something here." He closed his notebook. "You're right. The boat *did* cross the deepest part on the return trip. But when the detectives went out to Hamblin Bay to tell her about her husband's death, Yolanda collapsed right on the spot. She was so grief stricken we had to tow the yacht back. I guess with the ignition off, none of the gauges would work. Ergo, no explosion!"

"*Ergo?*" I said. "Jesus!" I finished the juice, placed the cup on the table and told him in no uncertain terms, "I want to see Rachel, Lieutenant."

Oakley let out a long breath. "You've got to stay overnight. And so does Rachel until we check everything out." He tucked his notebook inside his jacket and gave me a friendly smile. "But it looks good. For both of you."

A light knock sounded. The door cracked open and Julius Contini poked his head through. "Hey, Ace," he called brightly. "How're they hangin'?"

"Don't ask, Mr. Contini."

"Can I come in?" He noticed Oakley sitting there. "Oh, hey, I'm sorry. I didn't know you had company."

The lieutenant got up from the chair. "It's okay. I was just leaving." He rested a hand lightly on my shoulder. "And Morgan, I meant what I said. If everything checks out like I think it will, you'll be having dinner with her tomorrow."

"I sure hope so, Lieutenant," I said sincerely. "Because if not — *ergo*, big lawsuit!"

Oakley was studying my baby blues, patting me on the shoulder. When he finally finished his examination, he squeezed hard a few times with those big mitts of his until I winced, just to show me who was still in charge. "See you soon, Jake."

Big Julie took the seat when Oakley left. He was dressed for work, in a silk suit and tie, and he was wearing the best of his toupees. He leaned over, whispering in a conspiratorial tone, "I heard what happened from downtown. Is it all over?"

I told him it was, or would be very soon. After filling him in on all the details, he clapped his hands once loudly. "You did good, my boy!" he beamed. "Real good."

"Thanks, Mr. Contini."

"No, thank *you*! I'm just glad it was someone from outside the —" He stopped midsentence, clearing his throat. "Uh, what I mean is, I'm glad it wasn't Rachel. It's in the best interest of the hotel — if you know what I mean."

I was feeling charitable. I also wanted my new job as a poker dealer when I got out. "Oh, sure, Mr. Contini. I knew what you meant all along."

"Good boy, Ace." He lifted his bulk from the chair and stretched, thus completing what was probably his exercise for the day. "Well, I better let you recuperate." That seemed to remind him of something. "By the way, McClusky says hi. He was really worried about you."

"That's nice of him." I tried to smile, but it hurt too much.

He held out his hand and I took it. "If there's anything you need, Morgan, just ask."

I took his hand and pumped thoughtfully, then I came right out and asked him for it.

Chapter

"Oh, Jake," Rachel cried. "It's absolutely beautiful!"

I squeezed her warmly. "After a jail cell, I bet even my apartment would be a welcome sight."

She hugged me back and smiled sweetly. "Not quite."

Rachel and I were standing in the marble foyer of one of the best suites the Oasis had to offer. And it was all on the house, comped by Contini for the part I played in saving his hotel's reputation.

I hadn't told him I didn't give a damn about his hotel or its rep, that my only real concern had been for the lady I was now holding in my arms. But what the hell, truth be told, I really did deserve it.

Rachel just stood there, lapping up the luxury. "This room must be costing you a small fortune!"

"*Rooms*," I corrected. "But you're worth every penny!"

Sure, it might have been deceitful that I hadn't bothered to explain the suite was free, but I felt strongly that it was best Rachel didn't know about Contini's ulterior motive behind my working for him. She had been through enough. I was also hoping my knight-in-shining-armor role had cemented my chance at a permanent relationship with her, and the thought I'd spend some bucks on her might go a long way too.

It was around ten o'clock, Saturday night, and Rachel and I had been together since late afternoon. Lieutenant Oakley had come to visit me in the hospital prior to my release, saying he had a surprise for me. He did.

He left the room momentarily and came back in with Rachel. He had the good sense to leave us alone for a few minutes, then he returned and filled me in with the missing details of my adventure with Yolanda Valentine on Lake Mead.

The police had located the dinghy thirty feet down off Burro Point, along with a plastic bag containing burglary tools, maps, combination codes and the missing death threats and photos. Divers also found the detonator responsible for the explosion and, once all the pieces of the puzzle had been put together, Oakley had been quick to release Rachel. The possibility of a huge lawsuit for keeping her locked up longer than necessary might have had something to do with it, too.

All in all, it had been a memorable day, and I planned to make it an even more memorable evening. I had just finished a profitable session at the BJ tables downstairs while waiting for our suite to be made up. Julius Contini had relaxed the rules barring hotel employees from playing in house games, at least in my case, and now I was two thousand bucks to the good after only an hour of play. Rachel had wisely gotten me out of there after seeing poor McClusky twitching nervously at my good fortune. It was just as well. The black eye and bandages on my chin and nose were starting to scare off the other players.

On our way to our suite, I ran into Kenny and explained that I wouldn't be able to make it to his poker game tonight. He reminded me the two "loose cannons" from the previous game were scheduled to be there, but he took one look at Rachel and completely understood.

⋅

I took Rachel's hand and we walked toward the oak-and-brass spiral staircase. One entire wall was floor-to-ceiling glass, offering a spectacular, panoramic view of the busy Vegas strip. Rachel and I spent the next few minutes on a tour of the suite. All six rooms were magnificently furnished and looked like a feature out of *House Beautiful*. Maybe I should have worn a tie.

After treating her to a stunning rendition of "Chopsticks" on the music room's baby grand, I led her back to the living room. We sat down and studied the menus, then I lifted the receiver of an antique telephone sitting on the ornate bar.

"Yes, this is Mr. Morgan in suite 3501," I said easily, as if I'd been ordering room service all my life. "I'll have two of your thickest filets mignons, medium rare. One with baked potato, the other with rice, and both with vegetables and béarnaise on the side. Oh, and while you're at it, throw in the biggest steamed Maine lobster you have down there . . . What? Five pounds!" I held a hand over the receiver and looked at Rachel. She was too busy giggling to be of any help.

"The five-pounder will be fine," I said back into the phone. "And tell me, what's your best champagne? . . . Uh-huh . . . That sounds good. How much a bottle? . . . Three hundred and eighty-five!"

Rachel was laughing wildly behind a pink satin throw pillow covering her face.

"We'll have two!" I said indifferently. "With fresh strawberries and chocolate mousse . . . But of course, my good man. Two of each!"

I replaced the telephone and joined Rachel on the sofa, then proceeded to convince her forty-five minutes would be plenty of time to get to know each other better.

She smiled and said, "Wait. Let me get the lights."

"Forget the lights," I whispered, undoing the buttons of her blouse. "The clock's ticking."

Rachel seemed pleased Yolanda's vicious kick hadn't damaged any of my equipment.

It was the best forty-four minutes of my life.

·

By the time our order arrived, the two of us were lounging casually in thick white bathrobes. I gave the smiling waiter a healthy tip from my winnings, signed the bill over to Big Julie, and asked him to put the "Do Not Disturb" sign on the door on his way out. He gave me a knowing wink and told us to enjoy our evening.

The lavish meal was exquisite, as was the champagne, and we spent the next hour sipping and munching leisurely, enjoying the ambience of being bathed in soft candlelight and sweet music. It was as romantic as an evening could be.

When dinner was finished, we decided to have liqueurs on the sofa. We were so stuffed we barely made it there. We sipped our drinks and reminisced over the past week.

Eventually, I shut my eyes. Rachel rested her head lightly on my shoulder, and the two of us sat like that for quite a while.

"Jake?" she said later, in a sleepy, low tone.

"Uh-huh." I could tell she had something important to tell me. I wrapped an arm around her and held her close. There was a lot I wanted to say, too. "Rachel?"

She was still, her breathing deep. There was no need to call her name again. I kissed her hair. "You're welcome, babe," I said over her light snores. "You're welcome . . ."

I awoke alone a short time later. The soft glow from the candles cast surreal shadows around the quiet, darkened room. As I got up from the sofa I noticed a small sheet of hotel stationery propped against a vase on the coffee table. My hands shook slightly as I read.

I took the note, folded it cleanly and tucked it in my wallet. The unfinished liqueurs were still on the table. I picked up Rachel's glass and held it to my lips, taking in the warm anisette smells mixed with the scent of her lipstick. I closed my eyes and drank pensively.

After a minute, I walked to the bar and picked up the telephone.

"Hey, Kenny, it's Jake! Is the game still on?"

Want another hit from Jake Morgan? Try this sample from Rick Gadziola's *Dirty Laundry* — coming to a bookstore near you in the Spring of 2005:

Dirty Laundry

A Jake Morgan mystery
by Rick Gadziola

8:27 p.m. October 2, 1959
58 miles northwest of Las Vegas

The armor-reinforced Bugatti lumbered through the soft, shifting sand. Its long, bulbous nose rose, pointing to the apex of some distant mountain in the darkening sky; it sank just as abruptly, while finely tuned cylinders fought desperately to drive the rear axle. A low, howling wind buffeted the vehicle as it skimmed over a dune and set down on the other side.

"*Questo deserto maledetto,*" the driver muttered in Sicilian.

The passenger in the rear grinned at his trusted aide and countryman, then put a match to his thick cigar.

"Relax, Massimo." He puffed until the end glowed to his satisfaction. "You have driven this desert successfully many times, no?"

"*Sicuro,* Mr. Bonello. But not at such a late hour." And you never get used to the ridiculous whims of an old fool who claims he needs the quiet and solitude to practice his stupid cello, he wanted to add. The times they had ventured in the dark, from the neon-lit hotel to the star-lit desert, almost always meant some other occupant wasn't returning. Those excursions, at least, were capped with a sizable bonus, while bullshit assignments like this fell under his regular duties. But not for long.

A moment later they reached a familiar landmark: a broken-down wooden tower surrounded by scrub cacti. The driver brought the Bugatti to a stop and engaged the handbrake. Bonello didn't need to order Massimo to stay in the car, he knew better. This was a weekly ritual.

Carmine Bonello pushed the rear door open and stepped out. Sand whipped at his face and he forced his hat down harder on his head.

"Not so bad," he said to himself, pulling out a bronze-colored key on a finely linked silver chain from his vest pocket. He opened the trunk and took out a large black cello case. The weight caused the bottom end to drag slightly as he trudged around an eastern dune with a backhand wave to the driver watching through the side-view mirror.

Massimo cracked the window open a few inches and took a cigarette from a pack inside his jacket. He lit a match and it shook, badly. Looking at his right hand in the glow, he remembered the woman from only a few days ago. His knuckles were still scraped from causing so much damage, hitting her far too many times. He took in a lungful of smoke and held it for a moment before exhaling toward the window. He hadn't meant for that much violence to flare.

"Steady, Mass," he whispered, once again unwilling to acknowledge that his troubles were his own damn fault. He had gone over and over the plan for the last three days and now had no choice. If he did nothing, he was a dead man. If he failed at what he had to do, he was a dead man. If he made it to the airport and out, he might make it to his twenty-sixth birthday before they found him. And then, of course, he would be a dead man.

Massimo shot the cigarette out the window and swung open the door. He was downwind, and knew the sound wouldn't carry, but he still eased the door shut as a precaution. Out of habit, he surveyed for signs of an ambush or witnesses.

Nothing but broken rock, one-storey dunes, stumpy Joshua trees, and rolling sage. He would not miss this God-forsaken place.

Massimo reached inside his jacket and pulled free his Ruger Black-hawk. He had taken friendly teasing from some of his compagni because of his cherished weapon's old west, long-barrel styling as compared to their more stubby-nosed S&W's and compact Remingtons. He didn't care. He was in the old west, he reasoned. And besides, no one who had looked down the wrong end of the .44 Magnum had ever laughed.

Massimo checked the cylinder and cocked the hammer. He kept the pistol behind his thigh, pointed down, and made his way along the trail of footprints, staying close to the edge of each dune as he circumvented.

Although he knew his boss was doing more than playing his cello, Massimo had never chanced following Bonello before. If he had, and had been caught, he would have been buried right where he would have been shot. And up until now, he had valued his life. Still, he had a good idea of what Bonello was hiding, and it wasn't musical talent.

Massimo knew this area had been used for the American military's weapons tests, including the ones that produced the mushroom clouds, and the area was scattered with the occasional intact watchtower and bunker. It was the perfect place to hide what needed to be hidden — temporarily — from suspicious minds and prying eyes.

After a few minutes, Massimo heard the faint trill of whistling carried on the swelling wind. He hugged the side of the hill with his left shoulder and peered slowly around a piece of broken rock. Forty feet ahead Bonello was on one knee, fidgeting with a bronze clasp on the open case. Massimo was going to wait until his boss revealed the exact location of his secret hiding place. But then he noticed two things: a three-foot by three-foot wooden door against the side of the hill nearest Bonello, and the small mountain of cashier bags and elastic-bound packages of currency. He bit softly at his bottom lip and after a moment decided to proceed. It was all there for the taking.

Massimo stepped around the dune and walked briskly toward the bent-over man.

"*Ciao, bella,*" he called out from ten feet away.

Bonello turned on his knee. "Mass?" An astonished look filled his face. "*Ciao, bella?*" he asked incredulously.

"I was talking to the money."

Bonello noticed the gun. "Are you fuckin' nuts?"

"Yeah, probably."

"I'm going to stand up. Relax." Bonello slowly stood, wiping sand from his pants and then his hands. "Look, Mass, whatever it is, we can solve it. We'll be partners in this load. You and me."

"Mr. Bonello, don't treat me like a fool. We cannot go back. I can never go back."

The wind was picking up and both men used a hand to shield their eyes from the biting sand.

"If it's the money, no big deal," he reasoned. "I've heard. I know you're on the sheet for a few bad bets. We'll take care of it! I promise you, Mass."

Massimo forced a laugh. "Sure. Whatever you believe I owe, I probably owe ten times." His face went solemn. "And Clarista is dead."

"What are you talking about? She went to L.A. To visit her sister."

The gun barrel rose. The time had come.

"No, I passed that story around the hotel. It gave me a few days to clear this mess up."

Bonello spoke slowly and distinctly, "You hurt Clarista?"

Massimo laughed out loud this time. "You think you were the only one sleeping with her? She was a fucking dancer! A dancer with a big mouth I had to shut. I didn't know it was going to be permanently."

"You piece of shit!" Bonello shouted over the wind. "After everything we have done for you. Do you know how far back our families go? Your uncles and me? You lousy piece of shit!" Sagebrush tumbled against his right leg and he kicked it free. "I'll give you one more chance to put that gun down. Think about it."

Massimo wasn't going to think about it and Bonello never meant to let him. In an instant Bonello reached behind him and came out with his own weapon.

As he leveled the sight, a shot rang out. The white of his shirt went crimson, and he was thrown three feet where he fell on his back.

As Massimo Turito walked toward the fallen body of Carmine Bonello, he once again pulled back on the hammer of his pistol. Bonello had a gaping wound in his chest and blood was gurgling from his mouth. The shooter held out the .44 at arm's length, and when he stopped, fired two more bullets into the dieing man's head, just like he'd been trained to do.

He bent over the cello case and surveyed the contents. There were three casino cashier bags, which regularly held one thousand dollars in coin. Wrapped in individual denominations, and mostly twenty and hundred dollar, were twenty-five to thirty bundles of bills. A quick count put the cello case's contents at somewhere between sixty and seventy thousand dollars. Massimo let out a low whistle and closed the case. He was no accountant but he knew that they had been driving out here almost every week for over a year and that the combined amount of what Bonello had buried had to be at least three or four million. And Bonello had a driver or two before him.

He stood and again looked nervously around. The wind was picking up and already sand was beginning to drift on one side of Bonello's lifeless form. He would have to hurry before the trail back to the main road was lost. He had planned to bring the Bugatti closer to the bunker to make the transfer easier, but his emotions got the better of him. He had to see how much was really in there. He walked to the wooden door at the side of the nearest dune, reached out, held his breath, and pulled firmly at the rope handle.

The door lifted entirely from the earth and dangled in the air. Behind the door was only sand. What Massimo had thought to be the door to great wealth was just a piece of wood lying against a dune.

So, it had to be around here somewhere. He circled where he stood and counted at least twenty to thirty mounds over a couple of acres of land that were high enough to have been bunkers covered up by sand and time. As if laughing at him, the wind picked up its low howl as it raced across the desert floor and channeled through the dunes. The sand began to sting as it whipped at his exposed skin.

Massimo dug his hands furiously into the side of the hill where the wooden door had been, but nothing gave way. He moved down ten feet and did the same with the same results. He shouted something unintelligible and raced to another hill.

He located a broken piece of lumber and used it as a pick and shovel. He speared as hard as he could into the earth from one dune to another with no luck, and after ten minutes, fell back sweat-drenched against the seventh mound attempted, out of breath, and out of time.

"You stupid, ass!" he howled against the wind.

Glancing at his watch and knowing the sky would be totally dark soon, he was forced to abandon his search. If he should escape from the grips of those that would come, he might return at a later date. For now he would settle for what he had. He was still a rich man. He looked around wistfully one last time, and thought, "but I could be so much richer. . . ."

At the Las Vegas Airport, Massimo Turito turned the Bugatti into the darkest corner of the parking lot. He had discarded the bags of coins where he had found them, deciding their conspicuousness was more dangerous than their worth. The wads of bills were transferred into a suitcase he had brought in his own vehicle he had driven to the airport earlier that day. Leaving the Bugatti there would make it look like Bonello and Clarista had taken off from there to some secret locale.

Massimo started his vehicle and made his way onto I-95, heading northeast toward Utah. He had second cousins who operated a funeral home in Buffalo, and a brother-in-law with a small construction company in Niagara Falls, on the Canadian side. If he was lucky, stayed on the lesser-traveled routes, drove at night, and wasn't recognized, he might make it in a week.

If he was lucky....